JANE MACKENZIE has always had a love of languages and speaks fluent French. Much of her adult life has been spent travelling the world, teaching English and French everywhere from the Gambia to Papua New Guinea to Bahrain, and recently working for two years at CERN in Geneva. She now splits her time between her self-built house in Collioure, France and the Highlands of Scotland, where she has made her family home. She runs her own consultancy business, and is currently writing her second novel.

469 122 74 6

By Jane MacKenzie

Daughter of Catalonia

Daughter of Catalonia

JANE MACKENZIE

Allison & Busby Limited
12 Fitzroy Mews
London W1T 6DW
www.allisonandbusby.com

First published in Great Britain by Allison & Busby in 2014.

Copyright © 2014 by JANE MACKENZIE

The moral right of the author is hereby asserted in accordance with
the Copyright, Designs and Patents Act 1988.

All characters and events in this publication,
other than those clearly in the public domain,
are fictitious and any resemblance to actual persons,
living or dead, is purely coincidental.

All rights reserved. No part of this publication may be reproduced,
stored in a retrieval system, or transmitted, in any form or by
any means without the prior written permission of the publisher,
nor be otherwise circulated in any form of binding or cover
other than that in which it is published and without a similar
condition being imposed on the subsequent buyer.

A CIP catalogue record for this book is available from
the British Library.

First Edition

ISBN 978-0-7490-1578-7

Typeset in 10.5/15.5 pt Sabon by
Allison & Busby Ltd.

The paper used for this Allison & Busby publication
has been produced from trees that have been legally sourced
from well-managed and credibly certified forests.

Printed and bound by
CPI Group (UK) Ltd, Croydon, CR0 4YY

To my truly wonderful children Fiona and Alexander,
and to Morag, for her unfailing enthusiasm and support

PROLOGUE

November 1942

The small group of people trudged along the mountain pass from France. Above them rocky shadows loomed blacker even than the night sky. They were below the snowline, but it had started to rain, and Madeleine was shivering furiously in spite of her warm clothing. Elise held tight to her daughter's mittened hand and spoke reassuringly.

'Just keep going a little bit further, darling, and then Papa will be able to carry you again.'

Madeleine turned serious eyes to her, glinting white in this colourless world. She hadn't complained or even spoken yet on this slow, stumbling walk into Spain. They had told her she needed to be quiet so that the border militia wouldn't hear them, and her normal six-year-old chatter seemed to have frozen in the night air.

From the moment they set off in the car, on that tense, creeping drive along border tracks, edging towards the foot of the mountains and the pass that would take them to safety through the Pyrenees, Elise had thanked the clouded heavens for the shelter they had given them. They'd chanced taking the car as far as possible, headlights off, easing forward at a snail's pace for silence. The children couldn't walk the whole way, so they had no choice, they had to take the risk. They'd made it to the pass unchallenged, and Elise had breathed again, her chest sore from stupidly holding her breath. And they'd found their guide Enric waiting for them, urging them to get started, for they had fifteen kilometres to cover, and must arrive before daylight. With the children it would be slow going.

For the moment, at least, the greatest danger to them came from the natural landscape – the shingle which shifted constantly under them, and the boulders which caught their feet. A sprain would spell disaster. Occasionally a quick flash of a torch from Enric would show them a danger area, but for the most part they relied on their night vision.

Ahead the men stopped for a moment, and Luis lifted little Robert down from where he rested against his shoulder, and slid him back, swathed in his blanket, into the makeshift carrier Enric wore on his back. He'd taken him out when he began to whimper some time before, wrapping him against his body, hushing him gently into his ear, but now, miraculously, the child was asleep.

'We'll try him in here again,' Luis murmured to Elise. 'At least if he cries here there's less chance of anyone hearing him. I need to lift Madeleine for a while. She can't walk much further.'

He knelt down in front of his daughter. 'How are you doing, my little Amazon? Cold?'

She nodded, still soundless. Elise pulled another blanket from her bag, and wrapped it around her trembling shoulders. She hugged her and kissed her frozen cheeks.

'You're doing wonderfully, my darling.'

'She's a heroine,' asserted Enric. 'How old did you say she was? Only six? Well, little Madalena, your mother and father can be very proud of you.'

At his jovial Catalan words Madeleine gave her first smile, and held out her hands to be lifted into her father's arms.

They continued their slow progress, Elise shifting a suitcase from one hand to another. Luis had a heavy holdall slung over his shoulder. With no hands free, they all stumbled from time to time, but at last now they were on Spanish soil, and their goal was getting nearer.

They fell quiet again. The threat of meeting the militia on the French side of the border had receded, but even more terrifying for Elise was the possibility of being picked up by Spanish border patrols. With her British passport, she and the children would be protected, but Luis was carrying only his French residency papers. With his history, his Spanish passport was a passport to a prison cell in Franco's Spain, from where he might never emerge, and the further he walked, the more he walked into danger.

Ahead, Enric muttered something to Luis, and he stopped and beckoned Elise forwards.

'No noise now,' he instructed under his breath. 'There are houses ahead, Enric tells me. This is the village but we need to skirt round it. The safe house is on the other side, and we mustn't be heard.'

Elise nodded. She checked on Robert, who still slept restlessly in the backpack, and then gestured to Madeleine.

'You'd better give her back to me, Luis, so that you're free to take Robert. Enric will need to be free to move ahead and scout around, and we can't risk Robert waking up and crying again.' She stroked Madeleine's wet forehead. 'Can you walk, *ma chérie*, for this last little bit? We're nearly there now, darling. Hold my hand and we'll follow Papa and soon you'll be inside.'

They followed Enric onto rougher ground, wet with rain, and made a slow, edging progress around the village. It was still dark, but lights were lit in some of the cottages. This was farming country, and the people would be with their livestock before daylight. Elise held her breath again, willing them all to stay indoors until they were past. She gripped tighter onto Madeleine's hand, drawing the child in closer to her.

A dog growled, sounding frighteningly near, and Madeleine cried out in fear. Elise froze, and saw Luis and Enric stop dead ahead of them. Nobody moved. The dog growled again, and Elise crouched down and pulled Madeleine to her, her face close to the child's. She raised a finger to her lips, and Madeleine nodded, her lip quivering. They waited for the frenzy of barking which might follow at any moment. There would be other dogs in the village. Elise prayed that they were all chained up.

The seconds ticked by, and there was a blessed silence. Nobody came out to check on the dog. Perhaps his growl hadn't been heard inside. After what seemed like long minutes Enric gestured forward, and they crept on, even more slowly, for what seemed like an interminable fifteen minutes. The boggy ground was treacherous, and the suitcase felt like lead in Elise's hand as she hauled herself, the case and the child towards the goal which must now be so close. Twice she stumbled, and once her hold on Madeleine's hand was all that stopped the child falling to her knees. They kept going, following Luis who was following Enric.

A short way past the little village stood a cottage on its own, and Enric led them to the door. He opened it and went in without knocking, and gestured for them to follow. It was profoundly dark inside, and Enric lit his torch. It leapt eerily off the low ceiling, and then he was gone, leaving them by the door as he went into a second room in the cottage. After just a few minutes he returned, accompanied by a man in his late middle age, burly and hard skinned, who was pulling trousers on over his nightshirt.

The older man lit a lamp, and the simple room came into focus. He went to the fire and stirred the logs to uncover a glow underneath. Then he gestured to them to sit down. Luis greeted him in Catalan and his inscrutable face softened; he returned the greeting and made a remark about the bad night outside.

'Felip has a spare bedroom where the señora and the children can sleep for a while,' said Enric. 'In the morning Felip will take them in his cart down to catch the train for Barcelona.'

Elise sat with Madeleine on her knee, easing warmth into the child's frozen little body. Luis had lain Robert down beside her on the sofa, miraculously still sleeping. Luis and Enric spoke quietly by the window, but Elise felt too exhausted to talk.

Felip had disappeared but now came back and placed a steaming pan on the table. 'Soup,' he muttered. 'You should eat before sleeping.'

It was an excellent mountain soup, full of onions and beans. Madeleine ate hungrily, and the tight look eased from her little face. Elise tried to eat, fighting the knots in her stomach. Soon Luis would be leaving, with Enric, heading back to France, and she would go on to England without him. When would she ever return? When would they ever be together again?

Robert stirred on the hard little sofa, and Elise went across and lifted him.

'Come now, Madeleine, you should sleep for a while. I'll put you in to bed with Robert and then I'll come back and say goodbye to Papa.'

Fear returned to Madeleine. Her eyes shot towards Luis, and he came to her and lifted her and took her into the bedroom. Elise left them for a while, and then took in Robert. She found them lying together; Luis was asking Madeleine to look after her brother, and help her mother, and be a good girl, and soon they would all be together again.

'When you beat Hitler,' stated Madeleine uncertainly.

'That's right, my love, when we beat Hitler and send him and his soldiers back to Germany, then France will be free again, and you and *Maman* and Robert will all come home.'

He kissed her and made to rise, and she clung to him, and gave a tearless sob.

'And you won't die?'

'No, *carinyo*, I will not die.'

He rose and Elise laid Robert down beside her. Luis stroked his son's cheek, kissed Madeleine again, and left the room.

'I'll be back soon, Madeleine,' said Elise. 'Just cuddle under the blanket and I'll be in with you in a moment.'

She found Luis in the sitting room, clenching and unclenching his hands at his side. Enric and Felip had discreetly disappeared.

'We did pack everything?' he asked, for the hundredth time, gesturing to the suitcases. 'The money, and your pearls? Where did we put the passport and the children's birth certificates?'

'Stop, Luis. Everything is there. You know that.'

'Even your jewellery case?'

The attempt at a joke was almost heroic. They had argued over the jewellery case, Luis saying it was stupid to clutter herself with it on such a journey, and he'd insisted on removing the pearls and the children's birth certificates from it. 'That's the first place anyone would look who wanted to steal from you,' he chided her. He had been fiercely practical and positive these last few days. But he hadn't been sleeping. She knew, because she tossed and turned in the same twisted sheets.

I'm really going away, thought Elise. *This is it. He's going to leave us now.*

13

'Luis.'

He moved towards her and drew her into his arms, burying his head in her hair. She clung to him.

'You have to go now before it's light,' she said, as matter-of-fact as possible.

'I know.'

He looked down at her and her face was drenched in tears.

'Go safely, my darling. Stay safe for me.'

He kissed her and was gone.

CHAPTER ONE

March 1958

The upper floor of the house was hushed with the expectancy of death. Downstairs, in the drawing room, the hall, the dining room, daily routines seemed to continue as normal. The usual predictable menus at breakfast, lunch and dinner were served at the same set times as ever. Grandfather spent his days as always in his study muttering over the daily news, or in the garden, harrying the jobbing gardener. Grandmama moved within her small kingdom with her usual gentle grace, drank tea in her little sitting room reading the same society journals, and occasionally received well-wishers bringing flowers and small tokens for Elise. In the room above, Elise lay unheeding in her heavy mahogany bed, while nameless nurses came and went quietly on their shifts, so as not to disturb anyone on the floor below with the reminder of death.

Madeleine sat hourly by her mother's side, watching her, counting her laboured breaths, doing nothing because there was nothing to be done, nothing that was not better done by the nurses, brisk and forbidding in their starched collars. Once a day Grandmama would visit her daughter, wreathed in perfume, stroking Elise's hand with butterfly strokes as she made kind enquiries of the nurse. Grandfather never came.

Occasionally Grandmama would try to persuade Madeleine to leave her mother's bedside for a while, suggesting that she needed some fresh air and some company. Should she maybe not take a walk, or come downstairs next time there were visitors? This self-imposed vigil was surely unhealthy and unnecessary. But Madeleine conceded only a physical presence at mealtimes, eating without tasting, and answering questions posed by form with the standard answers they deserved. And after each meal she returned upstairs to her mother.

Elise spent less and less time awake now. When she woke, she would occasionally be fully conscious and vitally aware of her daughter's presence, and it was these rare moments which Madeleine lived for. At other times she would lie semi-comatose, her eyes unfocused, in a world between sleep and life, occasionally at peace, to Madeleine's eyes, but more frequently twitching involuntarily in a silent underworld of pain. As increasing pain drew her out of sleep, her face would constrict sharply, and she would come fully awake, her hands gripping Madeleine with an intensity which left small blue bruises on Madeleine's wrists. The nurse would then emerge from behind her desk, moving Madeleine gently aside, a syringe in her hand with some dose to help Elise back into the sleep of the near dead, to begin the cycle again. Did she dream, Madeleine wondered? Did her dreams take her back to younger days of sunshine and passion? Did that time still exist for her?

Today Dr Jenkins, musty as ever in his pre-war jacket with its newly sewn elbows, had made what might be his last visit to Elise's bedside. He had listened to her breathing, checked her pulse, and conferred in a hushed voice with the nurse, then had gone to break the news to Grandfather that his daughter would probably not live through the night. Robert had been sent for and was due today. At some point, Madeleine presumed, they would all come up to stand over the impending corpse. But for now she had *Maman* to herself. Even the brisk day nurse had gone downstairs to eat, and Madeleine sat alone in fragile stillness listening to her mother's shallow breathing, stroking the crumpled skin on her thin, tired hands.

The covers on Elise's bed were stretched so tight they appeared to constrict her uneven breathing even further. Leaning over the high bed, Madeleine loosened them, disturbing the marble finish of the sheets and wondering what reaction she might get from nurse. *Maman* lay quiet on the heavy pillows, her still beautiful golden hair framing ashen, sunken cheeks.

Only forty-two years old, and until last year the most beautiful English rose, in spite of her faded clothes and worn expression. She had been a broken rose for many

17

years, Madeleine thought as she watched her, and now no petals remained. She had done nothing to fight her illness, although it was hard to believe anything could have been done for her. Cancer was a word of dread and foreboding, and Elise had relieved the family of many months of fear by hiding the illness and her weight loss, appearing merely to be losing her youth as she had long since lost her hope.

The nurse came quietly into the room, checked swiftly on Elise, and nodded at her sleeping form. She turned to Madeleine. 'I've had my lunch, Miss Madeleine, and now I'll sit with your mother. You go down to lunch now. Mrs Hopkins tells me your grandparents are already in the dining room. Go down now, and then maybe your mother will wake when you return.'

'No, no thank you, I'm not hungry,' Madeleine said, with a quick shake of her head. 'She may wake any moment and I want to be here.' It may be the last time, she wanted to say.

The nurse pursed her lips. 'As you say, Miss.'

She moved over to the window table which now served as a desk and dispensary, and placed a new vial next to the syringe. The low-lying spring sun shone in watery shafts through the new leaves on the trees outside, and picked out the metal dish which held the syringe, and the plain glass jug of water on the table. Not a mote of dust floated in the sunlight.

'They've sent for your brother to come home from Oxford,' offered the nurse. 'I think the driver went for him, so he should be here quite soon.'

Madeleine acknowledged with a brief smile, but her throat constricted at the thought of Robert seeing their mother at the end. He was a surprisingly fragile creature, despite his youthful muscle and careful poise. He was at once commanding and childlike, and his last visit home had tested his hard-imposed self-control, flaying open old wounds which he had long ago sealed over with a studied British reserve. Madeleine had seen in his eyes the beginnings of fear, and the hands which held his mother's had trembled. *Maman* had come unusually awake for Robert, reaching out to touch him, each movement of her eyes a caress. Robert, who was the copy of his father, the closest living image of the dark, broad, handsome Spaniard who had defined Elise's existence. Only Robert's skin was fairer, and his hair a rich brown in place of his father's black mane, but still his colouring was not fully British and irked their grandfather. Madeleine shared this smooth Mediterranean skin which would not freckle and turned olive in the sun, with the same almond eyes, full lips and mass of dark hair, but her face was longer, slimmer, more like her mother's. It was Robert, with his broad, planed cheeks and electric smile, who personified Luis, their photos sitting side by side on *Maman*'s dressing table.

At Madeleine's side came a tiny flutter of movement, and Elise opened her eyes, gazing straight ahead, in the position where her sheets held her imprisoned. Madeleine leant forward so that her head was above her mother's.

'*Maman?*'

'*Petite!*' Her mother smiled, a half smile with the

merest shadow of the old magic. Madeleine reached for her hand.

'Robert is coming. You'll see him this afternoon.'

Another smile, then a sharp grimace of pain, and two words, 'Ah, Robert.'

'He'll be here. He's on his way.' And God willing you will be awake to see him. Let this not be the last awakening, thought Madeleine.

The grimace of pain had been enough to make the nurse act quickly. She approached the bed, a full syringe in her hand.

'Not yet!' Madeleine protested, then leant again towards her mother. She squeezed the shrivelled hand gently, and smoothed a stray lock of hair from her forehead.

'Would you like to drink something, *Maman*?' She offered a glass of water.

Again a precious half smile. 'Thank you.'

Madeleine put her arm around Elise's shoulders and raised her feather-light body a little. As she drank, a tiny, painful sip, Madeleine held her close. There was nothing she needed to say to *Maman* now. To have her awake was enough.

Elise leant back against her, and another spasm of pain twisted her face. This time the nurse stepped forward with iron determination, and Madeleine eased her mother back onto the pillows, and then watched helplessly as the syringe entered her arm and she sank again into oblivion.

'You might as well go and eat now,' the nurse repeated.

Madeleine sat for a further minute, then nodded

dumbly. There was no point in staying now. She picked up her cardigan and went downstairs.

In the gloomy green dining room, her grandparents were already seated at table. Thankfully this was Sunday, cook's day off, and a simple cold buffet had been laid out on the sideboard. Self-service lunch, and she could arrive late without a scold. Grandfather was dressed for church. A tall, bent figure, with skin as dry as paper and joints stiff and sore, he sat awkwardly at the head of the table, and glowered at the array of pills set out before him in a regimented line.

In the drawing room there was a photograph of her grandfather on the day of his graduation from King's College in Oxford, tall, lean and very serious in his robes, and next to it another silver-framed photograph of him some years later with Grandmama, during their courting days in London, Grandfather in a morning suit, looking very dashing next to the dainty, high-born Parisian *demoiselle* who had secured his future as a society lawyer. The grave young man in the first photograph showed hints of the determination which had allowed Paul Gresham to climb so fast, but no hint yet of the careful charm which won him his wealthy clients, and the grace and diplomacy he used to rescue them from their indiscretions. Grandmama opened the doors for him, and he treasured his elegant French bride and her connections like a fragile piece of antique lace, working endlessly to give her the social life she took for granted. As a child Madeleine had always been drawn to the silver-framed couple in that photograph in the drawing room: they were almost deliciously elegant but curiously superficial.

There were no photographs of the grimmer years of the Great War, but in the 1920s there were more pictures of them dancing and parading in Gay Paris. Where were their children, Madeleine wondered, during these visits to Paris? John and Michael, and little Elise, of whom a group photo sat on a different table, the boys in starched collars, Elise in little girl's ribbons, gravely posing together for a studio camera. There were no more photos of disgraced Elise, but there was one of John and Michael again, as young men, dangling an enormous fish proudly from a hook. Michael must have died soon after, thought Madeleine, in that road accident no one was allowed to mention. And then John: there was a final picture of John, in his uniform, handsome and serious, placed next to the DSO that had been awarded to him posthumously – just one more war hero who had never returned.

Had it been this final grief which drove Grandfather to isolate himself in the country, and turned him into the hardened fossil who crabbed at life, consumed by the iniquities of tied tenants and the outrages of socialism? Madeleine had known no other side of him. From the moment of her arrival in England with her mother and brother, three windblown, miserable refugees from occupied France, she had lived with her grandparents in this house, and Grandfather had required silence, conformity and above all 'Englishness' from these barbarian grandchildren previously raised in what he deemed a bohemian, Communist conspiracy. That

22

past was dead, and their lives were henceforth his to command.

Grandmama was different. She paid little attention to Grandfather's outbursts and simply arranged his small comforts, and at sixty-eight still radiated elegance. Amid her velvets and silks, soft leather gloves and laced corselettes, she stood out among her Berkshire neighbours in their tweeds and riding suits, but managed to be accepted, and even played a part in parish activities, provided nothing was too strenuous or demanding. She fluttered and murmured in French, and unlike him was happy to hear her grandchildren speaking French with their mother. But like Grandfather, she could never forgive her daughter for the crime of marrying Luis Garriga during a supposedly well-controlled visit to her aunt's family in Paris. Nor could she forgive her for being alive when her two beloved sons were dead.

And as for Luis Garriga's Mediterranean children, they had to work their way into a place in this family. Robert had achieved approval when he was picked for the rugby team at Winchester, and became his grandfather's pet when he later chose to study law at Oxford, following in Paul Gresham's footsteps. He rode well, talked fishing to Grandfather, and was popular among all their social group. Madeleine knew how hard he had worked at this character. Outgoing by nature, yearning for acceptance, and struggling with the elusive legacy and identity of a father he couldn't remember, Robert had found safety and refuge finally under his grandfather's gradually unfolding wing. Paul Gresham needed a new son, and Robert had won his wings as the family's future.

Madeleine had always been of far less interest. The family may have needed the little boy who came to them so young and unformed from France, but his brown, passionate sister was older, and spiky and unbending. Six years old, speaking Catalan and French in preference to English, her memories of 'home' were strong, and she spent her days with her mother, prattling endlessly about Vermeilla, and Papa, and Uncle Philippe, hiding from her grandparents.

When the news came of Papa's death in 1944, and *Maman* became so terribly withdrawn, it was decided it would be better if Madeleine was sent to school. The experience certainly cured her of her childish prattle and exuberance. School life surrounded by girls called Margaret and Audrey, Elizabeth and Susan, all with identical, insular backgrounds, was worse than living with Grandfather. None of the girls, in these post-war years, had ever left English shores. None had names like Madeleine, and they pronounced the name with exaggerated care, as something exotic and potentially suspect.

Madeleine reacted like a porcupine, curling her soul into a tight ball, with nothing but sharp quills directed at all around her. The girls learnt to keep their distance, and Madeleine learnt to keep hers. She wanted to shout at them. 'Madalena! My real name is actually Madalena!' She could imagine them murdering the name in their upper-class accents, and called up memories of her father's deep voice, his laughing face inches from her own as he swung her in his arms. 'Madalena,' he would say, 'Madalena *bella*. Your beautiful eyes will win all hearts.' But now Madeleine learnt to stay in the background, and nursed her memories in private. At weekends she was allowed home, and would cling to her silent mother, willing her to get better.

As the years went by she mended her manners, learnt to play tennis and the piano, forgot her Catalan, and kept her French for *Maman*. She had her passions well hidden, and moved through life trying not to stir any waters. She lacked Robert's easy good humour and brilliant smile. Where he was popular and sought after, she was happy to live in the shadows.

She hoped to be unnoticeable today as she entered the dining room, and quietly helped herself to some salad and a little cold meat. Grandfather lifted his head from his pills and grunted a greeting, but Grandmama rose to kiss her on both cheeks, and led her to her chair. She had changed, Madeleine noticed, from the green silk she had been wearing this morning to a sober grey jersey suit. Not yet full mourning, but just the right touch for a house on the verge of a death. Madeleine's pink cardigan looked both shabby and uncaring in contrast.

'My poor girl,' intoned Grandmama, pouring a small quantity of wine into Madeleine's glass. 'We are all going to have to be very brave.'

'She's sleeping again,' Madeleine replied, not bothering to keep the weariness from her voice. 'I hope she wakes for Robert.'

Grandmama inclined her head, and gave a small sigh.

'I must go to see her after lunch. My last remaining child. It will be so very hard.' Grandmama's sigh was perhaps genuine, thought Madeleine. It was maybe just her style which seemed so insincere.

'Nurse will tell us when we need to go up,' muttered Grandfather. Then, as if it would solve everything, 'We'll wait for Robert.'

And after lunch he came, striding through the doors and wafting in the cool, crisp air of the world outside, where normal people lived and worked and walked in the spring sunshine. He kissed Grandmama on both cheeks, clasped Grandfather briefly, then took Madeleine in his arms.

'Is she really going, then?' he whispered.

'Really, yes, Bobo. She's more and more drugged – hardly wakes. But she smiled at me this morning.'

She drew him up the stairs, and hesitated by her mother's door. 'She's in a lot of pain now, Bobo. It's hard to watch at times. You'll see. It will be best if she goes quickly now, really it will.'

Robert nodded impatiently and put her aside to open the door, entering the room with the almost offensive vigour of the young and healthy. He slowed, though, as he approached the bedside, and then stopped, reaching for Madeleine's hand. His face was leaden as he surveyed the ashen face, thinner even than the last time he had visited, sunk in deep sleep.

He was silent for several minutes. Madeleine watched him rather than their mother, trying to read his thoughts. She was so unsure of how he would react, but until he spoke his face gave little away. When he did speak, his bitterness was fierce. Bitterness at the illness, but especially at Elise. It was unlike him and it shocked Madeleine to the core.

'It makes me so angry to see her lying there like that,' he muttered with real fury. 'It just seems to sum up her life. Lying there so passive, so stupidly passive. Giving in as usual. Suffering as always. Why couldn't she ever live? She might as well die of cancer. She doesn't even *want* to be here with us.'

Madeleine flinched at his anger, but heard his pain and the years of loss he was trying to express. For a young man eager for life, Elise had been a poor role model, meek, submissive and inactive, too rarely laughing, too frequently placating.

She thought carefully before replying. 'She loved us, Bobo. She lived a lot through us, I know, and should have got more from life, but she wasn't always passive. She could be quite fiery at times, especially when defending us – defending you mainly, when Grandfather wanted to punish you for breaking a window, or for wrecking the plant border with your cricket games.'

Robert smiled briefly in acknowledgement, and she pressed home her point. 'Do you remember how she would laugh with us later, up here away from the rest of the house, and she would produce some chocolates from the hidden drawer to calm you down. You used to get so mad when Grandfather told you off!'

'I know, I know,' he acknowledged. 'There were some special private moments. But what a life overall, in the

27

end. Was she ever really happy, do you think?'

His hand was still in Madeleine's, and she squeezed it. She noticed out of the corner of her eye the nurse quietly leaving the room, and was relieved at their solitude.

'I think so, Bobo. Oh yes, she was happy. I have memories of her laughing so freely, so gaily. Teasing Papa, teasing me too. She was really alive then.'

'I don't remember anything from those early days. I don't even remember Papa.' His voice was bitter, anguished.

Madeleine stood for a moment, conjuring up memories. They came, but with time it was taking longer and longer to retrieve those memories. Maybe it was part of losing your childhood. But the memories were so important.

She shook herself slightly, and squeezed Robert's hand again. 'I don't remember much myself. Just some images which come back to me. Papa in a kind of blue overall, and Uncle Philippe, and they both smoked tiny little cigarettes which they rolled themselves. I don't think there was much tobacco available. And *Maman* in a flowery apron. We had a big wooden table and a fire in a stove in the corner. I wasn't allowed to touch it.'

'A fire? It was the south of France, Madeleine!'

'There was a fire, with logs, and a really old black stove,' Madeleine insisted.

'I wish we knew more. I wish I had asked more.' Robert removed his hand and moved restlessly to the other side of the bed. Madeleine held his gaze across their mother's sleeping body, wanting him to listen.

'She wouldn't have told you anything. Not after he

died. We used to talk about home all the time when we first came here, but after she got the letter she stopped talking.'

'She didn't have the right to be like that,' growled Robert. 'Loads of women lost their husbands in the war, but they still helped their children to remember. They still talked about their husbands. It wasn't fair to us to stay so silent. She just excluded us and left us with nothing!' It was a poignant cry, and Robert shook his head as if to shake away imminent tears.

'*Maman* wasn't allowed to, you know that! None of us were allowed to remember. Poor *Maman* was a family disgrace, come home to do penance. Don't ever blame her! When did she ever let you down? She loved you and protected you and helped you to be happy here. How can you judge her? Look at her! Look how tired she is! And yet she smiled for me this morning!' Tears were in Madeleine's eyes for the first time. Robert came back round the bed to her side, and put his huge arm around her shoulders and hugged her.

'Sorry, Lena. Sorry. I know, I know. She loved us so much. Will she wake again, do you think?'

'I don't know. They give her so many drugs now, and when she wakes she's in pain.'

'Then I hope she doesn't wake. Look how peaceful her face is.' Robert stroked his mother's cheek, and freed the hand which the nurse had again tucked severely under the stark white sheet and grey blanket. 'We should let her go now.'

'Will you be all right?'

'A strange question from you, Lena. What about you? What are you going to do here without *Maman*? Join the bridge club? Or marry one of the worthy young men that Grandmama keeps throwing your way? What's that doctor's name – Peter, isn't it? The one who only does dried-up research and runs away from real patients? He'd marry you tomorrow and bottle you up and label you like one of his experiments.'

Madeleine smiled. 'Peter's all right, Bobo. He's interesting, at least, and doesn't talk about land laws and foxes, or stupid village gossip. He's been nice too while *Maman*'s been unwell – coming round in his car and making me go out for some fresh air sometimes. And never putting me under any pressure. That's pretty human behaviour, isn't it?'

'Not very passionate though, either, is it?' Robert grimaced. 'You surely wouldn't marry him, Lena?'

'No. You can rest assured. I don't want to marry him or anyone. I just want to get away from here. If all else fails I can get a job as a secretary. That was *Maman*'s only success with the elders as far as I'm concerned – getting them to fund my studies. So I'm employable if only I can get away. But I don't have a bean to get started with.'

'Fund your studies!' snorted Robert. 'Is that what you call it? With your brain it should have been you at Oxford, not me. And all they would allow you to do were secretarial studies! You're not going to live any life at all as a secretary. You should run away to Paris, that's what. I was thinking about it on the drive here. You should go to

30

Tante Louise. You'd get a real life there – the kind of life you'll never have here.'

Madeleine could only gape at him. What was he saying? Paris? She tried to digest the idea. He might have been suggesting she go to the moon, for all she could imagine it.

She looked again at Robert, his intense eyes all lit up. *Oh, my God, France,* she thought, and the idea was suddenly electrifying.

'Could I?' she questioned, more to herself than to him. 'Could I really go to *Tante* Louise? But how? I can't live without money, and if I don't work I only have what Grandfather gives me.'

'I don't know. We need to write to *Tante* Louise. Maybe if she invites you the elders will stump up the cash to send you there.'

'Are you joking? After *Maman* went to Paris as a girl and disgraced the family by running off with Papa? They've hardly even communicated since, the elders and the Paris family. They blame *Tante* Louise for everything.'

Robert took his time replying. 'All right,' he said eventually. 'So you find the fare somehow and then get a job in Paris. There must be people there who want a bilingual secretary. You could make more money there than here, surely? And Lena . . .' Robert's voice took on a new urgent edge.

'Yes?'

'Maybe once you are in France you could find out something about us. About Papa. Maybe *Tante* Louise can help answer our questions about him. You could even go south to Vermeilla and find Uncle Philippe.'

Madeleine stared at him blankly, her head spinning. So many possibilities opened up before her, but it took such a leap of faith to believe them achievable. Robert had a child's imagination, unlike her. They'd sapped her imagination, the elders, with their restrictions and inertia.

But as she looked again into Robert's impulsive, hopeful face, it came to her with complete certainty she would leave, and that if *Tante* Louise would have her, she would go to France. But the money. How to get the money? She looked down at her mother for inspiration, and was surprised by a smile on her face. The merest whisper of a smile, in sleep.

CHAPTER TWO

Elise Garriga died early the following morning, without regaining consciousness. A rather timid sun was nudging over the horizon, and Robert had opened the curtains and the window, to the nurse's dismay, so that a fresh breeze caressed her cheeks and hands. Grandfather and Grandmama had visited the night before, after dinner, and Madeleine had been surprised to see a rim of tears in her grandfather's eyes as he gazed down at his daughter, and held her hand in the sombre gloom.

But as day broke only Robert and Madeleine were with their mother, and when she stopped breathing the change was so subtle it took them time to realise that she had gone. Before they called the nurse, they unearthed her favourite flowered bedspread from a cupboard, and put it back on the bed, and brought the vase of roses from the dressing table to the bedside, so that their mother slept as she had always slept, surrounded by flowers.

'Say your goodbyes now, Lena,' Robert had said, as they stood together looking at Elise for the last time alone. 'Her burial won't have much to do with us, if I know Grandfather. She has peace now for the first time in years, but they won't give her much peace from now until she's finally in the ground.'

Robert stayed until after the funeral. It was strange to be burying *Maman* from the gloomy, Gothic village church which she had refused to attend ever since her return to England. This was another aberration for which Grandfather had blamed the atheist Luis Garriga, but now the English were fully reclaiming Elise, burying her in the local churchyard after a decently low-Anglican service, followed by sandwiches at the house, in the large, musty, front drawing room. The funeral and reception, and all the condolence visits which had preceded it, were a dreary trial dominated by the rural genteel, their faces set in platitudes, their feet in sensible shoes. The rector hovered around them, benignly haughty, drinking sherry in painstaking minuscule sips. Having barely known Elise, he focused on his more amenable parishioners, talking in soft tones about the prospects for the summer weather and the best dates for the pruning of roses.

Four figures enlivened the day, descended from London to give some family representation. An uncle, aunt and two cousins from Grandfather's family, they came from another world, from the world of restaurants and cinema and theatre and London shops. From the world of work and colleagues and gossip and movement.

Grandfather had climbed further in society than his brothers, but had paid heavily with his middle-class soul. His brother's son, a prosperous trader, mocked gently the studied gentility of life at Forsham, while his two daughters talked of rock and roll and Marlon Brando, of cabriolets and American fashion. Forsham society looked on, bemused, and Grandfather glowered as his beloved Robert blossomed. Cousins Cicely and Eve enfolded Robert in their casual sophistication, and made clear their admiration of his charms, rendering him almost sheepish by their side. Cicely had a particular radiance, with her dark hair loosely curling inside the enormous raised collar of her tight-waisted jacket, and her slender pencil skirt skimming her calves. She lived with another girl in an apartment in Chelsea, and worked for a property agency.

'Not much of a job, really,' she laughed, 'And just a tiny apartment, you know, very modern – such small rooms they give you these days. But it's so close to everything I want in London, and it's so *dusty* to live at home with the parents, don't you agree?'

Madeleine could only murmur in what she hoped was easy agreement. For her Cicely and Eve were a revelation, they were so vibrant and pleasure-seeking, people whose conversation bubbled and who wanted to amuse and be amused. The way they embraced modern fashions and ideas was electrifying Robert and shocking Grandfather, but for Madeleine it held out a simple glimmer of promise. Could she be like this, she wondered, if she made it to Paris? It seemed a million miles away. Get the funeral over first, and finish sorting *Maman*'s affairs, then think about the future. Cicely had thrown her an easy invitation to stay 'any time you are in London'.

Madeleine also overheard her saying to Robert, 'Your sister has such sultry looks, so sexy and Mediterranean. It's the eyes, of course, and that amazing mouth. I'm so jealous. Does she live buried down here? No boyfriend or anything? Surely she needs more than this?'

How right you are, thought Madeleine. *How very right you are.* To hear herself described as sultry and sexy was a little mind-blowing.

Peter was at the funeral, of course. He was a good-looking young man, tall and very slender with long, elegant hands and a face which Grandmama described as being 'full of refinement'. He came up to Madeleine while she was talking to Cicely, and it amused her to see the play between him and her London cousin, Cicely interested and full of smiles, Peter quite ruthlessly dismissive. He was the type, Madeleine thought, who pursued single-mindedly whatever was his current objective, and didn't even notice what was in the periphery. It made him successful, but rather narrow of vision.

Right now his objective was clearly Madeleine, not some shallow London cousin.

'I'm sorry I couldn't call round before the funeral,' he said, holding her hand. 'I've been away – a conference – I only heard yesterday about your mother's death. I hope the end was as easy as possible, for her and for you.'

'She went peacefully, yes, thanks, and Robert was with me.'

'I'm glad it was peaceful.' Peter's hand shifted slightly in hers, his fingers tightening slightly as he held her gaze. 'It'll take you some time to adjust.'

Was he calculating how long, wondered Madeleine? A month, two months, before he could make his move? She wasn't sure what he saw in her, but something had settled in his mind that she was a suitable wife. He certainly wasn't passionate – Robert was right about that. But he was keen. She wondered what he would say if she asked him why. All of a sudden she wanted him gone. She wanted to talk to Cicely again – happy, frivolous Cicely.

Let me out, oh please, God, get me out of here! The thought was so vivid she wondered if she had spoken aloud. She drew her hand away from Peter, and muttered her excuses as she turned to attend to other guests. He followed her.

'I'll call to see you tomorrow,' he said. 'Maybe we can go for a drive.' His voice was gentle, but confident and dominant.

'Maybe,' she replied. 'Maybe later in the week, though. Robert is still here, you see.'

'Yes, I can understand you want to spend time together. I'll telephone and find out when he has gone.'

The words were fine, but the faintly smug tone was unbearable. Madeleine simply nodded and made her escape, looking for Robert and finding him happily surrounded by the cousins. As he and Cicely turned to smile at her, at once the day seemed brighter again, and she could even imagine her mother taking comfort. These cousins were perhaps shallow, but they were from the world she yearned for. Their laughter was a comfort and their insouciance for now seemed infinitely more real than Peter's careful sympathy.

The next day she wrote to *Tante* Louise. It was the first time in her life she had ever written to her. As she sat with her pen poised above Grandmama's best inlaid paper, she conjured up a picture of the tiny Parisian woman, with her deeply lined, very mobile face and expressive kohl-lined eyes, topped by expertly dyed hair tied back in a heavy French chignon, and the whole head perched on a bird-like neck which seemed too thin and fragile to support her. The last time Madeleine had seen her was in London, when Louise and her daughter Solange came on a visit, and Madeleine had gone with her mother and grandmother to tea with them at the Ritz. Grandfather had, of course, refused to come, and also refused to invite them to Forsham. They'd had the most elegant English tea, she remembered, and *Tante* Louise seemed to dance verbally among them, while Grandmama rigidly tried to control the conversation. But after a while, Louise had woven a spell over Grandmama as much as the rest of them, and she had unbent, and begun talking hungrily about the old days in Paris. Louise was Grandmama's cousin, a few years younger than her, but they had partied their way through the twenties together in Paris, in the days when they were the closest of cousins, before *Maman*'s disastrous visit in 1935.

Madeleine had watched Grandmama's transformation with wide eyes; this elderly woman emerged from a tired life in rural England, her soul taking flight once more under the influence of the little, wrinkled Frenchwoman with incessantly mobile hands and a tantalising smile. Louise was quite simply bewitching. Even *Maman* had come alive with this woman she had always known as her beloved *Tante*, and gained the confidence to talk about her summer in Paris, for once forgetting the cloak of shame which her parents had thrown over the whole episode. For *Maman* the summer had been a turning point in her life, and a period of liberation. Solange and she had gone to parties and fashion shows, theatre premieres and the ballet, part of a fashionable Paris set following a determined social scene which defied Europe's financial and political troubles. They had been girls together, and for a while *Maman* had been a girl again that afternoon in London.

At fifteen, Madeleine couldn't remember ever seeing her mother like this, so happy and free. Later that day, as they returned to Forsham by train, as *Tante* Louise's personality receded and Grandmama became her normal controlling self, Madeleine watched with a sense of loss as her mother withdrew inexorably again into herself. She had a sudden burning vision of her mother in earlier years, and thought that just as she had stored away jealously the memories of moments from her childhood, of her mother laughing alongside her father, so she must store the memory of *Maman*'s extraordinary blossoming this afternoon. But at fifteen she hadn't imagined herself writing this letter to Louise nearly seven years later.

'*Tante* Louise,' she wrote in French,

I need you. Maman *loved you, and the only time*

I have seen her blossom in recent years was in your
company. I know so little about her days with you in
Paris, but now that she is dead I need to leave here
or I will stay imprisoned all my life. Robert believes
that if you invite me to Paris I may be able to get
away. It is presumptuous to ask you, but could you
possibly write to Grandmama inviting me to stay with
you? Grandfather is unlikely to agree, but they've
been worried about me becoming withdrawn and
depressed, so they may at least talk about it. If they
don't agree, I may have to leave home without their
approval, and I could perhaps get a job in London,
but I would have to sell Maman's *jewellery to pay my*
way at first. Without their approval I couldn't come
to Paris, because I know they would blame you, and
it wouldn't be fair.

The letter written, and quickly posted before she could
worry about her words or what she was doing, Madeleine
had nothing to do but wait for an answer, breaking the
idleness of the imposed period of mourning at Forsham
by frenetic walks on her own through the Berkshire
countryside, largely soaked by a spell of prolonged rain
which sluiced through raincoats. Madeleine welcomed
the rain which spattered her face under her rain hat, and
tingled her ungloved fingers. It was a sign of life, a world
of sensation outside the dead interior of her grandparents'
house. What she would do if she didn't hear from *Tante*
Louise she could no longer imagine. The yearned-for
letter had become her link of hope to the future.

And when the letter finally arrived it was so simple, so astonishingly simple. *Tante* Louise replied,

Ma chère Madeleine. Your mother loved us and we also loved her. It would be the greatest pleasure in the world to get to know her daughter. I remember you being born, such a beautiful baby. How proud your parents were. I cannot believe that your grandfather will permit a visit to us, but I will write anyway, as you suggest. But if he does not approve, and if you want to come here, we urge you to come anyway. The opinion of your grandparents is of no significance to us. I will most certainly not come again to London, and without your mother, England has little appeal for Solange. Your mother found happiness in France, and no one could have known Luis would die. Your grandparents didn't know him, and could never have appreciated him. Come to us, ma fille. I do not go out as much as before, and we do not have a young girl to keep you company, but I am sure that life here will be more amusing for you than in that terrible English countryside. You were a beautiful girl seven years ago. I am sure you are a truly beautiful young woman now.

As she read the words Madeleine surprised herself in floods of tears. Here were people who had loved *Maman*, and who had known and appreciated her father. 'I remember you being born,' *Tante* Louise had written. Suddenly Madeleine felt a hunger she could hardly contain for this acceptance and belonging. Whatever happened now she would definitely go to Paris, with or without her grandparents' approval.

But first she had to run that particular gauntlet, whatever the outcome. She just wanted it to happen now. Soon her grandparents would receive their own letter from Paris. She could barely eat and certainly not sleep as she waited for the storm to break.

Tante's letter to Grandmama arrived the following day. Madeleine saw it arrive, but at first all was quiet. No one said a word to her, and by the end of the day she realised that the elders were going to ignore the letter completely. She could appreciate the strategy, but her need to bring the issue into the open was now stronger than any fear of confrontation. So she waited until lunchtime the following day, as they sat over a beef casserole, and with hammering heart she brought it up herself, pouring the words out in one breath.

'I had a letter from *Tante* Louise,' she said, trying desperately to keep her tone light, 'inviting me to Paris. She said she was writing to you as well. Have you had the letter?'

There was a long silence. Then Grandmama looked at Grandfather, who wiped his hands painstakingly on his napkin before replying in a deep rumble of impending thunder. 'We had a letter. There is no question of sending you to them, though. What an impertinence even to suggest it. Typical of Louise!'

'But I would like to go.' Madeleine clenched her hands under the table and made her voice as natural as possible. 'It's been such a long, hard time recently, and I won't get back to normal life while I'm here in the same house where *Maman* died. I needn't stay there long, but I would like to go to Paris.'

She encountered Grandfather's severest frown. 'I said it's out of the question, Madeleine. I agree that you need a change, and we can maybe look at a trip away for you and Grandmama. Or you could take up a secretarial post locally. It would give you something to do. Both Grandmama and myself agree that you should have some occupation.'

Madeleine armed herself, and continued. Force came from somewhere, maybe from Paris, and her voice came stronger. 'You know I don't need your permission to go, don't you? I just don't have any money, that's all. But if necessary I could sell *Maman*'s jewellery to pay for my ticket.'

There was an astonished silence. Then the storm really broke, lashing at her across the table. What on earth did she think she was going to get up to in Paris? She was nearly twenty-two years old. It was about time she thought about settling down, not gadding about. She was ungrateful. How could she even think of selling her mother's jewellery? Such a terrible thing to think of doing.

Madeleine sat tight through the storm, finding it all surprisingly easy. She could hear Robert's voice, very calm and positive, and it pushed her grandfather's rantings into their proper place. Her own voice when it came was equally calm. 'All right,' she answered them. 'Then I'll go to London first and stay with Cicely or Uncle, and work to raise my fare. I'm very sorry, but you can't stop me.'

And still the storm raged. That girl Cicely! Fast and cheap, that's what she was. What kind of people did Madeleine think she would meet in her company?

'I don't know!' Madeleine spat the words, no longer calm. 'That's the point! I don't know any other company than the people I meet here. I'm twenty-one and have no experience of life at all. I wear tweeds and flat shoes, and the world is passing me by. You *lived* when you were young. You didn't think *Tante* Louise was unsuitable then. You seemed to spend most of your lives in Paris.' Madeleine shivered involuntarily, shaken by her own anger, and deliberately paused, calmed herself. 'It's my turn. I want some life, and I'm going to stay with *Tante* Louise – with my own family. What could be more normal?'

There was silence then, which was eventually broken by Grandmama. Her voice was surprisingly gentle.

'So much heat, Madeleine! It's been such a short time since your poor mother passed away. You are not yourself, and I can fully understand that you want a change of scene. You must miss her so much – we all do. Leave us now, and we'll discuss it some more. There's no need to be hasty.'

Madeleine looked across at Grandmama and tried to speak, but her throat constricted and no sound came. She brushed tears from her eyes and walked blindly out of the room, out of the house, onto the small patch of lawn in front of the house. There she stopped, the cold March wind whipping the tears from her eyes, chilling her wet cheeks. She took deep breaths, gulping the cold air, feeling it cooling her throat, opening her lungs, expelling the dead, suffocated air of the dining room. She walked through the trees to the little stream which ran to the side of the house, and followed the path to the bridge, and to the road. The trees were bare of leaves, hard and angular, and their barrenness suited her mood. As she reached the bridge, the deep chill of the air by the stream was wonderful, crisp, unsullied. She walked down to the stream, and bent to wash her face. The icy water hit her cheeks and she laughed out loud, for the first time in months. She crossed the bridge and walked briskly down the road, heading for the open fields, every step a liberation, and skipped like a child as she looked up at the leaden sky, allowing the wind to tousle her hair and blow around her uncovered neck.

Whatever happened now, she knew she would go. They could rant and rave but she had breached the ramparts and Grandmama's tone alone told her they knew it. For years she'd let *Maman*'s quiet submissiveness be her guide, watched as *Maman* saved her energy and held her ground only for her children, only for the biggest, most momentous things in their lives. She'd copied her, but it had never suited her character, and now she was a new creature. Her father's daughter! *Tante* Louise's niece! Cicely's cousin! All of these people, yet more importantly, she was herself, and she was about to find out who that person really was.

She walked for hours, not thinking too much, just content to know that she herself had made this move. It was enough for the moment. Later they could tell her what they had decided in these further discussions of theirs. Either they would pay her fare and send her, in which case she would have to put up with tiresome weeks of interference before she finally boarded any train, or they would remain immovable, in which case she would simply go around them and sell the jewellery her mother would never have grudged her. The latter would be simpler really. She could then just leave, maybe stay with Cicely while she arranged tickets, a passport, then go independently to Paris. The mere thought was as exhilarating as the wind.

Night fell early in March, and by the time she made her way back along the too familiar country roads to the house a half-moon was trying to show itself through the clouds. She'd left the house without a coat or gloves, and only by tucking them into her jumper could she keep any feeling in her hands. Her feet were also as cold as ice, and she knew that the rest of her would feel the chill as soon as she went indoors. But the cold was like a triumph, vital, rejuvenating. It quickened the breath and strangely fired up the heart.

She entered the house by the side door, looking for the first time at her watch. They would already be at dinner. Life was marked at the moment by a series of mealtime encounters, it seemed, by the monotony of the round of breakfasts, lunches and dinners all served in that same green dining room with its oppressive mahogany sideboards and the huge table of which the three diners occupied one tiny end. Casserole for lunch, what would it be for dinner? Fish, probably. Grandmama liked to eat light foods in the evening. They never ate badly at Forsham, Madeleine acknowledged. Grandmama was French, after all. It was the predictability of each meal, and the repetitive conversations, and the long silences, and the criticisms hovering in waiting for any misplaced word which had annihilated Madeleine for years. Now she went in head high and smiling. Who cared, after all?

CHAPTER THREE

The Gare du Nord was teeming with people at the rush hour as Madeleine and Robert hauled their cases off the train from Boulogne and looked around for a porter. At first sight the station looked just the same as any busy London station: dark, grimy, metallic, smelling of oil and dirt. Even the passengers looked the same with the harried look of passengers everywhere. Madeleine felt a pang of disappointment, but as the porter reached them, muttering in French, pulling on a chewed cigarette, a whiff of French tobacco came towards her and she felt a surge of excitement. Further along the platform café tables spilt into the alleyway, and as she followed the trolley towards them she was hit by the smell of intense, freshly ground coffee. Men in work clothes leant on the café bar's counter drinking what she thought must be pastis, cloudy and yellow in thin, straight, painted glasses. Workers in overalls stood alongside raincoated office workers with an eye on their watches, not a word passing between them. Madeleine slowed to pass the tables, stepping around a child playing on the grubby floor, his mother in furs, gazing intently at her companion over something long and mint-coloured in a tall glass. Her husband? Her lover? Madeleine felt as though she was moving in slow motion through a long-lost world.

Robert strode along before her alongside the porter. She'd made it to France more easily than she could have imagined after all, but the elders had insisted she mustn't travel alone, and had sent Robert with her on the outward journey. Not that she was complaining. It was wonderful to have Robert with her, and he too had a past and a present to discover in France.

At the end of the platform, behind the barrier, she could already see Cousin Solange, standing out in an elegant cream suit in front of all the rest of the waiting crowd. Beside her, with a hand lightly holding her elbow, stood a rather round, pepper-haired man with a small moustache, whom Madeleine supposed must be Solange's husband Bernard. She waved, and Solange surged forward until she was nearly touching the barrier.

As Madeleine came through, Solange wafted her into an embrace. 'Madeleine. I would hardly have known you. How wonderful to see you. And this must be . . . oh!'

Solange's eyes gaped, and as Madeleine looked from her to Robert she suddenly realised why. Solange had never met Robert, who was so much the image of the young Luis whom Solange and her family had known. They could expect this level of astonishment from everyone who had known their father. She hastened to explain, with an extraordinary flush of pleasure.

'This is Robert, Solange. He is very like our father, I know. Is that what surprised you?'

'Surprised me? It's astonishing!' said Solange. She reached out to Robert and smiled rather shakily. 'Robert you are very welcome. My mother will be incredulous when she sees you. Your father was such a distinctive-looking man, so . . . so *broad*, and dark and handsome. Oh, I sound stupid, but you are Luis. You are simply Luis.'

Robert smiled, and allowed himself to be enfolded in a perfumed embrace. Solange kissed him on both cheeks and then turned to her husband.

'Bernard, these are my cousins Madeleine and Robert. You know their history, but you just *can't* know what it means to see this young man, so much the image of that astonishing father of his.'

Bernard came forward, gracefully manoeuvring past Robert, and first kissed Madeleine on both cheeks. 'No doubt, Solange, but my first welcome must be for this beautiful young woman. How do you do, my dear Madeleine? I have heard so much about you ever since Solange visited London and met you. She has always talked about how much of your father she saw in you also, as well as the beauty of your mother. I only met your mother once, but I will never forget how lovely she was.'

He turned to Robert, and shook his hand. 'Robert, it is good to meet you at last. You are very welcome. You are both very welcome.'

Madeleine drank in the moment, not wanting to move. These people welcomed them because of their parents, not in spite of them. There were memories here which they could explore, and goodwill which radiated and warmed them. She looked across at Robert again, looking for the mirror of her excitement, and caught a reflected smile.

'Let's go,' said Solange. 'My mother is waiting anxiously to see you.'

A short taxi ride took them through some of the most famous streets of Paris. They swept down the rue Lafayette, and on into the Boulevard Haussmann. The evening was drawing in, and behind the avenue of trees the department stores were all lit up, revealing a quick glimpse of chic luxury as the taxi followed the slow-moving evening traffic. The Arc de Triomphe loomed ahead.

'Look!' Madeleine breathed at Robert, as they drove past the arch, and on into the Avenue Victor Hugo.

'I know,' he replied, with suppressed excitement.

On down the Victor Hugo and into the sixteenth arrondissement, where *Tante* Louise had her apartment. Madeleine had known that the family lived in the heart of fashionable Paris, but was awed now that she was here.

'Don't be too impressed,' said Solange, as they drew up outside the beautiful old stone apartment block, with its elaborate wrought iron balconies framing every window. 'This apartment has belonged to the family for a very long time, and those who had the money to buy it are long dead. Even the furniture, which is quite beautiful, was mainly bought by my grandfather.'

Access to the second-floor apartment was by an

ancient lift with a grill which had to be pulled across and clicked shut before the lift would move. In previous times, Madeleine guessed, there would have been a man operating the lift for residents, just as the desk in the entrance hall would have had a permanent concierge. The hallways were still perfectly maintained, with immaculate black and white tiling on the floors and lovely green glass tiling on the bottom half of the walls.

As the lift doors opened onto the second floor, Bernard stepped out ahead of Madeleine, and held out a hand to guide her quite unnecessarily over the lip of the grill door. She took the hand with a rush of feminine pleasure. He led her to a panelled wooden door and rang the bell. A maid quickly answered, dressed in a black dress and white apron, and ushered them into a high-ceilinged entrance hall. Madeleine took in the marble flooring, a side table from the early nineteenth century, possibly Bourbon, she thought, and a Sèvres vase painted in gold. There was an old landscape as well, a hunting scene with graceful, long-limbed hounds. The whole scene was so elegant, so impossibly French, that it reminded Madeleine of idealised Hollywood visions of Paris, except that here was *Tante* Louise, emerging from a door facing them, busy and tiny and mobile as ever, her face a mass of tiny lines which framed her thin lips and nose, and almost seemed to be holding her bird-like little face together.

'My children!' she cried, both hands outstretched as she took Madeleine then Robert into her arms. 'My Robert, oh my goodness, Robert! Why, I haven't seen you since you were just a baby. I knew then that we didn't need to worry about Luis's heritage. You were his image then as you are now.'

She smiled triumphantly at Solange, who was murmuring agreement. 'You didn't ever see Robert as a baby, did you? You must have had a surprise when you saw him today. I remember Elise had a photo of Luis kneeling on the floor in the apartment in Vermeilla looking down into Robert's eyes. Robert was just a baby and lying on a rug, looking up at Luis – the two of them in profile. The likeness was stunning. I don't suppose you remember your father, do you Robert? No? Well then, we have much to talk about. But first, come in all of you. It is the aperitif hour, and we have much to celebrate.'

She led them into the drawing room, ushered Madeleine to a cream-coloured *chapeau de gendarme* armchair, and drew Robert down next to her on an embroidered sofa on ebony legs, which looked as though it would never carry his weight.

'We'll have a glass of champagne shall we, my dears, to celebrate? Or would you prefer a whisky, Robert?'

She talked effortlessly and without pauses, about their journey, about the weather, about what Paris could offer them as entertainment at this season.

'Maria Callas is here, at the Opera House. You must go. She's so much at her best just now. Rossini's *Tosca*, that's what you must see. And, of course, you must go to the cinema. There's that amusing little film by Jacques Tati that everyone's so delighted about. Solange must find you some young people to go to that with. Such a lovable character, Monsieur Hulot. I saw the last film, a few years ago. The style's really rather modern for me, but terribly clever and such fun.'

'And then, of course, you have to see Paris. Do you like art? Oh, I am glad. So sad to come to Paris and not love its art. We are just coming into the season of major exhibitions. Such a good time for you to visit. And the weather is improving daily. It felt almost like summer yesterday. Robert, how long can you stay with us?'

'No more than ten days, unfortunately, *Tante* Louise. I'm on holiday just now from Oxford, but the new term begins at the end of April.'

Tante Louise nodded approvingly. 'Of course, you are at Oxford University! Clever young man. Well, we'll just have to make the most of your short time to do all the essential things, then later we can do fashions and the like with Madeleine. Not so, Solange? We've been looking forward to having a young lady around again to shop with. Oh, we'll keep you busy, never you fear.'

Over a delicate dinner of fish rich in wine and butter, conversation became more serious. Solange wanted to know about their mother's illness. Had there been warning? How come the news of her illness had only reached them in Paris a few weeks before her death? They would have travelled to see her. There was so much still to be said between them. It filled Madeleine with anger, because she knew that although her mother's illness had been diagnosed very late, the elders had taken even longer to communicate the news to Paris, leaving no time for any new rapprochement. But there would be no purpose served now by telling them this, so she explained simply how no one had known until very near the end, how Elise had kept her symptoms hidden from them all.

'I don't think she really wanted to know what was wrong with her, or to be treated,' she said. '*Maman* was such a private person. She said so little and imposed so little that I don't think anyone thought to question why she was fading away before our eyes. She just didn't want to fight, you see.'

Louise was astonished. 'But Elise was a fighter! She was an Amazon. She may have looked soft and pink and feminine, but she could take on the world!'

Robert put down his coffee cup with a start. He gaped at Louise, and she looked back at him with equal surprise. Robert flushed rather self-consciously, and straightened his little cup, which had landed at an awkward angle. He paused deliberately and then smiled at *Tante* Louise.

'Forgive me, *Tante* Louise. We didn't know this Elise,' he explained. 'My mother in later life was not the same person we think you knew. She seemed to be a beaten person after my father died. But we know there was more to her than we knew. We have so much we want to learn about her. We don't know anything, you see. Nothing about her youth, or about her and Papa, or her life in France. She didn't talk about it, ever.'

'She used to talk, though,' Madeleine interposed. 'When we first arrived back in England from Vermeilla we talked all the time about Papa, and France, and all of you, and all the people we'd left behind in the village. We talked about when we would go home, and I used to make up stories about what we would do, and she would laugh at me a little. Robert doesn't remember.'

'And then it stopped?' Louise wanted to know.

'Yes, when we got the letter telling us Papa had died. It's all a bit hazy to me, because for a few weeks I didn't really see *Maman*. She was too ill to see anyone, I think. Nobody told me anything, but I wasn't allowed near her room, and I spent all my time with Robert and his nanny. I didn't know then that Papa had been killed. *Maman* told me that later, and she told me he had been very brave and we should be proud of him, and she let me cry, and held me, but that was all. After that, all our little chats about Papa and the friends stopped, and if I asked any questions she would just smile – you know that soft smile of hers – and change the subject. And I soon learnt not to ask any more.'

'And her character changed as well?'

Madeleine nodded, and Louise nodded in her turn.

'It doesn't surprise me so much. I wondered, that day in London, to see Elise so quiet at first, and sort of faded, almost. But then she became more animated, and more like her old self, so I stopped asking myself questions.'

Madeleine sighed. 'It was wonderful that day. It's the only time I can remember since I was tiny that *Maman* came to life again. But it was only with you, and it was over as soon as we left you. You even managed to make Grandmama human that day.'

Solange looked towards Robert.

'And you weren't even with us that day in London. You don't even have any memory of your mother as the happy woman we knew. For you that's very sad.'

Robert took time to answer. 'She was good to us, don't get us wrong. *Maman* always loved us and looked after us. And we loved her. She was still a wonderful woman. But sometimes I feel she deprived us of our roots, and she even died without leaving us anything. No letters, no token even, no link to our past. She left us nothing but questions.'

Tante Louise and Solange exchanged glances. It was Louise who spoke.

'And you would like us to give you some answers?'

Robert nodded. 'It's what we've been hoping for.'

'And what we were expecting, *n'est-ce pas*, Solange? We knew you would want to hear about Elise and Luis, and we've been talking about them a lot ourselves, knowing you were on your way here. It's such a pleasure to talk about them and bring back their memory. But we don't know anything about what happened to them in the war, you know.'

'Can you tell us about Paris, about that summer here in your house?' asked Robert. 'It was the start of it all, wasn't it?'

Solange looked across at Louise. 'Yes, that much we can certainly tell you. So, who tells, *Maman*? You or me?'

'You tell, my dear. I'll listen, and maybe add something if I feel it. But first the cognac, Bernard. Let us be comfortable.'

Bernard, benign and leisurely, rose from the table and brought a tray with two heavy crystal decanters and glasses from a corner table, offered cognac and chartreuse, and waved his cigar box towards Robert, who declined. The cut glass reflected little glimmers of light from the chandelier, and gave off small chinks of sound as decanter touched goblet. There was hardly a word spoken, just the simple words of service and acceptance. Then Bernard leant back in his chair, raised his glass to them all, and once more to Madeleine, then settled back unhurriedly to light his cigar. Louise waited, took a sip of her own little glass of green chartreuse, and then turned to Solange.

'Now start, my daughter.'

Madeleine felt quite breathless, like an excited child at story time. She leant forward in her chair, and Solange caught her eye and flashed her a conspiratorial grin.

'Once upon a time,' she began, '*il était une fois*. There was a lovely young woman, half English, half French, who looked English but moved like a Frenchwoman. She came to Paris as part of her "coming out", to widen her social circle, to learn a little sophistication. She was so funny, Elise, always laughing – laughing at the French and at the English, at any stuffiness, at French men and their flattery. We had a lot of fun, and I suppose we were as silly as most girls our age at that time. I was two years older than Elise and thought I was much more mature, and I used to tell her off for giggling so much.'

'But she was intelligent too, and she knew she'd been brought up in a narrow British circle, and she wanted to learn. It was 1935, and Hitler had just become Führer and begun militarisation, we were still in depression and there was so much poverty, and nobody knew whether to be fascist or communist. *Maman* always had a lot of artists and writers among her friends, and mostly they were communists or liberals. But we also knew a lot of diplomats and financiers living in this *quartier*, and some of them toyed quite openly with Fascist ideas. It was a revelation to Elise because her own parents – your grandparents – were simple, old-fashioned conservative thinkers, and she had never before taken part in much debate. She never stopped asking questions, and still knew how to laugh at some of the more fanciful ideas our friends came out with.'

'Maryse was just the same, though, when she was young,' Louise interjected.

Madeleine started. She'd been lost in thoughts about her mother. It had been a long time since she had heard her grandmother called Maryse. Everyone in Forsham called her Marie. Madeleine wondered what her grandmother really thought about her English adopted name. She looked up at *Tante* Louise, focusing on her eyes as if the answer would be there.

'Oh yes,' continued Louise, 'Maryse was just like Elise. Always laughing, teasing, testing people a little. Never taking them too seriously. Nobody listened to young ladies then, but Maryse would say things which floored people, and then when they looked at her she would smile so sweetly and move on as if she hadn't said anything at all. Nobody ever knew whether she was really an impudent young madam or just an innocent. You can imagine how I adored her. I was four years younger than her, still a child really, and there was this beautiful, fashionable cousin who seemed to hold the whole world in the palm of her hand. What fun she was. And she stood up for us children, too. She made us feel we could have a voice.'

'What on earth did she see in Grandfather, then?' Robert's voice was bitter.

'Oh, he was just wonderful! No, really! He came back with her to Paris after her London season, in 1906, I think, or was it 1907, and we children were completely captivated. He was older than her, of course, and quite serious, but he was so handsome, and tall, and held himself so upright, and we loved his funny way of speaking French. He didn't mind when we giggled, and he gave us sweets and presents, and he treated me like a young lady, which was wonderful at the age of fourteen. Everyone was in love with his English manners and that tantalising reserve. Maryse's *Maman* and Papa were not fully convinced about him at first, because he didn't have family money, you know, but everyone knew how dazzling his career was, and they allowed themselves to be won over. And Maryse was head over heels in love with him. You see, he listened to her, unlike all the so gallant French men we knew, and he didn't just pander to her like some wayward child. He was really proud of her intelligence and she loved it.'

Madeleine watched Robert's face, his frown of concentration, and thought they must both be following the same thought process, trying to match the young couple being described with the elders they knew. But it made sense, she realised. She'd always known about the elders' romance and some snippets of their times in Paris. She hadn't realised why Grandmama had been attracted to him, but of course, he must have seemed so different from the complacent Gallic suitors who surrounded the young Maryse. And that deferential seriousness could so easily turn over time into the crotchety, captious old man Grandfather had become. And as for Grandmama, she pandered to her husband but she mainly pleased herself in her life, and was not at all dominated by him. And she still charmed their neighbours. She was just a little lacking in heart. Madeleine voiced her thoughts.

'Wasn't she always a bit self-centred, though, the Maryse you knew? Was she warm or was she a bit cold at heart?'

Tante Louise took time to reply, deep in thought, perhaps casting back for memories.

'I suppose she may have been a bit cool. She was good to us children – fun, you know. There was joy in her. And when I came out into society she was wonderful about advice, fashions, shopping, how to handle my mother; all that kind of thing. And she adored her children when they came. The two boys were her idols. She didn't spend a lot of time with them, but that was so normal in those days. I think they felt loved. Your mother came later, of course. She was born during the war, in 1916. I was already married by then and had Solange. When your mother was born it was Paul who was over the moon. He loved his little daughter, and when she was little he lavished attention on her. But Maryse preferred the boys. She loved their cheek and their decisiveness. She used to tell me she really pitied me for only having a daughter.'

She sighed and shook her head. 'Losing her two sons dried her up, I think. All that joy was extinguished. But I wish you had known that side of her.'

Solange interjected, 'But Elise was all warmth and heart.'

'Oh yes,' Louise's face softened, 'Elise was a very loving child. She was always my favourite niece. She gave and she gave and she gave. And she still had all of Maryse's joy.'

'Yes,' she repeated, with a wistful smile, 'Elise was wonderful.'

The evening was now growing late. The coffee on the table was cold, the decanter stoppered, but still nobody moved from the table. Bernard sat at the head, comfortably silent, the drift of smoke from his cigar almost stationary above their heads. Robert sat opposite, leaning back in his chair, and between them the three women had drawn in their chairs, and sat forward, arms on the table, *Tante* Louise's hands fluttering as always when she spoke.

With curtains drawn and side lamps shaded, the dining room was softened from its usual sharp, classic elegance to a space of intimate secrets, where the corners of the room were unknown shadows, and only the rounded centre breathed warm and alive. They had all fallen silent now, each lost for a moment in their own private bubble of thought. Madeleine longed to ask more questions, but was afraid to disturb the stillness and break the spell. Finally Robert leant forward and took Louise's hand softly in his.

'How did Elise meet our father?' he asked simply.

Louise looked across at Solange who took up the thread again, equally simply. 'It was here. In this apartment. Everyone knew Luis that summer. It was 1935, remember. Everyone was talking about Spain, and Luis was the revolutionary, the one everyone wanted to listen to.'

'Why was he in Paris?'

'You don't know?'

'We know nothing. That's what I was telling you. We've never been told anything.' Robert's voice was edged with frustration. 'We know he fought against Fascism, but 1935 was before Franco, before the Civil War. Why wasn't he in Spain, helping build the Republic? Why was he in a Paris drawing room?'

'Not any Paris drawing room, Robert. My drawing room! But you are right – he didn't want to be here. Oh, my good Lord, no, Luis was only here because he was driven.'

CHAPTER FOUR

'Why am in a Parisian drawing room?' Luis asked himself for the twentieth time that month. It had all seemed so different before, Paris, so charming, so elegant. And this house, Louise's house, was a haven of good taste and intellect. He'd always loved coming here, and a young, handsome Spanish journalist with a secret smile at his own charisma was guaranteed a place among these silks and knotted cravats. But that was when he was in Paris before. Before Spain had stood up and declared her freedom, before Alfonso had gone, and De Rivera, and the people's pact had set them all on that mad path of hope and betrayal, and Luis had gone home to join the madness and the dream, that genuine, hard-earned dream. How had it all gone rotten so quickly? Only three years into the Republic, and the right wing were stripping his country, his Catalonia, of its new identity. Like teenagers, they were all still trying their new muscles, striking poses, practising being independent, and then it was gone, and it all became deathly serious, fighting now with adult fear and resolve for what they had only just come to know, and the army turning on them, killing, beating, putting the constitution behind bars. And yet there was still a republic, still elections to come, still so much work to be done. But not by him – that was the bitterest pill. The newspaper was gone, Miquel and Felip were in prison, others had disappeared, and Luis was on the run, back in Paris, not by choice this time, but in exile. He would go back. By God he would go back! This band of right-wing butchers would get their comeuppance soon. But meanwhile, he was here, and the Catalan dream was somewhere on the road behind him, in the ditch, hiding and biding its time as it had done so often in the past.

A young Italian diplomat came towards Luis and then spotted him, and turned to one side, keeping a careful distance. Why did Louise invite these fascists into her house? It was all very well embracing different views of the world, but Mussolini's lackeys?

'Hail, fellow!' a voice boomed in his ear from behind, and Johnny Denton was by his side, large and fat and untidy. He grasped Luis in an eager grip, and Luis grimaced ruefully as he pulled his hand away from the yellow-stained fingers. He grinned.

'Unhand me, you oaf! I can't be seen shaking hands with a raw-faced American who believes that Clark Gable and Mickey Rooney are the new leaders of world culture!'

'Ah,' replied Johnny Denton, 'but some of us journalists

have to earn a humble crust writing about the modern day idols! Not all of us can get away with writing long political tracts and calling them newspaper articles. Which you do, and I'm glad that someone can, though I don't suppose it pays as well as my drivel! I liked your piece today, Luis. You're right about the polarisation of the left and right in Madrid. But the right is weakening, and if the left and centre can work together they'll bring the Republic back on track.'

'Let's hope so,' Luis's voice was grim. 'It's the "if" that worries me. We don't only need all the factions to work together, but the geographical groups as well. The right isn't really weakening, you know. It's weaker in the polls, but that's not necessarily going to stop them. They've got Hitler's example to follow. When someone doesn't agree with you, eliminate them, and damn democracy.'

'But you're not there yet, and there's a spirit in Spain for freedom. It's not Germany!'

'But it's not America either. The Church, tradition, intolerance, corruption – we've got them in spade-loads, and it makes democracy damned hard work.'

Denton smiled. 'Ah yes! Democracy! In America we have democracy, but believe me, there's a whole heap of intolerance hidden among the Hershey bars, and Mamma's apple pie, and God and country!'

'But it's a country that openly embraces sex icons like Mae West and Marlene Dietrich!'

'Mae West from afar, but you wouldn't really introduce her to your mother, not if you were from homely Ohio!

Talking of which, have you seen Louise's young niece, who's just come over from London?'

'More Shirley Temple than Mae West, surely?'

'I don't know, but she has something, a little something behind the eyes that spells passion to me. And believe me, Luis, I know these things!'

Passion? She had passion, Luis discovered. But first the eyes just looked a question at him, an open, conspiratorial question which invited him to answer. It was the openness of a child, through eyes that gazed unprotected as can only those who have never known fear, but there was delicacy there, and understanding, and the instinctive maturity of a woman, and a voice which caressed him unknowingly as she spoke. It seemed to wake his soul.

He'd been asleep for a long time, he realised, as he returned Elise's smile.

'Luis, this is my darling niece, Elise, who has come to visit us from London, to keep Solange company and have some fun this summer.'

She had a perfect smile – soft rose lips, nothing pouting, nothing painted, but the softness made you want to touch, to taste. And there was a sweetness which reached the eyes, deep blue eyes in an English face. She held out her hand and Luis took it and held it.

'You are English, Mademoiselle? I didn't know that Louise had family in England?'

'My cousin,' Louise nodded. 'Dear Elise is her daughter – not a niece at all, I suppose, are you my love? And nor are you English. We have you back here now, and we will send you back home a Frenchwoman!'

Elise laughed. 'Goodness knows what I am, Señor Garriga. A half-breed in both countries, but my mother wishes at least my manners to be French, and so has sent me to live for a few months in the most elegant home in Paris, n'est-ce pas, Tante Louise?'

She didn't speak like a debutante, despite her age. Was it her English education which made her so at ease, or just her nature? And the voice resonated, soft and mellow, like the vibrations of a viola. Luis couldn't resist laughing with her, but then she became serious.

'I read your article today, Señor. Tante Louise tells me you have been a mainstay of the Republic. You make one feel it in your writing – the power of what is there to defend, and the work to be done. You must hate being here.'

No one in Paris ever referred so directly to his exile – the French were so tactful. But Elise's words held a mixture of compassion and interest which held him.

'Not tonight, Mademeoiselle. Tonight I am unexpectedly glad to be in Paris. But you are right about what I am trying to say when I write. If I can make one person feel my urgency, then I have been successful.'

He was still holding her hand, he realised, and she made no move to remove it.

'Will you tell me?' she appealed. 'I believe there's food in the other room. Will you take me through, and tell me?'

'It was a lost cause between those two when they met,' said Louise. 'Within days your father was almost living in our house, and they played no games, made no pretence. We could be around the dinner table, and Luis would look at her, and it was as though he was touching her. He told me she made him feel all things were still possible. "I'm a journalist," he told me, "but with her I am a poet." I didn't really have any reply. But I did worry about what Paul and Maryse would think. They would hardly see him as an eligible husband for their daughter. And there was no doubt that was what Luis and Elise were thinking about, within just a few weeks. They were both essentially such serious people. There wasn't much chance of either of them changing their mind.'

'So what happened?' asked Robert.

'Maryse happened.' Louise's shrug was as eloquent as it was Gallic. 'Maryse came out to Paris to visit, and there was no disguising the romance. Luis made no attempt to hide his feelings. He set out to charm Maryse, and did his best to present himself as a serious, important journalist! He might have succeeded, but she read some of his left-wing work, and then called Paul, and the next thing we knew she was arranging tickets to take Elise home. And then Luis and Elise disappeared.'

'Eloped?'

'Yes, in the best old-fashioned tradition. Paul arrived from England raging, and blowing all colours of hot air. I've never seen anyone so angry in my life. What a scene! I, of course, was completely to blame. They should never have left their daughter in my care, he said. She could ruin herself for all he cared. He would never agree to a marriage, and more and more of the same!' *Tante* Louise allowed herself a wry smile.

'I can just hear him,' Madeleine muttered.

'Yes indeed. There was nothing anyone could do, of course. We had no idea where they'd gone, and gradually it dawned on Paul exactly how powerless he was. Then there came a letter from Elise. She wrote that she and Luis had travelled south to the French border with Spain – to French Catalonia, and that from there Luis was going to continue his writing. He still had contacts, and could write even better from there about the situation in Spain. And she finished the letter by saying that she wanted to marry Luis, but while she was too young to do so without permission she would simply live with him, and indeed was already doing so. I don't think I ever saw Paul as speechless as when he read this. Elise had sent a poste restante address in Perpignan, and Paul went down there and caused all kinds of ructions, but he got nowhere and found no one, so eventually he came back here and gave me a letter to send giving his consent to a marriage. He couldn't bear to contemplate the idea that his daughter was living in a state of sin, let alone that she might have a child out of wedlock. You can have no idea how outrageous your mother's behaviour appeared in those days.'

'Oh yes I can!' breathed Madeleine.

'Yes!' *Tante* Louise gave a small chuckle. 'Well your grandfather couldn't bring himself to send the letter himself, and he told me to send it, and then never to darken his door again, and to tell his daughter the same! Such wonderfully old-fashioned language. Anyway, at last they left, and we were able to contact Elise.'

'My God!' Robert's voice was awed. 'Imagine *Maman* being so bold.'

'Not just bold, joyously so,' Solange assured him. '*Maman* and I went down to Vermeilla to witness Luis and Elise's wedding, and they were ridiculously happy. They'd found this tiny apartment in a little street in Vermeilla, one of those streets where the sun never gets between the buildings, and the apartment had just three rooms, and they cooked in the same room as they lived in. What a muddle everywhere, as well – Elise had never had to take care of herself, or cook, or clean, or wash clothes, and she was hopeless at it. But Luis didn't care, and they had already made friends, and he was in contact with his people over the border, so he felt involved again, and was happy. Elise was simply glowing, wasn't she, *Maman*?'

'Yes.' Louise was less enthusiastic. 'I would have preferred to see them in better circumstances, I must admit. They were so impractical. And soon afterwards Elise became pregnant. I went down to see them again, without Solange, not long before you were born, Madeleine. I was worried, and I begged Elise not to have a baby in that mess.'

'You're surely not going to stay here once the baby is born?'

'But Tante *Louise, you surely don't expect us to move now? What would we do with everything?' Elise waved a hand vaguely around the apartment's one main room, in which every corner was crammed with books and papers.*

'But if you had a bigger apartment you needn't have the mess! There'd be room for all this!'

Elise laughed. 'Yes, but how long do you think it would be before Luis filled the extra space, and it all looked the

71

same? If we can't go to Spain, we may as well stay here!'

Then she laughed again at Louise's expression. For Louise nothing could be worse than to think of them moving to Spain. Elise allowed her mind to drift back to that too short visit, just when everything had come right again, and the Popular Front had united and beaten the right wing in the elections, and Catalonia had been declared free again. Luis had been so hopeful for a while, and so happy not to be an exile. They had roamed the streets of Barcelona together hand in hand, Luis introducing her to friends, buildings, shopkeepers, landmarks, comrades, and Elise sometimes hardly knowing which was which, depending on who he was speaking to and in which language. It was exciting, Barcelona, always moving, edgily political. This was the spring of hope, and everyone wanted to believe.

'Could you live here, vida meva?' His eyes had coaxed.

'If you help me, I could live anywhere. But you'd have to teach me Catalan, cariño! And I haven't exactly been gifted so far.'

He smiled, and his hand just touched her belly. There was no sign of the pregnancy yet, but the baby was there, a bud of hope, he called it. Their love child, Elise called it.

They walked along the beach by the port, and the early winds of spring pulled at her hair and made her want to run, and pull Luis down onto the sand. But there were morning walkers, and the city moved behind them, so she leant back into him, reaching her hands up and behind her to cradle his head, and he nuzzled her neck, touching his lips just where her hair met the back of her ears.

'Temptress!'

Elise chuckled. 'Wait a few months and I may tempt you less!' She drew his hands around her stomach, and he trailed them from her breasts to the line of her thighs.

'What would your mother say?'

'That the siren had corrupted her son.'

'I've always wanted to be a siren!'

'Well you failed, my temptress, for you are Hera, and you bring nothing but love.'

They visited his mother, in the mountain village of Sant Galdric, where their car was the only transport except for the baker's van. One long, steep street bordered by faded stone houses, and brown, blistered paintwork which Luis swore had never changed since his childhood. Children played in front of open doorways, but otherwise the place seemed lifeless to Elise. Where was everyone, she wondered? In France, in Vermeilla, everyone moved, and met outside, and gossiped, and intrigued.

'Oh, there's plenty of that here, don't worry!' Luis told her. 'But times have been troubled, and nobody knows who to trust. People have learnt to do their gossiping indoors.'

His mother, thin and wiry, with his deep eyes, shed tears and clung to him, touching him compulsively throughout their visit.

'Now you can come home,' she repeated again and again, fluttering around him, and around Elise, talking about the baby, the future. 'But keep him away from politics. It does no good, and these Republicans, they just want to close our churches, and nothing is any better than the old days.'

'No, Mòmia,' Luis's voice caressed her as he disagreed.

'Don't be fooled into thinking that way. That's what the right-wing parties in Madrid want you to believe. No real Republican will ever interfere with your religion, but they want the people to run the country, not the clergy and the army. We'll make mistakes in the Republic, but they're honest ones, and we will always put people first, and Catalonia first.'

'He always spoke like that,' Señora Garriga told Elise. She touched her son again and smiled. 'Always so passionate and so political! Maybe one day you'll be proved right, my son. Your brother seems to think so, but all I can say is, it didn't do your sister any good, all that politics.'

A shadow crossed Luis's face. As they'd roamed the Barcelona streets a few days before, he'd told Elise they had to find Vigo's ghost. 'He'll be here somewhere,' he'd insisted – the comrade and best friend who'd married his sister Maria. While Luis escaped Barcelona in 1934, Vigo had been captured, and soon after his release his heart had failed. When they passed the apartment where Vigo and Maria used to live, Luis held Elise's hand compulsively, letting it go with a long breath as they turned the corner. 'They tell me he died at home,' he explained.

And now Maria was in Sant Galdric, and appeared at her mother's house, trailed by her two children. Luis reached out to hold his niece and nephew, and the children looked up at him with a yearning in their eyes which seemed to Elise to sum up Spain for her.

Luis gave Maria money, such as he had, and talked to her about a future together here in Spain. Maria smiled, her *intelligent eyes almost teasing her brother as his infectious enthusiasm rained down on her.*

'Elise is with me in thinking we could move back to Barcelona,' he urged. 'And then you could come back to join us, you and Joana and Josep here.' Luis caressed his niece Joana, a budding blonde beauty who gazed silently at Elise with large, questioning blue eyes. And Elise, who understood only parts of what she heard, smiled back at her and thought, if we come to live in Barcelona, these are people I could learn to love. Together they ate rice soup and mountain cheese, and amid the noise of talk she couldn't follow, Elise felt the peace of Luis's homecoming . . .

'You won't go to Spain now, will you?' Tante Louise's anxious voice penetrated Elise's reverie, and brought her back to the present. She shook her head to clear the memories, and reached down to feel her swollen belly.

'No, don't worry. Six months ago we would have gone, but Luis had work to do here so we had to wait, and now . . . what to do now that Franco has declared war on the Republic? It's Civil War, and in two weeks I'll have a baby. Luis would go still, but I won't go.'

'Thank God!'

'Yes, but it's tough for Luis, finding himself an exile again. So we won't disturb his mess and his books, and we'll let him stay in his little apartment! And now, it's too hot and I'm too fat to cook, so we're eating at the café this lunchtime, meeting Luis and Philippe. But Tante Louise?'

'Yes, my love?'

'Don't pester Luis about moving house. Please?'

'Don't worry, I know when I'm wasting my time. I'm

*outnumbered by a bunch of idealistic fools, and there's no
point in appealing to your friends either. Philippe is as bad
as the rest of you! But I won't drink their hellish local wine
at that café!'*

Elise enfolded her in a hug.

*'Don't worry, ma Tante, Philippe told me he was going
to buy you champagne.'*

'*Tonton* Philippe,' murmured Madeleine, smiling.

'You remember?' asked Louise. 'Your *Tonton* Philippe?
How he loved you, child. You were never off his knee.
Such a kind, lovable man. He was deeply in love with your
mother, of course. Oh, no need to look like that. She wasn't
even aware of it. He was just like a brother to her always,
but I could see it in the way he looked at her.'

'Who was Philippe?' Madeleine asked. 'I remember
him, his face, and his brown jacket and tie, and he had
brown hair and he seemed really tall to me, almost bent
and very thin. But I don't know what he did, where he
came from, whether he was married, or anything.'

'He was the schoolmaster in Vermeilla,' Louise
explained. 'He was your father's greatest friend there. They
were both passionately intellectual, and I think Philippe
had been a bit starved of such company before your father
came to the town. It was just a village, really, but it was big
enough to have its own primary school, and Philippe was
the headmaster. He wasn't from Vermeilla. He was from
Burgundy, I remember, and had discovered Vermeilla while
on a painting holiday, and said he never again wanted
to live without the light of Catalogne. That whole coast

always attracted artists. Anyway, I think Philippe had come to the village a few years before Luis and Elise. He wasn't married, but I often wondered if he was having an affair with the owner of the Café de Catalogne. I can't remember her name.'

'Colette,' cut in Solange. 'I'm sure she was called Colette, and her husband had been injured on the railways.'

'That's right, it was Colette. A real Catalan woman. Handsome, rather than pretty, and olive-skinned. But a nice woman, I thought.'

Madeleine stared at the table, conjuring up images in her mind.

'Was there a floor of brown and yellow tiles with green flowers on them?' she asked.

'My goodness, I don't know! It was certainly very Catalan. Spanish in style, rather than French, really. Can you remember it?' Louise was surprised.

'I don't know. I remember a long bar, and I couldn't see over the counter. It must have been above my head. I don't remember people in it, funnily.' She shook her head. 'Was it a busy place?'

'As busy as every bar, I suppose, my dear. I only went there once or twice. In those days not many women went to the café.'

'Except Colette.'

'Except Colette, of course. And I'm sure that's why people talked about her. It should have been her husband running the bar, of course, but he was an invalid. I think that's why they took on the café, to provide an income after he was injured. Do you remember Colette's little boy?

He would have been a couple of years older than you.'

'I don't remember anyone except Uncle Philippe. Even Papa is really vague to me, and I think I mainly remember him from *Maman*'s photo of him on her dressing table. I do remember holding his hand, though. I think we must have been walking along the street, and then I remember him helping me up the stairs. Was our apartment up some windy stairs?'

'Too many stairs!' Louise's voice was eloquent.

'Then that's it. And we had a stove that burnt wood. Tell Robert we had a stove, because he doesn't believe me!'

'Yes, my dear, there was a stove. It could be pretty cold in that street in winter. And the winds! The Tramontane blows down from the Pyrenees, and freezes the bones. Or the sea wind comes off the Mediterranean and brings rain and everything gets damp, even inside the house.' *Tante* Louise shivered. 'I was always glad to get back to Paris.'

'That's not fair, *Maman*!' Solange was indignant. 'When we went down for the wedding it was September and it was beautiful, after the summer heat, and everyone so happy, with the grape-picking under way, and a good harvest. And there were no smelly fishermen because they were all in the vineyards helping out! There were even some holidaymakers, remember? And artists painting by the beach.'

Louise smiled. 'Solange is right, of course. It was later that I was there in winter. It's a beautiful place, and you all had a real life there. I just used to worry about Elise and you children, but I knew I had no right to interfere.'

Madeleine watched them, smiling in return. Elise and

Luis, Philippe and Colette; they were all so near, it seemed.

'How old would Philippe have been?' she asked.

Solange considered. 'Around the same age as your father, I suppose, or no, perhaps a few years more. Maybe in his mid thirties by then, or a little more. Why?'

'That means that he must be in his late fifties now. He may be still working as a teacher, and perhaps still in the same school. He'll be someone we can find. Philippe and Colette!' Madeleine felt a growing excitement. 'I bet they're still alive and still in Vermeilla. And it's just a village. They'll be easy to find.'

'Find?' Louise was stunned. 'You want to find them?'

'Of course we want to find them! We've spent our whole lives to date in ignorance about what happened to our parents. We left France in a hurry in the war and left Papa behind, and all we know is that he was killed. As Robert said, *Maman* didn't even leave any letters. Robert and I need to know, *Tante* Louise. We need to know about our father. Please, you must understand. Robert has to go back to England soon, but after he leaves, I want to go down to Vermeilla, just me, on my own, and find our past so that we can simply know.' The room was silent. Louise's hands were suddenly still and her eyes frozen in what could have been horror, while Solange just gazed at Madeleine, her face emptied of all expression. Then Bernard leant forward, shifting his comfortable weight in his chair, and spoke for the first time since serving the cognac.

'Of course you must, my child. I can quite see why you want to go,' he said, his voice interested and thoughtful.

'It is quite normal that you should want to know more. Louise, I think we should help the child.'

Louise turned on him.

'What are you saying, Bernard? You call her a child, and that's the only sensible thing you've said. Madeleine, my dear, you have just today arrived in Paris, and your grandparents kept you tied very close to their home, didn't they? You've been very protected and I don't think you understand anything about what you're saying. You can't just head off, a girl alone at your age, to look for people who may no longer exist, without any contacts or invitation. It's such a strange idea! Stay here with us. You can discover Paris, make some friends – even work, if you like. But to head down to Vermeilla now? It's just not feasible. Wait a while, if you like, and maybe Bernard could go down with you, when he has time, or better still, we could write to the village mayor at Vermeilla to ask if Philippe is still in the village. But to go down there now, on your own? My dear, it just won't do!'

Madeleine felt her heart sink. *Tante* Louise's view of her didn't seem to differ much from her grandfather's. Was she really so useless, so unformed, so incapable? The glow of the evening, and its easy, companionable reminiscences, shrivelled cold before her. Cousin Cicely came to mind, with her worldly independent life in London. And Peter, with his serenely arrogant assurance. Madeleine felt like a silly child caught trying to buy cigarettes, unfit to join the adult world.

Was it so stupid to want to go to Vermeilla? But why not? Why was this so difficult? To *Tante* Louise Vermeilla was an insignificant, coarse fishing village a thousand kilometres from the sophistications of Paris, but for Madeleine Vermeilla was her birthplace, her only real past, and she felt more strongly than ever that she needed to stand on its soil in order to grow.

You want me to grow up? Then let me go. And let me go now, while I have escaped from England and no one is looking for me. I've been imprisoned – don't do it to me again.

She struggled for the words to make them understand.

'*Tante* Louise, I would love to discover Paris. I don't mean to be ungrateful. But I have something else I need to discover first, for me and for Robert. It has become very important to us now that *Maman* is gone. And I know I am inexperienced, but I can as easily take a train as anyone else and visit a small village which holds my roots.'

'And if they don't want to know you?' The question was from Solange, not hostile, but concerned. 'If after all these years the Garriga family has been forgotten in Vermeilla, since your mother never returned there? What will you do then?'

'Why, then I'll come back! I'll behave like a tourist for a few days, see the area where I was born, and then return to Paris. I only have money to go for a short while, anyway. I'm not planning to set up house!'

It was Bernard who spoke up again now, measured and reflective as before.

'I don't think a small village will quite have forgotten your family. After all, it has only been fourteen years since the liberation. But they may not know anything much about how Luis died, if he was up in the hills with the resistance, as I think he was. You say it was Philippe who wrote to tell your mother? Then they know at least the bare bones, and to my mind enough people will still be there in Vermeilla to talk to you about your parents. Your father did a lot of high-profile work down there. It's that you want, I think, more than anything else – to hear about your parents, and to feel your roots again? Well, I think you're right.'

Louise shook her head in dismay, and Bernard moved smoothly on to change the subject. But later, as Bernard and Solange were leaving, Madeleine overheard more agitated discussion in the hallway. Bernard's very rounded tones sounded loud and clear.

'Those two children have been deprived of all the history and background most people take for granted. And that girl has eyes which are shaded for fear of defeat. But in this she has determination, and that's why we need to help her. You've got a couple of weeks to work on her if you want to, but I don't advise it. She'll go anyway. But if you help her to go, she'll come back to you, and who knows, she may have some of the light of the Mediterranean about her.'

Through the open doorway Madeleine caught a glimpse of Bernard holding Solange's coat for her to step into, and then Solange turned her head, and said with wry amusement, 'The light of the Mediterranean seems to have got into you tonight, Bernard! But I am glad you have fallen for Elise's daughter. If we can make her smile like Elise, then you'll be right and I'll be grateful. So we'll do as you suggest, and if she falls into the sea, we can always send you down to fish her out! *Bonne nuit, Maman*. Have fun with the children. We'll make the most of these two weeks, and then we'll be very brave and let the little Madeleine follow her mother, *n'est-ce pas?*'

CHAPTER FIVE

The little, old-fashioned train rattled through the hills of southern France, wending its way past deep canyons and strange rock formations, opening out to give broader views of the mountains occasionally, green and hazy in the late afternoon sun. They had passed Toulouse, and Carcassonne, with its medieval city, and according to Madeleine's map she should soon be able to see the sea. She had been travelling since dawn, and had become almost part of the rat-a-tat, rat-a-tat of the train's motion, bracing herself with her fellow passengers automatically when they swung corners around the mountains, shifting her buttocks uncomfortably from time to time on the hard, leather bench.

She had changed trains twice, and walked platforms whenever stops permitted to breathe in the sun on sleepy platforms with troughs of flowers and empty benches. The

84

further south they reached, the sleepier the platforms, and the less baggage and shouting and engine noise. Her fellow passengers also changed. The commuters and harassed mothers were replaced by peasant women in grey-black skirts and flowered aprons, their square, weathered, rather beautiful faces expressionless as they sat next to their husbands, mahogany-skinned farmers of lean build and bent legs. Conversation between them was muttered and almost incomprehensible to Madeleine, heavily nasal and guttural, and with their mouths hardly seeming to move. It was depressing to think she was heading further south, to Catalonia, where her correct Parisian French might turn out to be quite useless.

Her seat was next to the window, and she was hemmed in by canvas bags of shopping and farm produce. Her neat, old-fashioned suitcase, brown leather with black stitching, sat on the rack above her head, lost among the jumble of country possessions which spilt over onto the floor. There was no chance of leaving the carriage to walk in the corridor. She shifted once more in her seat, stretched her legs between a large black trunk and the legs of the woman opposite, who smiled at her with surprising friendliness, and closed her eyes to the Cathar country outside. She was weary, and anxious to arrive, and wanted above all to see the Mediterranean appear before them. Soon, soon . . .

Only yesterday she had said goodbye to Robert at the Gare du Nord. Ten days with him in Paris, and they had packed the days full of sights and sounds. They had eaten at St Michel, taken coffee at the Café Procope, strolled down the Boulevard St Germain and along the banks of the Seine, visited Notre Dame, the Louvre, the Eiffel Tower. All of the obvious tourist attractions, plus all the galleries, and the obligatory visit to the Opéra to see Callas sing. They had bought horrendously expensive, handmade, violet-centred chocolates at a *salon de thé*, soaked up smells in a cheese shop and charcuterie on the left bank, and everywhere they went they stopped for coffee, to sit on the terraces and pavements and watch Paris go by.

At Montmartre Robert had insisted on running all the way up the steps to the top, and Madeleine had followed, protesting but laughing, for once happy that her unfashionable skirt and shoes were so much easier to move in than those of the chic Parisian ladies who watched her with haughty amusement. From Montmartre the whole of Paris fell around them, a panorama which was nevertheless small enough to cup in your hands. The city noise was distant, and the little web of streets around the church was an intimate village. If ever she lived in Paris, Madeleine thought, it would have to be here. They drank aperitifs in the square, bathed in sunshine, surrounded by the artists who peddled second-rate portraits. Lunch was disappointing – tourists' fare at inflated prices – but it didn't matter. The moment was as perfect as it needed to be.

Tante Louise had wanted Madeleine to stay at least long enough after Robert's departure to plunge into Paris fashions and meet some more of their Paris friends, but she was determined to make the trip south before her grandparents started asking any questions. Already she had received a letter from Peter, wanting to know when she would be returning to England, and suggesting that he might come to visit her if she decided to stay on in Paris. She had replied to put him off, but there was no time to lose in making this journey. She didn't need high Paris fashion to visit a small Catalan fishing village, but she bought some dresses for the sun – sleeveless dresses with narrow waists and swirling skirts which made her feel strangely daring and feminine. And she allowed Louise's chic hairdresser to tame her long hair into gentle curls which swept off her face and over her shoulders, and which Robert, almost awed, said made her look like Grace Kelly. Then she left most of her belongings with Louise, bringing only enough clothes for a few days, and her mother's jewellery case, which now never left her side. This was just a quick trip, she told herself whenever she felt nervous.

Bernard had taken care of all arrangements, with admirable efficiency, discovering what hotels were available in Vermeilla – one or two new tourist hotels, it seemed, now that the French had discovered the Mediterranean for holidays, and a couple of older hotels, one of which, the hopefully named Hotel Bon Repos, had accordingly been booked for her. She was armed with phone numbers of everyone back in Paris in case she got into difficulty – 'I can be there in a day,' Bernard had said to her, at least three times, as they stood at the station this morning.

It wasn't the travel, or managing on her own, which

bothered Madeleine. She was so nervous she could hardly breathe at times, but it was the task ahead, the searches and introductions, the probable failure, the fear of the unknown. It's just a holiday, she kept telling herself, without any real conviction. But now her nerves were numbed to the point of exhaustion, and she closed her eyes and listened without hearing to the mumble of voices around her and the rumble of the little brown train.

She woke to a rush of blue. Blue sea, blue sky, and as they curved to follow the coast, she could even see blue waters ahead on the other side of the train. She was startled, but then remembered that this was an area of flatlands and inland lakes. The train was passing between a lake and the sea. Then she could only see the sea again, impossibly blue and still, with a low evening sun shimmering gently on the water. This was not the sparkling, choppy Mediterranean she had expected, but a quiet sea, deep and reflective, purple-fringed, with a pink mist drawing in the evening sky. Not a postcard but a painting, with all the colours of Matisse in one simple panorama. Still half asleep, she drank in the dreamy vastness, gazing towards the horizon as the evening light darkened in the distance and shrank the sea.

Then it was gone, and they were in suburbs, among houses, and all around her people were gathering together belongings. They were coming into Perpignan, and here most people would leave the train, but she had some more miles to go, further yet towards Spain, down towards the Pyrenees, away from the flatlands and the plains of Roussillon towards the rocky coastline around Vermeilla.

There was a ten-minute wait in Perpignan, and she got off the train briefly to stretch her muscles, stiffer still from sleeping in an awkward position. So close now to her goal, she was terrified of missing the train, and hung around the door to the corridor by her carriage, waiting to see doors being closed and hear the bangs and clatters as the train prepared to depart. A conductor came by her and spoke to her, not in French, she realised with a rush of excitement, but in Catalan. Then he saw her incomprehension, and repeated, in carefully polite French, 'On board, Mademoiselle, if you please. The train is about to leave.'

'How long until we reach Vermeilla, Monsieur?' she asked him.

'Just twenty minutes, Mademoiselle,' he reassured. 'You are nearly arrived.' He was middle-aged, she thought, maybe forty or so, but he gave a very male smile as he looked at her, and opened the door wider to allow her to re-enter the train.

'Which carriage are you in? This empty one? Let me take down your suitcase now, then, since there is no one here to help you when you arrive.'

'Thank you,' Madeleine smiled at him.

His gaze swept over her again, not disturbing, merely appreciative. 'The pleasure is mine,' he twinkled, as he left. Her first Catalan admirer: Madeleine chuckled and settled down for the last twenty-minute ride to her destination.

The train again followed the coast, but it was now

growing darker, and the lights were on in her carriage, so she had only the impression of a deep, dark space on her left from time to time as they headed towards Vermeilla. Three small stations, almost empty of passengers, and then they had arrived. A station like any other in France, almost half a mile from the village, and not a taxi to be seen, so Madeleine picked up her small suitcase and headed down the single road to look for her hotel. Nerves on end, she refused to feel daunted. Soon ahead was a square surrounded by plane trees, carefully trimmed in their camouflage colours. Gentle street lights illumined the square, a rectangle of shingle with sections for playing boules, and little shuttered shops all along one side.

Then she could see the sea, to her left, just yards away at the end of a cobbled street with a couple of restaurants and, she hoped, her hotel. She headed towards the water, here lit by the lights of the bay. There was a promenade, a sea wall, and then the bay, now moonlit and serene, with a few boats at anchor, several more tied to a stone jetty at the end of the shingle beach. It was the most peaceful scene Madeleine had ever seen. The bay curved round, with buildings all around it, soft and pink in the low street lighting. A stone church stood watching over the bay, timeless and sober. Behind her a bar was doing good business, but the sounds receded from the waterside, and the still, purple waters captured the silence.

She stood for what seemed a very long time, not wanting to move. Not much would have changed here, she was sure, since she had left over fifteen years ago.

Turning, she looked back at the village, the thriving bar on the promenade, the little streets leading away in a fan from the bay, wooden shutters on small windows designed to keep out the sun, tiny balconies with their spectacular views of the bay and the sea beyond. Everything was in miniature, a tiny world to itself on the fringes of France. Tears welled up, and she blinked them back. Where had their apartment been, she wondered? Where had she lived, with her Papa, *Maman* and Robert? And was there anyone here who would remember her? Her nerves from earlier in the day returned, and she felt suddenly very alone.

She looked further along the promenade and saw a little sign above a doorway, lit by a tiny lamp above it, *Hotel Bon Repos*. So her hotel was on the seafront. The sheer magic of this made her smile; her tears receded, and she walked towards the hotel.

The entrance to the hotel was an old archway, with heavy wooden twin doors opening outwards, and now held open to the world, with a small porch inside and an inner glass door through which a small flood of light glowed amber on whitewashed walls and a floor of beautiful Spanish tiles in a riotous pattern of orange, yellow, blue and green. The hall was a narrow corridor, leading to a steep staircase in the gloom beyond, while by the entrance was a dark wooden counter, a small reception area behind it, and then a door to a room which looked, from the glimpse Madeleine caught of it, like an office and sitting room combined. Two rickety old chairs in Spanish leather stood in front of the counter, and, shining silver in the light of the single bulb, on the counter was a tiny push-button bell. Madeleine put her case gratefully down onto the tiles, and rang the bell.

There was a flurry of movement from the room beyond, and the sound of a kindly, hectoring voice, and then two people crowded into the small space behind the counter. Monsieur and Madame Curelée, her hosts at the Hotel Bon Repos. Madame Curelée dominated the tiny space, an elderly, matronly landlady in a black dress and rumpled apron tied over an ample waist. Almost tucked behind her was her husband, a small man with a few wispy grey hairs, who stood in her shadow, wordless but nodding. Madame Curelée was voluble in her welcome, a woman, Madeleine was sure, who would have her life story from her in hours. Her strong accent indicated she was a local woman. She might prove useful. After all, Madeleine had nothing to hide, and was here to learn and discover. Madame Curelée would undoubtedly be a mine of local information. For now, she allowed the elderly woman's words to flow over her, enjoying the feeling of being at her destination. It was the end of the first stage of her journey, and it was good to have arrived.

'Welcome, Mademoiselle Garriga. We have your reservation, of course. And the best room for you, with a view of the sea, and next to the bathroom. I am sure you will be very happy. How long are you staying? At least a week? Well, welcome. Have you travelled far? From Paris? In one day? *Mon Dieu!* You must be exhausted. You will sleep well on our bed, but first I am sure you want to eat something. Alain, come here, take Mademoiselle's suitcase to her room. Quickly now, the poor young lady is tired. Go with my husband, Mademoiselle, and then, when you are ready, I have some purée with a nice piece of beef for you, just waiting for you to arrive. Our dining room is there behind you, and there's a little sitting room as well. You'll be comfortable, oh yes, very comfortable.'

Madame Curelée waved a hand of dismissal at her husband, almost pushing him towards the stairs, still nodding and smiling at Madeleine, who found herself following wordlessly in his hapless wake, like a piece of flotsam drifting in a strong shore-bound current. Madame's words followed them up the stairs.

'You will find your towel in your room, Mademoiselle. You will want to wash before some supper, I'm sure. And there is a new lavender soap in the bathroom laid out for you on the washbasin. As soon as you are ready I will have your supper ready for you, so late as it is, and you most likely starving on that long train journey. And a glass of wine to warm you. Oh yes, oh yes, a glass of our good Vermeilla wine will set you to rights, no doubt.' And she gave a satisfied nod which brooked no argument.

It was approaching ten o'clock, and Madeleine was far from hungry, provided as she had been all day with the picnic prepared for her by *Tante* Louise's housekeeper. But to say so to Madame Curelée seemed all but unthinkable, so she gave a fleeting smile backwards down the stairs towards her hostess, then followed Monsieur Curelée meekly along the upper corridor to her room.

Upstairs the floors were tiled with the same tiny patterned tiles, the long corridor lit by brass wall lights which gave the floor a soft glow. There was just one small skylight window halfway along the ceiling, and Madeleine guessed that the corridor would be better lit now than by daylight, when the hot sun would be ruthlessly excluded from the house. Her room was small and simply furnished, with a high single bed in the centre of the room, and a huge, old, wooden wardrobe occupying a whole wall. Above the bed was a painting of the Virgin Mary in rather startling reds and blues, and on the opposite wall was a crucifix. A rather beautiful rug in fine cream and pink wool softened the tiles by her bed, and on the far wall a window stood open to the sea.

Even from the door the view through the window was breathtaking. The shore lights gave just enough glow to touch the pinks, yellows and creams of the stone buildings, while the beach beyond was a black softness leading to the waters of the bay, still and deep like liquid mercury in the light of a bright crescent moon. Madeleine edged past the bed to stand closer to this miracle of light and dark, and from the window she could hear the soft movement of the sea, a few distant voices, and then stillness. Stars unknown to her were emerging into the newly dark night sky, and she wanted to know their names. She turned to Monsieur Curelée, half intending to ask him, then smiled as she saw him hesitant and shifting, waiting to attract her attention, intent on completing his errand to his Madame's satisfaction.

As she turned he moved, muttered to her, with a gesture of his hand, 'I put your suitcase here, Mademoiselle, on the low table by the door. Now I need to show you the bathroom. It is next door, very close.'

His voice was hesitant, almost childlike, the voice of a man who spoke few words. Madeleine followed him and duly admired the simple bathroom. 'I am sure I'll be very happy here, Monsieur,' she assured him. 'My room is lovely, and in such a wonderful position. Please thank Madame Curelée for me, and tell her I will come down for supper in just a few minutes.'

Monsieur flushed and smiled, and hurried off back to his wife to report that all was well. Madeleine returned to the window, and lost herself for a while in the night, thinking about her mission in coming to Vermeilla, and the answers which now lay hopefully quite literally round the corner. She was here. She had made it. A few weeks ago it had seemed an impossibility, but the soft-lit bay of Vermeilla lay before her, so real she could smell the sea, and her past was just as real and tangible, embedded in the village behind her. The thought was as invigorating as the sharp salt air, and suddenly she was hungry, and ready for that glass of wine. It was time to begin, thought Madeleine with a smile, and headed downstairs to the talkative Madame Curelée.

Madame's steak was simply prepared and perfect, tender and pink, sitting on its bed of puréed potatoes. A green salad followed, richly dressed with old, scented olive oil, then Madeleine turned down a small cheese from the Pyrenees in favour of a delicate *tarte aux pommes*. Madame pressed her to take a second glass of the heavy, fruity local wine, made, she assured her, by an uncle in his own *cave*. Madeleine complimented the meal, but refused a second glass.

'We don't have any wine as rich as this in England,' she told Madame, laughing. 'I feel wonderfully mellow after one glass, but I don't think I could dare to take two!'

Madame was amazed. So Mademoiselle was English? But she didn't sound English. Had she not come from Paris today? And yet her name was Spanish, surely?

Why yes, Madeleine explained. She was half Spanish, on her father's side, and her mother was half French. But she had been raised in England from the age of seven, so she wasn't used to drinking too much wine.

Madame nodded, drinking in the information. And was Mademoiselle on her way to Spain, therefore, to be stopping in Vermeilla? Such a difficult country to visit, Spain, with that dreadful Franco in charge. Surely not a place for a young girl from England to visit!

Madeleine paused a moment, then took the plunge.

'If truth be told, Madame, my whole purpose in travelling from Paris was to come to Vermeilla. You see, I lived here when I was a small child. My mother, my brother and I returned to England during the war, and we never came back. I've returned now, hoping to find some old friends of ours, who I hope may still be living here.'

Madame's eyes sparkled with curiosity. Who might these friends be? Philippe Lemont? Why certainly he was still here. 'Such a good man, Philippe, and he has done so much for the school.'

Monsieur Curelée at this point raised what seemed to be a rare voice in this establishment.

'A good school?' he muttered. 'Perhaps, but there's too much politics behind it, if you ask me. He's a political man, that one, mark my words.' There was presumably not much worse you could say about anyone.

Madame was instantly dismissive. 'Political? What nonsense. Just because he wanted to reform the school? You are talking about a man who supported De Gaulle during the war, and now we are going to have De Gaulle back, God be praised, to put some backbone into this stupid government of ours. Don't you listen to my husband. He doesn't trust anyone who isn't from here. No, I tell you, Mademoiselle, Philippe is a good man, a very good man, and if he was a friend of your family then you can be sure he will be pleased to see you.'

A frisson of pure excitement ran through Madeleine, and relief – relief that Philippe was still alive, still living in Vermeilla. Would she find him at the school, she asked?

'Why no, not now,' Madame replied. 'Philippe only works at the school now when the new schoolmaster is sick or away for some reason. He took early retirement last year. He had some problems with his health, you know, and now he mainly plays chess by day at the Café de Catalogne. He takes his meals there most days as well. Colette has always cooked for him, him being alone as he is.'

'Colette? Why Colette was the other name I was looking for, though I don't know her family name. I remember Colette in her café. So she is still here as well!' Madeleine's excitement was electric. She couldn't believe these two pivotal people were waiting for her in Vermeilla, still living the same lives as they had fifteen years ago. She had spoken of it with such faith in Paris, but in her heart she had hardly believed she could find them so easily. But then, why not? Village life doesn't change much, and those who survived the war and stayed put were not too likely to have moved on later, as they grew older.

Madame Curelée was in full flow. 'Colette? Oh yes, Colette is still here. She has the Café de Catalogne, not that she speaks as much Catalan as she should, Colette, though she's a born Catalan herself, but she keeps a good café – you'll have passed it in the street coming down to the harbour. There are two bars in the village, apart from the tourist cafés on the front. Two bars for locals, I mean – Colette's and the Bar du Soleil.'

Madame's tone of disapproval spoke volumes about the Bar du Soleil. A bar for rough men, she said. Not somewhere Mademoiselle would want to go. But Colette kept a better house. All on her own too, or as good as, with that husband of hers unable to work since before the war.'

Monsieur interjected again, with another point of order. 'She's not on her own now, not now that she has the two sons to help,' he said.

'Yes, indeed,' Madame acknowledged, 'Although Daniel is busy fishing. But when not fishing he helps his mother. He's a good boy, I've always said so. And his brother, too, though younger and still at school – young Martin. Fancy, they say he could well be accepted one day to study to be a doctor. Such a proud thing it would be for the village, to have a young man at the university. Of course, Philippe has helped him all the way. He saw his brains and fostered them, and insisted he stay at school, and go on to the *lycée* as well, in Perpignan, even when Colette said she couldn't afford the travel. Philippe insisted, and I think he helps her as well, financially.'

Monsieur Curelée muttered something in Catalan, and Madame spoke sharply to him, an apparent rebuke, also in Catalan. Madeleine understood nothing of this quick exchange, which seemed designed to exclude her.

Madame turned back to Madeleine with a dismissive gesture towards her husband.

'Oh yes,' she continued rapidly in French, 'it will be a wonderful thing to have a son of this village as our doctor one day. If he comes back, of course, when he has such a bright future in front of him. But he will be the first, they say, the first ever from the ordinary folk in the village to go to university. And his mother and father simple bartenders!'

'And Philippe never married?' Madeleine asked. 'He has no family?'

'No, no. Not even brothers and sisters, I think, or maybe there is one brother. There was one visit years ago from an older brother, or a cousin or something, but Philippe never visits any family. He came here long ago from somewhere in the north, and never went back. Just stayed here on his own all these years. Colette's boys are his family, in a way.'

Madeleine sat entranced, absorbing this information so simply given. It was all too easy, really. She cradled the dregs of her glass of wine, turning over what she had learnt.

Madame Curelée moved around the table in the little dining room, preparing the other tables for breakfast in the morning, and sending Monsieur running to the kitchen for more knives. She paused, and looked across at Madeleine, her eyes questioning, suddenly very alert.

'Tell me, Mademoiselle.' she said, wonderingly. 'Your name, Garriga. It's Spanish, you tell me. Was your father Luis? Are you the daughter of Luis Garriga?'

Madeleine nodded, suddenly unable to speak. This woman had known her father.

'Well, then,' said Madame, slowly, with a curious note in her voice which Madeleine could not quite understand. 'You are very welcome in Vermeilla, my dear, very welcome indeed. And you most certainly need to talk to Philippe Lemont.'

CHAPTER SIX

Despite her travel fatigue, it was a long time before Madeleine fell asleep that night. She lay in the narrow little bed with its overstuffed mattress, and listened to the sound of the sea through the open window. It moved sluggishly under the stilling influence of the moon, occasionally slapping gently against the quayside. The rough, blue-painted shutters shut out the moon and the stars, so she opened them to the night, and stood for a long time before returning to bed, poised halfway between the domesticity of the Hotel Bon Repos and the deep dark of the bay, her mind unfocused, lulled and weary, yet the night lights of Vermeilla twinkled a promise, or possibly a challenge, and stirred her beyond sleep. The sea felt close and intimate here in the bay. We all feel moved by the sea, she thought, especially at night. It can bring its melancholy into any room. She looked towards

101

the darker shadow of the sea wall, imagining the bigger swell of the sea beyond the bar.

Sunset and evening star, and one clear call for me! Tennyson's words came from nowhere, from out in the bay, triumphant words of death and resurrection. How did it continue? *And may there be no moaning of the bar, when I put out to sea. But such a tide as moving seems asleep, too full for sound and foam.* In Madeleine's melancholic state, the words spoke not of resurrection but only of loss. The ache of loss for her mother, and, suddenly, piercingly, as she gazed out to sea, a sense of loss for her father, whom she would not find living his life here in Vermeilla – who was beyond finding.

Confused and, as she realised, overtired, she lay down again on the bed, and willed herself to sleep. Better thoughts came to her. Memories teased her mind of a row of tables, fishermen gossiping over coffee, her father playing cards with Uncle Philippe, and Colette offering her childhood treats of leftover sticky doughnuts and furry, juicy apricots. I'm here, she thought, and found the warmth she had been looking for, dropping at last into sleep.

She woke the following morning from a deep, dark sleep, dreams hovering around her consciousness, troubling dreams which she couldn't bring back to mind. She lay for a moment bemused and lost, until a rattling sea breeze and the sounds of the morning in Vermeilla brought her awake with a jolt. Through the open window came the sound of boat engines and oars, and men's voices, calling out to each other in Catalan.

Madeleine had heard snatches of Catalan on the train, and of course the hurried exchange between the Curelée's which had so efficiently shut her out the previous evening, but now she lay drinking in the noise and chatter in this language which was so elusively familiar, so frustratingly no longer her own. It was a strange mixture of Spanish and French, unembellished; 'pagan', her father had called it, laughing as he caressed her with its deep, guttural syllables. Always, when alone with Papa, she had spoken Catalan, even though it was officially banned by the government then, for fear of the Catalan independence drive wafting towards them from over the border in Spain. *Maman* had never learnt. She and Papa spoke French, always. And with the children *Maman* spoke English, a language Madeleine loved to make her father speak, with his halting accent and slow understanding. Three languages, one of which she had not heard again until now, and the rush of pleasure she felt was quite physical.

She rose from the bed and went barefoot to the window, relishing the cold scrape of the tiles under her feet. Below on the quayside were several open boats, like long rowing boats. Some had masts, which leant forward in a strange triangle, and thick sails now furled in loops underneath, orange and brown. Most of the boats had motors, small outboards at the stern, and a few of these had removed their masts. The rough wooden hulls were curved in shape, curved above, below, to the sides, all curves and grace, and brightly painted in greens, pinks, blues. They had clearly just returned from a night's fishing, and

Madeleine could see floats with lanterns attached, which she seemed to remember were lit at night to attract the unsuspecting fish to the surface. The men were hauling the nets off the boats and laying them along the quayside to dry, attached to wooden posts. And beyond them were a group of tradesmen and black-skirted fisherwomen, inspecting the baskets and waiting to take the fish away. Madeleine couldn't see inside the baskets. They were too far away. What did they catch here, she wondered? She had no memory of that. It made her feel like an outsider. That and the language – her language, which she no longer understood.

It must be quite early, she realised. The sky was blue above but still purple in the distance, and the sun was too low on the horizon to be visible. The air was freshened by a brisk breeze which rattled shutters and rustled around the boats. The wind came from along the quayside, Madeleine noticed, not from the sea. It whipped the water into small white peaks, and the gentle stir of last night was now a steady crash around the sea wall. She'd read of the Tramontane wind which blew from time to time from the heights of the Pyrenees down to the plains below. Swirling and dry and achingly cold in winter, as *Tante* Louise had testified. Now, at the end of May, the morning was crisp but not cold, although the fishermen below were dressed in thick wool jerseys below their blue cotton jackets.

Madeleine dressed quickly in a new white skirt and a cotton blouse in deepest Mediterranean blue to match the sea, and threw a white cardigan over her shoulders before heading downstairs for breakfast. There were a few others in the dining room, a young couple dunking croissants in their coffee, and an older couple eating bread and olives. Both couples looked at her curiously, and Madeleine greeted them all rather shyly, aware of her youth and single status as she hadn't been yesterday evening. This is 1958, she reminded herself. Women do many things on their own, even young single ones, and surely even in traditional, rural France? She sat down decisively at the little table laid for one, trying to look composed and mature, despite her twenty-one years. She would feel even younger and even more alone, she was sure, before the day was over.

A young girl, even younger than Madeleine, was serving breakfast, but Madame Curelée was hovering behind, and surged forward to greet Madeleine with more questions than she could answer. Had she slept well? Did she feel rested? Would she like coffee or chocolate? Or tea? The latter was said hesitantly – it was such a barbarous idea to drink tea for breakfast. Madeleine opted for coffee and spread some home-made jam on a croissant. She wanted to ask Madame about the Café de Catalogne. What time would it open? When should she visit? She was eager to go and yet terrified inside at the thought.

Madame was encouraging. The café would be open from early morning, she told her, serving breakfast and coffee to the fishermen coming in from their boats. Just wait a little while, was her advice. The bar would be too busy just now, but would be quiet again soon, and then Philippe Lemont would come down for his own breakfast, after the rush. Madame squeezed her arm in a comforting gesture. She was Madeleine's sole acquaintance in Vermeilla for now, and a warm, motherly figure whose gossipy tongue was the only familiar thing in a bright but unknown world.

So Madeleine sat over her coffee, listening to the tourists planning their day, and practised dunking her croissant like the French (it was disgusting, and left crumbs and jam floating in the cup). Then she went back up to her room and carefully brushed her hair and tied a coloured scarf around her neck. She was Luis's daughter, making a first entrance for fifteen years. She wanted to do credit to the handsome Spanish Catalan who had made this village his last home. She opened her mother's heavy jewellery box and fingered the precious pearls which were her mother's only significant legacy to her. Her grandmother had resisted them being taken out of England, but Madeleine hadn't wanted to leave them behind, especially not in her grandmother's control, so they had come to France, and would stay with her. But they were not for today, she decided, as she shut the box and passed her fingers as always over the intricately carved flowers on the lid. *Wish me luck, Maman*, she thought.

Then she went outside. And walked up and down the quay, past the now deserted fishing boats, past the shingle beach, still empty of tourists at this early hour, past two restaurants just opening their doors. And back again, then to return, and back again. Anything rather than walk up the little cobbled street which led from the sea to the market square, past the little café where Uncle Philippe might even now be sitting, coffee in hand.

But then she began to be afraid that if she didn't make a move now Philippe might finish his coffee and move on, perhaps to the school, or to play boules. Suddenly she found herself hurrying up the little street, and standing at the door of the Café de Catalogne, hovering between the little metal tables in the street at the front, and the interior of wooden tables and polished tiles. She wondered whether to sit and order a coffee herself. There was no waiter in sight, just one or two young fishermen still sitting at the bar, and further back, a rather stooped figure alone at a table reading the morning paper. Madeleine looked at him for a long time: grey hair thinning at the temples, angular limbs and long hands with oversized knuckles visible even from where she stood. She couldn't see his face but she knew it was him.

Breathing rather hard, she entered the café and moved past the tables to stand before him, waiting for him to raise his head. He was engrossed in his paper, but eventually her presence, and the shadow she was casting, penetrated his immersed mind, and he looked up at her. She was aware that she must strike a rather strange figure, hands twisted in front of her, gaze fixed on him with uncomfortable concentration, so she found her voice.

'Monsieur Lemont?' she said, her voice a question. He nodded, his wide-boned face benign but indifferent.

'Yes, Mademoiselle. I am Philippe Lemont. What can I do for you?'

She licked dry lips, and swallowed, trying to lubricate

her mouth and throat. There was only one thing she needed to say. Her voice cracked a little as she spoke.

'Monsieur, my name is Madeleine Garriga. I came here to find you.'

There was just the slightest delay while Philippe took in her words, and then he froze, his eyes fixed intently on her face. She couldn't read his expression at all. His face seemed closed, almost elsewhere. The long pause, the stillness, hung intimidatingly in the air. Feeling slightly sick, Madeleine met his gaze, and willed him to speak to her.

'Madeleine Garriga,' he repeated, eventually, with a long sigh. *Mon Dieu*. At last! Our little Madalena.'

And as he said her name his bony face opened into a broad smile. He reached out his hand and just touched her arm, then took her hand. At the words *'La petite Madalena,'* tears had come to her eyes. He remembered her. Not just her father, but herself, the real herself, the little girl who had left here to run away from war and danger, leaving her father behind.

She smiled back at him, and squeezed the hand in hers. There didn't seem to be anything to say. No words she could think of. Then suddenly he found his voice and his energy, and surged out of his chair and folded her into an embrace. His words came in a rush.

'Little Madeleine. My God, you've turned into a very beautiful young woman. You look like your mother and your father. Like them both. *Mon Dieu, Mon Dieu, Mon Dieu*. I can't believe it. Is it really my little Madalena? It's so wonderful to see you again. I want to know all about

really tall, and always lifting me up above your head. I loved it, and then sometimes I was scared. I know Robert always loved it. He used to squeal and chuckle.'

Philippe laughed. 'You were already getting too big for me to lift you when you left,' he replied. 'And now . . . well now you're a young lady. How old are you? Twenty-one? My goodness, but that would be right. Fifteen years. Is it really fifteen years ago?' His voice dropped, but then he smiled again. Colette, returning in time to hear the hint of depression in his voice, took his hand as she sat down.

'Enough now, Philippe,' she chided, but very kindly, as to a child. Then to Madeleine, 'We need your news, Madeleine. We've known nothing about you since you left. We wrote to your mother but never had any replies. So tell us, please. Just in your own way.'

So she told them, about the years at the grandparents' home, about Robert's studies, her own genteel incarceration, about hers and Robert's silent questions and lack of answers, about their mother, her silence, her death.

'She just lost hope,' she told them, 'after we got the news about Papa being dead. Was it you who sent that? That's what I understood, but I've never seen the letter. But then *Maman* became a different person, and we just grew up under my grandfather's orders afterwards. But I never forgot. Robert finds it frustrating that he doesn't have any memories. This was our real life, and it was so short. It was just so short.'

Her voice was becoming rather ragged, she realised, so

111

she slowed down, and took a breath. She looked across at Philippe, and smiled again, uncertain how to continue. He had been watching her very seriously throughout her narrative, his coffee going cold before him. Now he sighed, and spoke very heavily.

'We never knew. Never any news. And poor Elise is dead. But when I look at you, there is hope, surely? Nobody is dead after all.'

'And you?' inserted Colette. 'How do you come to be here? Are you all alone?'

'Why yes. Do you remember my mother's *Tante* Louise? And her cousin Solange from Paris? They visited here a few times, I think, after my mother's own family cast her off. Well, I escaped to them after *Maman*'s death. I still don't know why my grandfather agreed, since it was at *Tante* Louise's house all those years ago that my mother and father met. He sees her as the worst possible influence.' Madeleine chuckled. 'I think he just wanted rid of me for a while. I've never been a favourite – Robert has that honour. So they let me go, and I've felt so free ever since. And *Tante* Louise and the family in Paris helped me to come here. They could hardly believe that Robert and I knew so little about my father and our lives here, and they could see I needed to find out.'

'So your family in England know nothing about you being here?' Philippe was clearly rather startled.

'They are not my family!' The bitterness in her voice surprised even Madeleine. 'Until *Maman* died she and Robert were my family. Now there's just Robert and me, and some new beginnings of family in Paris, who loved my mother, and who've done more for us in a few weeks than my grandparents have ever done.'

'And us, *petite*.' Philippe gestured from himself to Colette, and then around to the bar. 'You have a family here who have been waiting for you for a long time.'

He looked across at the two fishermen still sitting at the bar. 'Daniel, Eric, you need to meet someone very special.' His voice was celebratory, almost jubilant. 'Let me introduce you to one of the most beautiful young women this village ever gave birth to.'

He took Madeleine's hand and pulled her towards the bar. 'You young men won't remember this girl's father, Luis Garriga, but he was one of us, a real friend. Madeleine, meet Daniel, Colette's son. Do you remember him? He would have been about eight, perhaps, when you left?'

Madeleine looked with interest at this young man from her past. He was perhaps a year or two older than her. A startlingly handsome young man, whippet-like with fine angular features which bore no resemblance to his sturdier mother. Deep brown eyes studied her for a long moment from a face tanned by the sea, and she had the immediate impression that everything he did was measured in careful steps. He seemed to study her for a long while, then his lips parted in a very sweet smile as he held out his hand. His fellow fisherman, Eric, was a year or two older, with an already toughened body, and a long scar on his cheek which was presumably a legacy of his craft. His hold on Madeleine's hand lingered longer than necessary.

'Surely we should remember someone like you?' he murmured, his voice a caress.

Madeleine laughed. 'I would have been six years old, just a scrubby child at the time. I don't suppose a bunch of boys would have deigned even to speak to me.'

'True enough,' mourned Eric. 'So you went away and didn't come back until we'd all grown up. How very wise.'

Daniel jabbed his friend in the ribs. 'Don't be listening to this fool,' he urged Madeleine. 'He talks nothing but nonsense, and anyway, he's only been married a few weeks. I'd like to hear what Sandrine would say if she could hear him right now.'

'She should be glad to have a full-blooded male for a husband,' swaggered Eric, but with a grin that robbed his words of any arrogance. 'Anyway, I'd better be getting back to her, perhaps, if she's to stay as adoring as ever.'

He shook hands again with Madeleine, wished a general 'Bonne journée à tous' to the four of them, and sauntered out into the street.

'Don't pay any attention to him, Mademoiselle,' grinned Daniel. 'He actually runs around after Sandrine more than you would believe. He just likes to keep up his reputation, that's all.'

Madeleine smiled. 'The village playboy?'

'Every village needs one!' agreed Daniel. He looked at Philippe, still standing at her side, and seemed to consider his words carefully before he asked, 'Have you known *Tonton* Philippe for a long time? Have you come back to

114

visit us? When did you arrive? Will you be with us for a while?'

It gave Madeleine inordinate pleasure to hear someone else say *Tonton* Philippe. It made Daniel seem part of her family. She remembered Madame Curelée's comment that Colette's boys were like Philippe's family.

'I just arrived last night,' she answered. 'I've booked into the Hotel Bon Repos for a week, but I may stay longer. I've wanted to come back for a long time, and I can't tell you how happy I am to be here.'

'And we too.' It was Philippe who spoke, still with the same festive air. 'Daniel, if the boats aren't going out again today you should get some sleep, and then this evening you can take Madeleine down to the beach and show her your boat. For now, I am going to show this young lady our village. There's time for a stroll before lunch.'

He looked across at Colette, who was still seated at the table, strangely still, watching her son, her expression inscrutable.

'What do you say, Colette?' Philippe's voice coaxed. 'A special lunch today?'

Colette didn't move, and Madeleine murmured about having lunch at her hotel, but then Colette seemed to emerge from a private reverie. She lifted her head to Philippe, as if monitoring his face, and there was a moment's hesitation. Then she stood, pushed away her coffee cup, and came briskly across to them, taking Madeleine's hands in a firm grasp.

'Don't even think about it, my dear. Today is, as Philippe

says, special. And it's Saturday. Daniel will not be fishing tonight, I think. We'll eat late to give him time to sleep, and you'll eat with the family. We must give you some of our own anchovies. And a taste of our own wine as well.' She smiled again, the smile lighting her tired face. 'Believe me, we are really very happy to have found Luis's daughter.'

CHAPTER SEVEN

Philippe was like a man possessed as he propelled Madeleine through the cobbled streets of Vermeilla, calling out right and left to passers-by, to women arguing over the vegetables in barrows in front of narrow shop front, to an old man whittling wood on a stool in the street, to workmen in small workshops with doors wide open to the streets.

'Look, Serge, Jean-Claude, Alain, Claudine – look who I have here! It's the daughter of Luis Garriga, come home to see us at last!'

Daniel and his young friend might not remember Luis, but it seemed everyone over the age of forty remembered the name at least. People stopped what they were doing and stood to watch, their gazes curious but non-committal. But Madeleine could hear them murmuring to each other, her father's name, small mutterings, which could have been equally good or bad. Philippe towered over most of the townsfolk as he called out his news like a schoolmaster calling his children to class. Beside him, held firmly by the hand, Madeleine felt uncomfortably exposed.

At the corner of the market square Philippe came to a halt, and a small group formed around them. Philippe's enthusiasm seemed to pierce the Catalan reserve, and they began to exclaim, gathering round Madeleine, and again she felt excluded as the language passed her by. But Philippe spoke in French, and some replied in French, looking at Philippe, men speaking to each other rather than to her, sharing their own memories.

'Luis, hey? Now there was a man.'

'I remember now, there *was* a family, and they left when the Germans came.'

'That's when we all left, surely?'

'No, they left before, remember? The Germans were looking for them. Luis had to get them out.'

Then a few women who had been in deep conversation behind came forward to Madeleine, women dressed in espadrilles and cotton skirts, some with flowered scarves tied round their heads, and one dressed all in black, perhaps in mourning. One extended her hand with a gentle formality, and Madeleine found two hands enclosing hers.

'You are Madeleine Garriga. We remember you as a child. You used to play with my niece, Louise, who lives now in Port Vendres. You are welcome, welcome to Vermeilla, Mademoiselle.'

'Your mother, too,' added the second woman. 'I hope

she is well. She helped us so much when my son was sick before the war. She knew better when that fool of a nurse from Argelès told us we had to keep giving him that foul medicine, remember, Anne?'

'Yes indeed, a good woman, and not above any of us, for all her fine education and her Parisian family.'

'And Luis was a good man.'

'A handsome man, too. You look just like him my dear.'

'It's like you to say that, Anne Morales, with your husband standing just behind you!'

There was good-natured laughter and suddenly the crowd became almost merry, tribal caution set aside as the mood of reminiscence gripped them.

'I used to play boules with Luis. He could rarely beat me, though.'

'So you say, Alain, but nobody ever saw you win.'

There was much jocularity, in Catalan and in French. The growing crowd gathered around the open doors of a stone wine cellar. The smell of maturing wine was heady, and the group demanded a tasting. The vintner's protests that his wine was not yet ready were swept aside, and Madeleine found herself sipping a very fruity, sweet wine rather like port, which they called Banyuls. She had never before taken wine at eleven o'clock in the morning, but this morning was an intoxication all of its own. She stood passively in the midst of the crowd. In the flow of reminiscences nobody asked her any questions or even really talked to her. She was a mere young girl, an audience for their memories.

Next to her, the man called Serge, a large, squat man

119

in his fifties, leather-skinned like all the men around him, finally raised his glass to her and spoke to her through the chatter. His voice was strangely subdued, as though he didn't want to be heard by the motley crowd. But he caused a small silence around him nevertheless.

'He was a good man, your father. One of the few who could really hold his head high during the war. Those you see around you here, we all know what we did during those years. No one has anything to be ashamed of. But there aren't many who did as much as your father. You should be proud, Mademoiselle.'

Madeleine looked back at him attentively. Philippe, she noticed, was listening keenly to his words. A quiet murmur of agreement came from his companions. She nerved herself to reply in the same calm, steady tones.

'I am proud. And I have come here hoping to be more proud. To learn what he did. So that you can all tell me.' She raised her glass back to him. 'I'm here on a voyage of discovery. I hope you will all help me.'

Serge was silent for a moment, and then replied very seriously. 'We will tell you all we can. But the war was a complicated time, Mademoiselle. Not everything is easy to discover.'

He nodded towards Philippe. 'Start with Philippe here. He knows more than anyone, and was your father's closest friend. But here in Vermeilla, Luis Garriga had many people who would wish to call themselves his friend, even if he was more lettered than we are. And we are glad to know his daughter.'

There was a gallantry to his words which seemed

to take even himself by surprise. Madeleine reached up instinctively and kissed him softly on both cheeks, and around them hoots and clapping broke out. She could have sworn that she saw Serge blush beneath his olive tan. Philippe came over to her and said, 'You could quickly conquer some hearts here, my dear. Poor Serge hasn't been kissed like that since his wife mistook him for the postman. Now, these folk are either going to go about their daily business or stay here far too long, and you and I have things to do. Would you like to see where you lived, all those years ago? I don't suppose you remember, do you?'

Since arriving in the village Madeleine had been asking herself this question. Where had she lived? Would it still be the same inside? Would she recognise it? She agreed quickly, and they disengaged themselves from the group and moved away down what seemed to be the main commercial street running through the village, with several shops spilling goods onto the pavement – a motley jumble of vegetables, buckets, items of clothing, huge cans of olive oil, and bags of dried beans and lentils. A little way along they turned right into an even narrower street, where the roofs of the houses almost met overhead. Not an inch of sun would ever reach this street. Madeleine read the street name, rue Colbert, and her heart flipped in recognition. They must be within metres of her former home.

Philippe stopped in front of a weathered door, one step up from the street, and entered direct onto a narrow stone staircase which led upstairs. He led the way up three flights of stairs, emerging onto a little landing under the roof, with a small skylight making it quite bright after the gloom of the climb. There in front of them was a single door to the right. To her surprise Philippe didn't ring the bell, or even hesitate, but pulled a key from his pocket and opened the door.

'Welcome,' he said, with some shyness, 'to my home. Or rather to your old home, my dear. You see, I moved here after your father . . . after your father died. It was bigger than my old rooms, and I didn't want anyone else to sit in his chair, or cook on your mother's old range.'

Madeleine followed him in, catching her breath as she looked around. The flat was so much smaller than she remembered it. Tiny windows were closed in further by wooden shutters. The little kitchen and sitting area were divided by a thin wall along half the length of the kitchen. In the sitting area, sure enough, there was the stove she remembered, empty now, but with a small basket of logs tucked in behind it. A small sofa and one easy chair, and shelves built into the wall full of books. And a low coffee table strewn messily with papers, books, an old pipe in an ashtray, a small empty box with no hint as to its former contents. There was a minuscule bathroom, with a bath you had to sit up in. And there were the two bedrooms, one of which was now more of a junk room for Philippe's life possessions, but which had once been her room with Robert. There were still two small beds. Philippe seemed to have changed nothing at all in fifteen years, except for adding two rather fine oil paintings in the sitting area. Madeleine was sure these were his. They were recent views of Vermeilla, and her parents had never had any money for buying artwork.

She stood in the middle of Philippe's innocuous mess, drinking in her memories, which came crowding back. The wooden table in the corner of the room, with its three chairs, was where they had eaten every day all together, as a family. The room had always smelt of cooking, she remembered. And there were still only three chairs. Robert had sat in a high chair when they lived here, and she could recall as clearly as if it were yesterday her mother telling her father the child was now too big for his chair, and they would have to buy a grown-up chair for him. When Philippe had eaten with them, which he often did, Luis had pulled a stool out from the main bedroom. And if there were more people, well there was no room at the tiny table anyway, and they had eaten on their laps, perching wherever they found.

She looked across at the little sofa and the chair beside it. 'My father always sat on the sofa,' she said, matter-of-factly and completely sure of her memories. 'And *Maman* always sat in the chair. She would knit there in the evenings. Papa would be reading, or maybe at the table if he was writing. I don't remember where we children sat. On the floor, maybe?'

'You were always hemmed in for space here,' Philippe acknowledged. 'It is a perfect space for me, but with you children around, I was always amazed you didn't get stepped on.' He looked at her curiously. 'I didn't think you would remember so much.'

'I didn't until we came in here. Since I entered the

123

café this morning it has been as though nothing has ever changed. It's almost unreal, to return to Vermeilla and find things so unaltered.'

Philippe's face was very serious, his eyes almost painful as he replied. 'Yes, but a lot has changed really, my child. Rooms and buildings can stay the same, but so much else has changed.'

'You mean my father? Do you miss him?'

'Every day – and your mother. Nothing has ever been the same in this village since the war.'

Madeleine sat down on one of the old wooden chairs, and crossed her arms on the table. Her next question was so simple and obvious, and yet her throat constricted as she spoke.

'Serge said to ask you about my father. I don't know what he did in the war. Or how he died. Can you tell me?'

There was a silence. Philippe's eyes were fixed on the wall, but after a moment he nodded.

'Yes, I can tell you. Or at least I can begin to tell you, Madalena. None of us know everything.'

He squeezed his limbs into the chair opposite her, stretched his legs in an obviously familiar manoeuvre between the table legs, and brought his hands together almost as if in prayer.

'We'd better begin before the war,' he started. 'You must know already that your father came down here from Paris to be closer to his homeland.'

'Yes, and to elope with my mother.'

Philippe's rather anxious face softened into a reminiscent smile. 'Yes, indeed. I met them both as soon

124

as they arrived in Vermeilla, and I was a witness at that wedding. They were so passionate about everything, Luis and Elise. Luis and Elise . . .' His voice trailed off, and his eyes dreamt privately for a moment, then he shook himself and continued.

'Luis began writing as soon as he came down here, for a local paper in Perpignan. Nothing like the national papers he wrote for in Paris, but it was an income, and the paper here was glad to get hold of him. It gave him access to other journalists, of course, and to a political network which extended down into Spain. He would have gone back to Spain to fight, I think, when the Civil War broke out a few months later, but you had just been born, and he felt he should stay with your mother, so he carried on writing and fund-raising for the whole terrible years of the Civil War, and despairing as he watched his Spain and his Catalonia fall to Franco. And then he found real work, as he said, when Barcelona fell and Catalonia was overrun by Franco's troops, the last part of Spain to fall.'

The world was in trouble, this spring of 1939. Germany had withdrawn from its non-aggression pact, Mussolini had invaded Albania, and Europe was watching and waiting and arming its spirit. But more immediately in Elise's kitchen, Barcelona had fallen, the Republic was lost, and shattered, terrified civilians had fled in hundreds of thousands across the border to France.

'Nobody wants them,' Luis railed at Philippe. 'The villagers here call them troublemakers, spongers, illiterates, and if you could see where they've been incarcerated – the

camps – right there on the beach, exposed to the wind, no shelter, children dying of cold, and families forced to separate. All we do is what we can, and it saves nobody, but maybe we can change a few minds.'

Philippe ate less often at the house now. It was always full, he complained, and nobody spoke French any more. But he gave Luis a room behind the school where they put makeshift beds, and he drove endless kilometres as chauffeur without complaining. He was one of the very few people in the village to have a car. He and Luis. Luis's car was never still these days.

Elise moved among the refugees with a serene smile and made soup – 'I hadn't realised before that making soup was a humanitarian act,' she told Philippe. It amused Philippe to see how they all muddled around the little apartment. Little Madeleine, a toddler still but tall, slender and poised beyond her years, moving effortlessly around the Spaniards who now occupied her space, always with something to show them, a small toy she treasured, or a little picture she had drawn. She prattled in a mix of French and Catalan which they seemed to understand, and gave her hand into theirs with a smile which reflected her mother's.

Elise, her Catalan still weak, made herself understood with gestures and wrote down what she didn't understand for Luis to translate later. Her second pregnancy was a little complicated, Philippe knew, but she refused to complain.

'Look at the faces of the people who find their way here,' she would say to him. 'How weary, how physically beaten! We're so lucky, Philippe, and the baby is fine.'

She smiled again and Philippe was lost. He could never

126

withstand that smile of hers, and the light in her sky-blue eyes. The apartment was peaceful this morning, and Elise was alone, except for Madeleine, who was washing a doll in a bucket in the corner of the kitchen.

'At least there's no one here this morning, for once. Where is that husband of yours?' he said.

'Away with Henri to the camp.'

'You know there's dysentery in the camp now?'

'Yes, we heard. And with this cold spell people are dying – they've got no rations, and they're just so weak. How can we do this to people, Philippe?'

'We? You mean the authorities?'

'No, I mean the French. We're all doing it. If ordinary French people were all at the gates demanding entry, the camps would open up.'

'I know. It's all political appeasement on the government's part, and the worst kind of fear here in the village. And now that the word is out that there's disease in the camp, people will close their minds and their doors even more.'

'Not ours, it seems.' Elise smiled as the door of the apartment burst open and banged shut behind Luis, stalking in like a fury.

'Miguel's wife has fallen ill in the camp, and they won't let me bring her out! They say she's infectious and a danger to the community. Hah! I'll give them danger to the community! Anyway, I got their two children out, by telling the guard their grandmother was waiting for them in Collioure, and tomorrow I'll get the mother out as well. The guard Pierre's on duty tomorrow, and he'll help me.'

He flung himself onto the sofa by the kitchen, his legs dangling over the arm at one end, chafing his fingers together.

'By God, it's cold out there!' He reached a hand out to Elise.

She took it and rubbed it between hers. 'You need some soup. I know it's not lunchtime yet but some soup would do you good. Or would you prefer coffee?'

'Soup sounds wonderful, and it smells wonderful too. Philippe, my friend, how are you, and what have you been doing with my wife while my back was turned?'

'Planning her escape from your desertion, of course.'

'You can't escape from someone who has already deserted you, idiot. It's an oxymoron. And you a teacher! Come down and teach those guards something at the camp, will you? They're the most ignorant bunch of gorillas you ever set eyes on.'

'Tell me about Miguel's family,' Elise asked. 'Where did you leave the children? Do they need us? Is their grandmother really here?'

'Not the grandmother, but a cousin or something like who lives near Collioure. That's what makes the situation so stupid. Amongst all the people in the camps, Miguel and his family have no need to be there. They have a place to stay if they can get out. It's all because they suspect Miguel of having fought in the war. Well, what if he did? What's he going to do here now? The French have gone mad with suspicion.'

Madeleine appeared at his knee, holding out a wet doll which dripped on his trousers. He lifted her onto his lap, and helped her to dry the doll with a kitchen cloth.

'We need practice at this, angel. When our baby comes out of Mummy's tummy you'll have to help us bath her too.'

'It's not a girl, it's a boy,' Madeleine declared. 'Maman said he was kicking her this morning.'

'Is that what boys do?' Luis smiled into her eyes, stroking her hair back from her face.

Madeleine nodded vigorously. 'Daniel kicked me once. But then I hit him with Julie.' She waved her doll triumphantly.

'Amazon!' crowed her father, and kissed the top of her head.

'Soup, my love? Come to the table. Philippe? You're sure? But you'll stay to lunch! I got fresh fish from the market today.'

Luis rose from the sofa, carrying Madeleine, and kissed Elise as he passed her.

'Have we enough food for Philippe? He eats so much! Can we afford to feed him?'

Elise laughed. 'Since for once we don't seem to have anybody else, I think we can just about manage.'

'You hear that, Madalena? Tonton Philippe is staying for lunch. In that case we definitely need to eat soup first for there won't be much else for us!'

CHAPTER EIGHT

Listening to Philippe, Madeleine could almost see her parents in this room, and feel the heat of the little stove warming her father's hands. She watched him closely and waited for him to continue. He seemed to drift in and out of his private reverie, and then would emerge to take up his tale.

'The work became very serious for your parents,' he continued. 'They became part of an unofficial campaign group, and your mother learnt how to forge documents, identity papers to get people out of the camps, and they provided money, organised travel, and Luis wrote tracts and newspaper articles. When you came up the stairs to this apartment, if you didn't hear Spanish voices, you would be sure to hear Luis's typewriter rattling away.

'It all meant that in 1940, when France fell to Germany, your parents were already politically involved. You will hear a lot of rubbish about the war years, my dear, or maybe not, since nobody talks about it now if they can avoid it. But the truth was really quite simple. People were stunned and humiliated at the way France was just overrun by Germany. We'd all been led to believe our defences were impregnable. Well they weren't, and our "war" with Germany only lasted a few weeks, and then we were completely defeated, and humiliated, and scared, and at the mercy of the Germans. Then Maréchal Pétain stepped in as our leader and promised us a new France, new dignity, independence under Germany.

'Have you heard of Pétain? Yes, of course you have. Well, most people thought he was a saviour. No one knew what to do and he seemed to have the answers, and everyone assumed that Germany was going to defeat England in months as well, and just thanked their stars that our part of France had escaped occupation, thanks to Pétain. And of course all our news was censored and controlled. I must have heard a hundred people in this village saying well now at least the war was over, and this part of France was still free, and now we could start trying to rebuild France. All rubbish, of course, but no one had the heart, the faith or the information to believe anything else. That's what that sense of utter defeat and despair does to you.

'Only those who were already politicised had any notion of resisting. There wasn't any organised resistance, of course, not in the beginning, but people like your father were in action in any way they could be. Luis and Elise just seemed to carry on the same activities, with no change except that as well as helping Spaniards, they gradually began producing documents for people fleeing the Germans, trying to get over the border to Spain, where ironically they would be safe. Elise became a real expert.'

He paused. 'Would you like to see some of their old tools?'

Madeleine had been lost in his story, and the sudden question startled her.

'Tools for forging documents?'

'Yes indeed. Look!'

He manoeuvred himself out from the table and pulled down a tin from the top shelf in the corner of the room. Dust covered the lid of the tin, and he sneezed, then blew the dust on to the floor. It was an old, faded biscuit tin, and he brought it over to Madeleine.

'Take a look,' he invited.

Madeleine stared at the box. Then she gently lifted off the lid, which was only lightly pushed down. Inside were four wooden ink stamps, two round and the others rectangular. She picked them up and handled them reverently, and saw they were official police stamps, two marked *Ville de Montpellier* and two marked *Ville de Marseille*.

'Are these real?' she asked in an awed voice.

'Copies,' replied Philippe. 'But good ones. If you smudged the ink a little when making the stamp it would pass for the real thing. They used towns some distance from here because the local police would be less familiar with the style of documents they produced. They would type letters authorising travel, and stamp them, and of course, most important were the identity cards. See, there are some cards below.'

Madeleine lifted out the stamps, and below were some blank cards with *Carte d'Identité* printed on the top, the identity cards which had never existed in France before 1940, but which the Germans had imposed. There were sections for writing in all the relevant personal information, such as height and hair colour, and, despite the obligatory photo, more detailed information like shape of nose and face.

'These are real, I think,' said Philippe. 'I wasn't party to what they were doing, but by 1942 the Resistance had a good system going for "acquiring" – stealing – what they needed. The cards needed to be genuine, because by then the controls were getting tighter and tighter. But the Resistance had cooperation by then. The people had learnt to hate the Vichy regime, and all that old love of Pétain was dead.'

Madeleine placed the tools of her mother's resistance work carefully back in the box.

'You found these still in the flat after the war? Nobody lived here meantime?'

'As it happened, no. But the only reason they got left behind was because the stamps had changed, and these were old ones. There was a lot of other stuff, special inks and all sorts, but everything that could be important in creating more documents was passed on to another cell.'

Madeleine sat for a moment, visualising her mother sitting at this table, reproducing documents with painstaking delicacy, perhaps while she was at school. Presumably she had gone to school? She asked Philippe.

'Oh yes, you were in my school, one of my pupils! I taught you to read and write, although your mother had already taught you a great deal before you came, so you were the star of my class. You used to tell all the other children what you heard on Radio London. I used to come here to listen to the BBC broadcasts with your parents, because I didn't have a radio set, and you were often allowed to stay up to listen as well. I used to wonder whether you should really be telling the other children what you heard, but Luis used to say most of the village was listening in secret anyway, so what did it matter. By then the tide had changed – people were mostly only paying lip service to the Vichy regime, and waiting, hoping for things to change. The proudest man in the village was an old fisherman whose son was fighting with the Free French under de Gaulle in North Africa. The boy was actually a merchant seaman who had landed up in Morocco, and no one was actually sure he was really fighting, but we'd got to the stage where people wanted to believe it, at least!

'So there we were just surviving, but your father was coming increasingly under suspicion by the authorities. He protected himself by continuing to do work for the same newspaper he'd worked for before the war in Perpignan, which was now a Vichy mouthpiece. Then came the news in November 1942 that the Germans were moving in to take over from the Vichy government. They were scared by now of the possibility of an invasion from

North Africa, and wanted to secure this coast. We all knew things were going to get much tougher, and that's when things really did get much tougher between your parents.'

'*I won't go, Luis! I won't go!*'

'*Elise, my love, you know you have to! This village is going to be overrun by German militia, and our work is too well known. And you're English!*'

'*Half English!*'

'*Semantics! Everyone here knows you were brought up in England. It's bad enough being Spanish, but there are so many of us here now that I can probably pass. But you – you would be arrested straight away. We have to think of the children, Elise. If we get you over the border then you can go to the British Embassy in Barcelona. God knows, we've helped enough other people to do it! And they'll get you home.*'

'*And you? What are you going to do?*'

'*Well I can't go into Spain, that's for sure!*' *Luis's smile was grim.* '*I'll stay here, and keep on working. Enric or one of the others will find me a safe house, I know.*'

'*Luis, no! You never fought Franco! I know you've felt you can't go back into Spain, but they're not actually looking for you. Your battles in Spain happened so long ago, two years before the Civil War even started. Why should they be looking for you now? Surely you could come with us to Barcelona!*'

'*No, Elise. It's the same people running Catalonia now who were running it in 1935. Then they had been elected, and we could get rid of them the same way, but now Franco has given them all positions of power, and they've been told to keep us damned Catalonians under control. I can't run the risk of going into Barcelona. There are too many of them who would recognise me, and my name is on file.' He paused, and reached out to touch Elise's cheek.*

'And, carinyo, *I think you know that even if I could get away with it, I can't leave with you. God knows I love you, and I don't know how I'm going to manage without you, but I already ran away from one fight. I can't run away from this one.'*

Elise gazed at him in despair. It was because of her and the children that he had never joined the Republican army in the fight against Franco. She had kept him away from the cause closest to his heart. There was no way she could take him away from France now, and nor could she stay, not with the children. The logic was inescapable and more grievous than she could bear.

She nodded mutely and held his hand close against her cheek. Tears drenched it, and Luis pulled her into his arms, drying her tears with his lips.

'It won't be for long, Elise. The tide has turned in this war, and the only reason the Germans are moving in here is because they're sure the Allies are going to invade. It'll come soon, from one direction or another. And my love, as soon as that happens I will come for you.'

Day after day the plans were made, and Elise kept her fears hidden – fear for Luis, fear of the separation, and the horror of returning to her parents' home in England. The

136

time stretched before her as an endless ordeal, and she felt
she could have endured all the dangers of Luis's future life
far more easily.

As for Luis, he went about forming his plans for them
with a determined positiveness which would almost have
fooled her, had she not occasionally caught him looking at
her off guard, when she recognised her bleakness reflected.
That look made Elise even more determined to hide her
fears. And so together they smiled and made their plans
quietly, in secret from the world.

They would have to walk across the mountains. The
sea route was now impossible – the fishing boats were
watched and the beaches guarded, and no one had dared
use the boats for escapees for some time. But how to take
two small children on a walk of many kilometres across
a rough mountain pass in the cold of a November night?
The pass being suggested was over fifteen kilometres long,
and involved a climb of nearly a thousand metres. And to
get to it there were a further fifteen kilometres of heavily
patrolled country lanes to be covered. To avoid risk of
discovery, most escape parties went on foot to the pass,
across the fields. To take a car along the border roads at
night was to court arrest. Elise kept a smile on her face
because she had to, but was secretly aghast.

'Are we really going to try to cover thirty kilometres
with the children?'

'No, don't worry. Enric says there are evenings when the
militia are less likely to be out on patrol – he can watch and
tell us. We'll go as far as the pass by car, without lights. We'll
be OK. We have the benefit of inside knowledge, you see.'

'But there's still the pass to walk. Can we really do it with the children, Luis?'

'We'll be fine, don't you worry. It's already been done by other groups with children, and Enric has taken two families over before. He wants to help me carry the children – at least Robert – in a kind of makeshift backpack, and if he does so I can carry Madeleine for a good bit of the way. She'll have to walk some, but my Amazon will cope with that.'

'I just hope she'll cope with my parents as easily! Can you imagine my father's reaction when I turn up unannounced with two brown Catalan children with a war history to make their hair stand on end? It's almost worth going just to see his face!'

Luis grinned and kissed her. 'Attagirl! See it as a mission to enlighten the natives.'

'Yes, but let's hope it doesn't last too long, this war, or I may be murdered before I can make it back here.'

'Tell them you have a dangerous resistance worker for a husband, and I'll be coming to get them after the war! Tell me, dear wife, how does it happen that we have no children in this apartment this afternoon?'

'Serge told Philippe he has some apples, goodness knows where from, and so Philippe decided to take the children to buy some. He says this fine weather we are having can't last – well we know it can't, we're nearly in November – so he wanted to treat them both before we leave. Oh God, Luis, we're really going to leave aren't we?'

She reached for him, and he breathed into her neck.

'My love, you may leave, but we will always be together. It doesn't matter where we are.'

His voice deepened. 'How long will Philippe be gone?'

'He said he would take the children down to the shore afterwards. They won't come back for a while.' She gave him a smile of pure seduction.

'Show me how you will miss me, Luis.'

Philippe looked at Madeleine. 'Do you remember leaving? You probably know more about your journey than me. Luis went with you into Spain, and then left you, and we heard you got to the British Consulate in Barcelona, and from there to Gibraltar and then to England by boat.'

Visions came to Madeleine of a frightened six-year-old walking in the dark, wet and cold in the November rain, her parents and another man by her side. She remembered being squashed in the back of a cart, then a train, and what must have been a hotel room, and being even more frightened because she didn't understand anyone around her, or know where she was. She remembered her mother explaining to her that they were going on a boat, and that they were going to England, which she had heard of, but didn't want to go to. She had cried for her father, missing the man who had never been away from home, but she had no memory of her mother crying, only of her negotiating, arranging, discussing, always in the same quiet, patient voice, in English, French, bits of what must have been Spanish. The journey for her was a memory of confusion and fear and boredom, and always holding hard to her mother's hand.

139

'Yes,' she admitted to Philippe. 'I've always remembered the journey, just snatches, you know, and of course never fully understanding where we were or what was happening. Papa had told me I had to help *Maman* and look after Robert, so I just kept talking to Robert, and trying to keep him happy, because he was the only person I actually understood! And he cried a lot, probably because it was all so tiring, and nothing was familiar or routine. So I tried to feel superior to him and remember that I could tell Papa later how good I'd been. It sounds insufferable, but I suppose it was just a way of coping. I don't remember the boat, funnily enough, or arriving in England. I mainly remember the early bits of the journey. Maybe it all became a blur after a while.'

Philippe nodded. 'It was such a long time before we heard that you had arrived safely. Luis had left Vermeilla by then, and was living in a safe house, but he kept coming back whenever he could get transport, hoping to get news. In the end it was he who heard first, from the same *passeur* who had helped you across the mountains into Spain. He'd asked for information, and had it relayed back that you'd caught a boat safely. Luis kept hoping for a letter, but that was impossible, as he knew, really. We could get letters out sometimes with people crossing into Spain, and I know your father sent letters to Elise, but nothing ever came back. So you all just disappeared, and your father followed Allied movements with even more interest, and talked non-stop about when it would all be over, and you would all come home.'

'But we never did.'

'No,' sighed Philippe. 'You never came back, and we never again heard from Elise. I wrote to her, of course, as soon as Luis died, and then I wrote again after the liberation, thinking maybe the first letter would not have reached her. But she never wrote, even after the whole ghastly war was history, and letters were flowing normally. I wrote one last time in early 1946, and then gave up.'

Madeleine wondered what had happened to all these letters. Had her mother received them all? She knew the first letter from Philippe had got through, because the news of her father's death had broken over them at Forsham just as France was liberated. But letters from her father? Had any letters from Luis ever reached Forsham? It was impossible to know.

She told Philippe. 'Your first letter reached us, I know, with the news. The others probably did too. But my mother wasn't herself afterwards, you know. I doubt whether she would have had the will to write.'

Philippe shook his head in bewilderment. 'How strange,' he said, 'to try to think of Elise like that. How tragic. And Luis nearly made it, you know. He only died two months before the liberation. D-Day had just taken place and the allied forces were back on French soil. He was ecstatic the last time I saw him, talking about the end of the war being in sight.'

'So what happened?' Madeleine asked. Her question hung between them.

'He was shot, my dear. Shot by the Germans who found the camp where he was living. I can tell you a bit more, from the little I know; but not now. It's lunchtime, and we have raised enough ghosts for now, and should go out into the world and remember the present for a while. Colette will be waiting for us, and whatever she has prepared for us, I would hate to risk keeping her waiting.'

CHAPTER NINE

The streets of Vermeilla were deserted as they emerged from Philippe's home and headed back to the Café de Catalogne. Shopfronts were shuttered, and as they passed the entrance to the *cave* where they had earlier drunk Banyuls, the cavernous arch was filled by heavy wooden double doors. In something of a daze Madeleine realised it really was lunchtime, and the people of Vermeilla were already at table. She hadn't realised they had been so long in the little apartment, buried in the past.

'It's a good thing Colette told us lunch would be late today,' grinned Philippe. 'We would be seriously overdue otherwise. As it is, we'll get away with it.'

He set a fast pace which brought Madeleine briskly back to the present hour. She smiled back at him and answered, 'We may get away with it, but first we have to get there.

My legs are shorter than yours, remember. Could we walk just a bit more slowly?'

His lips twitched, and he slowed down infinitesimally, just as they rounded a corner and the café came into view. A few couples were eating at the tables outside, and one noisy family inside, but Colette was nowhere to be seen. A waiter and barman seemed to be in complete command. Philippe greeted them and then led her through the café, the length of the polished wooden bar, to a steep, narrow staircase hidden at the rear. Climbing it at his usual pace, two steps at a time, he halted before a door at the top and knocked decisively, then opened the door without waiting for an answer. Madeleine followed in his wake.

They were in a narrow corridor, with two doors off it at the front, and then it opened onto a large living area with more light than Madeleine had expected, coming in through double glass doors opening onto a large balcony with intricate wrought iron railings and the same tiny, dark terracotta tiles which ran through the rest of the building. On the far side of the living area another corridor led to more rooms. Later Madeleine was to learn that the front rooms were two guest rooms which had once been rented out commercially, while the back corridor housed the kitchen, bathroom and separate bedrooms for Colette and her invalid husband. The two sons had rooms up another winding staircase in the tiny attic.

A large table on the left of the simply furnished room was already laid for lunch, with a starched embroidered tablecloth, and a selection of chairs, none matching, all in differing shades of polished wood. It was overlooked by a picture of the Madonna and child, demure and saintly in a heavy wood frame.

As they entered the room a young teenager was putting some last articles on the table, overseen by Colette, who followed him around the table adjusting most of the places he had laid, scolding fondly the whole time. To the right, by the open balcony doors, Daniel straddled an easy chair, reading the local newspaper. He got up as soon as he saw them enter, and came across with a smile, ushering them into the room.

'Where will we sit, *Maman*?' he asked, turning briefly to Colette. 'Should we go onto the balcony?'

'No, my son. We are late already. We will take our aperitif at the table. Come, my dear,' Colette beckoned to Madeleine. 'Come and be comfortable, and meet my other son, Martin.' She caressed his hair as she spoke, and turned him towards Madeleine.

Madeleine looked curiously at this prodigy about whom she had learnt from the Curelées at the hotel. He was of a different build to Daniel, more like his mother, stocky and Catalan, with masses of dark curls and the broad cheeks and dimples which characterised Colette, but more masculine and planed. He might be thirteen or fourteen years old, she thought; a good ten years younger than Daniel. Colette's fingers still threaded his hair, an attention which he accepted without seeming to notice it. This, thought Madeleine, is clearly the cosseted darling of this household, the late-born child with such huge promise and his mother's greatest pride. She moved towards him, smiling a greeting, hand outstretched, and as she neared him Martin smiled back, a smile as endearing as Daniel's, but with an impudent sparkle his brother lacked.

'*Bonjour, Mademoiselle*,' said Martin conventionally. 'You have just arrived in Vermeilla? I hope you are enjoying our small village?'

'Very much, thank you. It is such a beautiful place, and I have been so happy to find old family friends like your mother and Philippe.'

'You can't be in Vermeilla and not meet *Tonton* Philippe. He is the heart and creative mind of this place.' He turned to Philippe and held out his cheek easily to be kissed. '*Bonjour, mon oncle*. How is your creative mind today?'

His manner was nicely deferential yet slightly teasing, his voice reassuringly still that of a child. This, thought Madeleine, was definitely not someone who lacked self-confidence. Philippe kissed him on both cheeks then laughingly took him lightly by the ear.

'Never mind my creative mind,' he retorted. 'How is yours? How is the Ovid translation coming on, young man?'

'Coming, *Tonton*, coming, I promise you, and even faster if I didn't have to lay tables and all the rest while my brother lounges around.'

Daniel was waiting on the other side of the table to seat himself when the others were ready, but at this he took a stray piece of string from his pocket and flicked it at his brother.

'Some of us work for a living, you little ass,' he said, though his voice was more amused than affronted. The resemblance between them was mainly in colouring, and in

146

their eyes, which in both were softer than the usual Catalan mahogany, with long, curling lashes.

Colette let Martin go, and turned to Madeleine with a shrug. 'For Martin,' she acknowledged, 'laying the table is hard work. He can write some fancy essay, but ask him to do any household chore . . .' Her voice was eloquent, but Martin merely grinned back at her.

Colette gestured them to the table. 'You must all be very hungry by this hour. Let's sit down. Daniel, could you go and fetch your father?' she asked.

Daniel nodded immediately then disappeared into the back corridor. Madeleine and Philippe sat at the table, while Martin went to the kitchen for the bread and the plate of anchovies which was to be their first course. Some minutes later Daniel reappeared with an old man leaning heavily on his arm. Or at least that was Madeleine's first impression, but then she realised that what seemed like the shuffling steps of an elderly man were actually the rather rigid, painstaking movements of a man who had only partial control of his legs. His face, too, seemed old at first, lined and set, with deep furrows around the mouth and on his forehead, and thinning grey hair completed the initial impression, but his eyes were a clear blue, and the skin on his arms and the backs of his hands was smooth. In reality Colette's husband was probably a great deal younger than Philippe.

Daniel had taken after his father, Madeleine realised, with his fine features and lean build. Only his colouring and eyes were Colette's. He settled his father into a chair at the head of the table, and once he was sure he was comfortable he took his own place next to him.

'Madeleine, this is my husband Jean-Pierre,' said Colette in a neutral voice, and then to her husband, 'Jean-Pierre, we have with us today the daughter of Luis Garriga, who has returned to Vermeilla after all these years. I am sure you will want to welcome her to our house along with the rest of us.'

The formality of the presentation made the man at the head of the table a stranger. At first he didn't react, seeming to take time to absorb the information. Madeleine felt the need to speak first.

'*Je suis enchantée, Monsieur*,' she said. She was too far from him to offer her hand, so she merely smiled.

Jean-Pierre Perrens contemplated Madeleine with a disconcerting stare, almost childlike in its directness. Next to him Daniel watched, waiting for his father to speak. The silence extended, and then Jean-Pierre Perrens turned away from Madeleine and muttered to his wife.

'Who did you bring here? Luis Garriga, you said? What has she to do with Luis Garriga?'

'I said she's his daughter, Jean-Pierre. You remember! Little Madeleine who used to come to the café before the war! She went away to England, and we haven't seen her since, but now she is a grown lady, and she has come back to visit us. We are all very happy to see her.'

Colette's voice was oddly emphatic, as though she wanted to imprint the information on his mind. Jean-Pierre gazed for what seemed like several minutes at his wife, although in reality it could only have been a few seconds, and then looked across again at Madeleine.

'Luis Garriga,' he said again, and his voice struck an unfathomable note. He looked at her for a few more seconds and then seemed to forget her and turned to contemplation of his napkin.

As the meal progressed, Madeleine couldn't figure out whether he was an intelligent man who had withdrawn into himself, or a man with a mind as damaged as his legs. Around him conversation flowed, and the rest of the family seemed to talk as though he wasn't there. Colette was clearly an indulgent mother, and Philippe the favoured uncle, and the sons therefore spoke and argued more freely than Madeleine had ever felt able to do in the presence of older adults. Her upbringing seemed so stiff in comparison. The conversation here was noisy and ceaselessly energetic, about the poor state of fishing, about the petition to the local council to build a bigger quayside so that they could bring in more modern fishing boats, about the iniquities of the council in not allowing new balcony railings on a neighbour's house.

'Just because they say the design is too modern,' Daniel snorted. 'They're dinosaurs, that's what they are! You watch, this council will turn this village into a dead place in the name of preservation. Port Vendres already has a new quay, and now they are going to have the latest fishing trawlers which can catch ten times what we can. What chance do we have? You know what will happen? All the fishermen are talking about moving their boats along the coast to Port Vendres, and all the buyers will go there too, and Vermeilla will become a place for picture postcards, full of old people and tourists.'

'But the new quay at Port Vendres is so ugly,' exclaimed Colette.

'Ugly but alive! What do you think Philippe?'

And all the while, as the arguments went back and forth, Jean-Pierre sat at the head of the table and ate what was put in front of him, anchovies, grilled squid, little meatballs in a rich sauce with beans, all local delicacies prepared especially for their visitor, and said nothing. Occasionally, though, Madeleine caught him looking at them all, one by one, seeming to measure them and discount them in one slow sweep of his eyes. The family ignored this, but Madeleine found his stare disturbing, and looked across at him several times to find his gaze upon her. He seemed to be especially focused on her, but she thought this might be because she was a visitor.

It was at the end of the meal, after a dessert of caramel flan, then coffee, that Jean-Pierre finally found his voice. In a small break in conversation he suddenly barked, not mumbling, but almost fiercely clear, 'That Luis Garriga. Where is he now?'

There was a silence, and then Colette replied, her voice sharp-edged.

'Luis Garriga is dead, Jean-Pierre. You know that. He was shot by the Germans during the war, just before the liberation.'

'I know, I know. But where is he now? Where did they put him?' His voice was querulous, demanding, and his hands were gripped tightly around his little coffee cup, as if it was too small for him to grasp properly. Madeleine found herself gripping her own cup just as tightly. She couldn't take her eyes off his contorted face.

'Put him?' The question seemed to surprise Colette as much as it did Madeleine. 'Why, you know what happened to him, Jean-Pierre. The Maquis took his body down to Philippe, in Amélie-les-Bains, and he was buried there in the cemetery.'

'Cemetery,' Jean-Pierre was still agitated, frightened almost, and his eyes were fixed on Colette. 'Not our cemetery, I hope. Not here? They didn't bury him here?'

Now it was Philippe who intervened. 'No, Jean-Pierre, in the cemetery in Amélie-les-Bains. He's buried in Amélie-les-Bains. I'm going to take Madeleine up to see his grave one day. But it's not in Vermeilla. You know that. Luis died up in the Vallespir, and was buried up there. He didn't come back to Vermeilla.'

His voice was steady and reassuring, insistent, and seemed to get through to Jean-Pierre, sitting twisted in his chair. Twisted, that's what he's like, thought Madeleine. He's like a tree that's got all twisted out of his shape, and his mind is all out of shape too. Why should he want to know where my father was buried? Why does he sound scared?

'Vallespir. That's right, up in the Vallespir! But she came here. Is she his daughter? His daughter!' Jean-Pierre laughed, a nasty, semi-triumphant laugh.

Colette spoke up, her voice quietly commanding. 'You can go through and sit on your balcony now, Jean-Pierre, and have one of your cigarettes. Daniel will take you through.'

Jean-Pierre held her gaze for a moment, and then his

head lowered, and he said no more. He allowed himself to be led away, head between his shoulders and his strange eyes hidden. At the door he grumbled something to his son, and Daniel made more room for him, and then they were gone.

There was what seemed like a long silence in the room, then Colette signalled to Martin, and he got up wordlessly to clear the table. Once he was in the kitchen Philippe let out a sigh.

'Well that was a strange outburst,' he remarked, almost idly. 'It's been a long time since he spoke like that. Not nice for the boys, of course.'

'And not very agreeable for you either, *ma petite*.' Colette's voice was troubled. 'I'm sure you do not want to hear your Papa's grave being talked about in that way. It must have been me mentioning Luis's name which set him thinking, not having heard the name for so long. He gets very confused, you know, since his accident, and strange things worry him. And the occupation frightened him because he felt trapped, and when so many other people were evacuated we were stuck here running the bar for the Germans.'

Madeleine eased her grip on her coffee cup, feeling rather stupid to have been so shaken, especially seeing how calm the man's sons had remained, although Daniel, she had noticed, had also frozen for a moment. Colette and Philippe were still watching her, their eyes anxious. They exchanged a glance and Madeleine thought, these people didn't need my visit. I'm an outsider here, stirring up memories and creating tensions. Had I not been here there wouldn't have been any outburst from Jean-Pierre. Above all she mustn't allow these people to worry about her. She spoke as brightly as she could.

'It's all right. Please don't worry about it. It was one of the things I was going to ask, anyway, where my father is buried. I had heard about people being buried where they died, and wondered if that was maybe what had happened to my father.'

'It did happen,' agreed Philippe, matching her tone, 'and quite often. But in Luis's case his team knew where to find me, and I wasn't far away. They brought him at night, and I was able to arrange his burial with the local priest. Not the best funeral, unfortunately, just me and a few people from Vermeilla who had ended up in Amélie-les-Bains as well.' He saw Madeleine's look of enquiry, and carried on, 'We only got as far as your departure, didn't we, when we were talking this morning? Well afterwards, the Germans gradually took over the whole coast, as we expected, and of course Luis left and eventually joined a small Resistance group up above Amélie-les-Bains, in the foothills of the Pyrenees – in the area known as the Vallespir. They were involved mostly in managing escape routes, being so close to Spain, but they did their fair share of sabotage, and they had a real mission to get information out about German movements and installations. Luis used to come down to Vermeilla in secret to gather information, since he wasn't really being looked for, unlike some others. Then a couple of months later the Germans evacuated most of us out of the village, as Colette said, and I ended up in Amélie-les-Bains where there was still a school and I could be of some use. We even had a few of our Vermeilla children in the school. That put me closer to Luis, and I used to see him quite often. He would stay some nights, and steal all my food, what little I had. Requisitioning, he called it! I used to tell him to save himself for his visits here, because Colette could always find some rations for him.'

'German rations,' Colette grimaced. 'It was good to be able to give him some of what the Germans should have had. It made me feel less like a collaborator.' She looked across at Madeleine, her face suddenly inexpressibly sad and tired. 'It was not a nice time, when the Germans were here, and there were only a very few of us kept here in the village to work, while everyone else was sent away. We felt so isolated, and that's what got to Jean-Pierre. At first after his accident he used to come downstairs to the bar sometimes, but when the Germans came he retreated upstairs and rarely came down, and became more and more strange.'

Daniel had come silently back into the room while she spoke, and she glanced across at him. 'He became obsessively worried about Daniel at that time, as well, and didn't want to let him out. Eventually we sent him up to Amélie-les-Bains to be with Philippe, since at least there he could go to school, and there were other children. There were no children left in Vermeilla, remember?' Daniel nodded.

'Luis's visits helped Jean-Pierre, at least at first. He would bring us news of Daniel, and tell Jean-Pierre not to worry, because the war was almost over, and the Germans would soon be gone. And of course, eventually they did go, but your father wasn't here to see it.'

Martin, too, was back in the room by now, slipping silently in from the kitchen, but no one spoke, and there seemed to be nothing to say. It was a peaceful silence, though, and Madeleine no longer felt such an outsider. Her father was a part of Philippe and Colette's lives, and remembering him was surely natural even if it did stir up painful memories. Eventually Martin moved away from his position by the door, and came towards the table. He went behind his mother and leant his head against the back of hers, his hands on her arms. Colette leant back onto him and stretched tensed shoulders. Philippe watched them with almost proprietorial eyes, a half smile playing on his face.

'We've been very serious,' he said, 'but all of these things were over a long time ago, and there's a lovely afternoon outside.'

'And a café to run,' Colette said, and she stood and faced her son. 'Do you have schoolwork to do? No? Then you can come down and help them clear up after lunch downstairs. Philippe, will you take another coffee downstairs? And you, *ma petite*, you must be tired. Shall Daniel accompany you to your hotel so that you can rest for a while, take a small siesta? Then we can meet again later on. You will eat with us again, no? And we will eat downstairs this evening, just ourselves.' This was said with emphasis, and a nod towards the corridor leading to Jean-Pierre's room.

'Thank you,' Madeleine mumbled, embarrassed. 'But

you've already been so kind. I should leave you in peace for this evening. Mme Curelée will be preparing food for this evening, I'm sure.'

'Mme Curelée! What does she know about cooking? No, you will eat with us, and taste what the café can offer you, and meet some of our people. We are here anyway, never anywhere else! As well be with us as eat on your own in that dining room of Anne-Marie Curelée's! It will at least be a lot livelier.'

'Me too, then!' chimed Martin. 'I eat downstairs this evening. I want some of Jules's pommes frites, and he was making a fricassee of pork this morning. I saw him!'

Colette's specially reserved smile softened her face. Philippe too was smiling, Madeleine noticed.

'My son,' purred Colette. 'You are without doubt the most precocious of young men, but yes, you shall eat with us this evening.'

CHAPTER TEN

The next two days passed in a whirl for Madeleine. It was a struggle to remember that on Friday morning she had been in Paris. The colours and sounds and people of Vermeilla were so forceful, so vivid, that even *Tante* Louise seemed discreetly tame in comparison.

With Daniel she walked, and sat on the sea wall, and learnt about fishing. They sat with groups of his friends, mainly young men with slicked-back hairstyles. Elvis and Ricky Nelson were all around her, Madeleine thought, with some amusement. But there were also some sharp-tongued girls of about her own age or younger, in long ponytails and wide skirts and long-sleeved blouses, all wearing the standard rope-soled espadrilles. They watched Madeleine warily, eying up her Parisian hairstyle and new fashion summer dresses, and then hunched themselves back into their groups, shoulders turned towards her. I've been an outsider all my life, she wanted to tell them, and I'm not here looking for you. Their little acts of exclusion amused her more than anything else. She preferred the company of the young men, whose badinage seemed uncomplicated and convivial, but even this was for the most part in Catalan, and beyond her grasp.

Daniel was one of this group, of course, and serenely at home with them, but different somehow, and it took some time for Madeleine to work out where the difference lay. In part it was his simple courtesy to everyone. He joked with his friends, but rarely at their expense, and seemed a shade serious next to them. And he spoke differently. He spoke the same French as his brother, educated and thoughtful, although not with Madeleine's Parisian accent. Daniel might be a fisherman, but he didn't speak like them, or even entirely like his own parents, and it was clear that Philippe's influence had been worked on him as well as on the scholarly Martin. Madeleine wondered whether fishing would be his long-term career. He was passionate about it in many ways, and it represented a way of life he believed in, but he seemed a very different, very private person when viewed alongside his robust group of friends.

And yet it was clear that they respected Daniel, and liked him, and they never made fun of him. He was one of them, a friend, and to be accepted rather than questioned. She noticed that they listened to him, and looked for his input. This village and its people were his home as they might not later be home to Martin.

At lunchtime on Sunday Daniel took her to visit his own personal vineyard, about twenty minutes' walk from the village, past some bigger houses with gardens, and then along a narrow lane which climbed gently up the hillside. Here all was vineyards, clambering up the slopes, their gnarled vines clinging to the hillside in narrow terraces built up using drystone walls. Daniel's was a small field tucked in among other smallholdings, all marked by their walled boundaries. From here you had a clear view down over the pink rooftops of the village below to the Mediterranean, blue to the horizon, clear as crystal in the Tramontane wind which freshened the air and cleaned the skies.

Daniel spent many Sundays here when there was no fishing, he explained, pruning and tying the vines, checking for pests, planting and watering new seedlings. Madeleine suspected that he came here also for the peace. The tiny stone *casot* shed in his vineyard held a little wooden chair and a blanket which she thought must be used for quiet siestas in the shade of the single fig tree. When she asked him, he turned on that smile of extraordinary sweetness, and didn't bother to answer. But he brought out the chair, and the blanket, and they sat and ate together next to the vines, bread with slices of *saucisson*, and little glasses of red wine from a cask stored in the shed, and cherries from the market.

She had bought the cherries with Colette that morning in the marketplace of Vermeilla, suddenly crowded with Sunday stalls selling fruits and vegetables, cheeses, fish, flowers, rolls of cloth in floral designs, espadrilles and earthenware. Colette had bought fish, and a small round sheep's milk cheese from the Pyrenees. At the stall where they bought the cherries, Colette introduced Madeleine to the stallholder, who had his own market garden beyond Perpignan. He was a tiny man in his late sixties or seventies, who hopped around with boundless energy and talked with everyone. He had been visiting Vermeilla to sell his produce for over forty years, and had known her father, but especially her mother.

'She had the sweetest face ever,' he told her. 'A gentle woman, and kind. I always saved her the best fruits in season. She was just one of the good people who were no longer around after the war. The last time I saw her or your father was in 1940, before the Pétainistes closed the market and began requisitioning most of my produce. We couldn't have got down here even if we'd had anything left to exchange so far from home. Colette tells me your mother died recently. I am sorry, Mademoiselle. Very sorry.'

Lots of people remembered and were sorry. Most, of course, had more to worry about in their lives now than old stories of the war years, but they liked to reminisce, and were pleased to meet Luis and Elise's daughter, whether in the bar, the street or the crowded market square. Everyone loved to talk, provided the conversation was kept off the difficult parts of the war. They'd rebuilt lives, here in Vermeilla, and old scars were not to be scratched. Philippe told her that most people in Vermeilla, as everywhere in Vichy France, had just tried to sit out the war and survive, but most of them had bitter memories of struggle and hunger, and some, of course, had things to hide. They were all, he told her, a mix of good and bad and heroic, just like every day today, but in the war it just mattered that bit more. There was an underlying silence which Madeleine could almost touch. You had to feel your way through each conversation.

It was easier with Daniel and his friends, who had only known the war as young children. They seemed to know little and care less, and that made things much less complicated. Daniel in particular seemed to take things just as they came, and reacted to everything with that ever serene smile. Walking with him again on the Sunday evening, on her way back to her hotel after eating the fish with Colette, Madeleine thought how easy he was to be with, but wondered at him too. Faced with a younger brother who was so academically gifted, and the cosseted darling of his mother, it didn't seem to occur to Daniel to feel jealous, or dissatisfied in any way. If Martin challenged or baited him he would always have a reply, but no more than was necessary. At no point had she seen Daniel initiate any teasing, or show any aggression.

With his friends too, as she had seen, he was equally unruffled and easy-going, if always a little reserved. She wondered how many people could claim to know Daniel really well. Philippe, perhaps? Did he have the key to what went on inside Daniel's quiet head?

With her, Daniel was like an elder brother, attentive and concerned without being overprotective. And he was one of the few who seemed unsurprised by her arrival in Vermeilla. Others in the village had made her very aware of the audacity of what she had done in coming alone to Vermeilla. This was a traditional society, and when they learnt that she had travelled alone from Paris and was staying on her own at the hotel, men's eyebrows would

161

twitch, and the women would exclaim in mock admiration.

After one such exclamation Philippe had suggested that she might like to come and stay with him, but reviewing his jumbled home in her mind, and the little room she had once occupied, which was now used as a store, Madeleine was not keen. She no more wanted the memories than she did the constant company, and was rather enjoying the independence of hotel life. She looked up at the placid young man walking beside her, and suddenly asked him.

'Do you think I have made a mistake in coming to Vermeilla, Daniel? I don't mean in wanting to meet you all, but in the way I've done it? I seem to have shocked some people in Vermeilla, being here as a girl on my own.'

They were nearly in front of the Hotel Bon Repos by now, nothing in Vermeilla being far away, and Daniel therefore stopped. He looked across at the sea wall and gestured, a question in his eyes. She nodded, and they went to sit on it, feet resting on the cobbles. Daniel took an inevitable look along to where the boats were again preparing to go to sea, and his crew mates would soon be waiting for him. Then he turned and gave her his usual smile.

'It's a funny place, Vermeilla,' he answered at last. 'It's just a village, set in its ways like other villages around here, but yet at the same time we get some tourists, and so people are more used to seeing different types here. And we always seem to have had people moving in from outside, like *Tonton* Philippe, and my father, of course. If you were a local girl, then you might be more fiercely judged, but since you are not, they just show some surprise, but then they'll get used to the situation. They just like to comment, that's all. You're the one-day wonder. There's not much new in this village most days. And you are pretty remarkable, after all.'

He smiled again as he finished, and his eyes flashed in the dimming daylight.

'Remarkable?' questioned Madeleine. 'Do you know, I've never known anyone more ordinary than me. I find this whole trip more testing than you could know. My mind's really overwhelmed at the moment, and I am unsure how to take things, so I don't want to get anything wrong. And I feel how alone I am, a lot of the time, but I am finding it liberating. I wish you knew how hemmed in I've been all my life.'

'Well, you're certainly not ordinary, Madeleine.' Daniel's voice was even more than usually gentle. 'I'm lost in admiration. I can't think of any girl I know who would travel outside this region on her own, let alone to Paris or London, not knowing what she would find, or whether there would be anyone to receive her. I'm not sure I would do it myself! I've never been much further than Perpignan in my life, which shows how adventurous I am.' There was a note of self-derision to his voice, but his smile returned, and he stood up from the wall a little self-consciously.

'You must be so tired, after all the travelling and then everything that's happening here. I hope you didn't find it too tiring walking out to the vineyard today. No? I'm glad. We can maybe do it again one day.'

He leant down and kissed her on each cheek. 'Sleep well, Madeleine. Is it not tomorrow that you are going with *Tonton* Philippe to see your father's grave? At Amélie-les-Bains? I hope that will not be too hard for you. But you'll have Philippe with you.'

He hesitated a moment, and reached out a hand half towards her, then withdrew it abruptly. His voice was less smooth than usual as he spoke, but the words were quite straightforward. 'We will see you tomorrow, Madeleine. Goodnight.'

'Goodnight, Daniel' she replied, strangely lost for other words. She watched him move off down the quay, calling to the other fishermen, pulling his packet of Gitanes from his pocket as he went, and then she herself slowly moved, towards the hotel and her little room with its old-fashioned bed and its patterned tiles, her tiny, private place of solitude and peace.

From this little haven she watched later as Daniel and all the fishermen put to sea for the night, and she began a letter to Robert, with so much to tell since leaving Paris only three days before that she hardly knew where to start. She would wait to send it until she had seen their father's grave, but for now she wanted to capture the treasured welcome and sense of roots, the daytime noise and the night-time peace, and the discoveries, the learning about Luis Garriga and his young bride, who had come to Vermeilla and made a life which was cut short but not forgotten.

'I think you should try to come here,' she wrote. 'It is almost impossible to describe to you all the people and the colours, and the Mediterranean, and the amazing landscape, and Colette's bar, and all the little streets around. And it was the strangest experience to be back in our old apartment. I remembered it so exactly, and Philippe had changed nothing – really nothing at all. There are some things here which are uncanny, and I don't fully understand why Philippe has chosen to live in the past in this way. He seems to hero-worship Papa, but I'm not sure that would be enough reason for me. He says he just found it easy to move in, and perhaps that explains things, since I don't think he has much interest in his material environment.

'I get hints from the Curelées, who run my hotel, that Philippe is thought to be perhaps a little too involved in the lives of Colette and her boys: quickly hushed little remarks that could mean a lot or nothing at all, a bit like *Tante* Louise's bit of gossip she'd heard. But basically Philippe is a darling, a genuinely lovely man who, I think, just wants simplicity and his close people. You need to meet him, Robert, and also to meet Colette and her family, except maybe her strange husband. Philippe and Colette would be so stunned to meet you too – the living Luis Garriga!'

It was hard to continue after this. Madeleine had such an image of her brother in her mind that she felt desperately adrift all of a sudden. She laid the letter aside to finish tomorrow, after the visit to Amélie-les-Bains. There was still so much to learn about her father and what had happened to him, and yet she was already so tired and saturated with information. She stood at the window and watched the couples walking along the quayside below her, laughing and together, and felt even more alone. As the fishing boats left the harbour the feeling intensified, and the quayside looked oddly deserted in spite of the people still strolling along it.

Melancholy is dangerous nonsense, she thought, and pushed her window open wider to the evening air. The world came closer, and as she breathed deeply her solitude receded and the safe sound of beaching waves reached out to touch her. I didn't ever think this was going to be easy, she thought. And yet it has already been easier and more fruitful than I could have hoped for.

Just as she turned back from the window to put away her half-finished letter, a knock came to the door. It was Madame Curelée, offering coffee, and a snack should she need it. She gratefully accepted the coffee and went downstairs to take it with them and a new young couple who had arrived that day from Toulouse, and who planned to walk in the Pyrenees but who were first seeking the grave of Antonio Machado, the most famous of all Spanish poets, who was buried in nearby Collioure. The young man was a researcher at the University of Toulouse, he explained, specialising in the literature of the Spanish Civil War. Madeleine vaguely remembered her mother talking about Machado, although she didn't remember ever seeing any of his work. It seemed that in this area, however, he was famous, and the young man was passionate about him.

'We're building him a proper vault for his grave now, and that's why we came at this time. I'm a member of the Friends of Machado, and we've got permission and money to build a fitting memorial for him. You wouldn't believe the people who are involved: Pablo Casals, who is still here in exile, you know, from Franco's Spain, and André Malraux – you know of Malraux, of course? So many senior figures of literature, music, art and even politics. And all giving freely and campaigning for this grave. They're building it now in Collioure, and we are going along tomorrow to be part of it.'

His passion struck Madeleine as odd for a Frenchman on behalf of a Spanish poet whose name was not exactly an international household name. She asked him why Machado was so important. His reply was both political and emotive. Machado had stood for Republicanism, had fled north ahead of Franco's troops to stay in free Spain, had left his country finally only when Barcelona was within hours of falling, and he himself exhausted and in poor health. He had loved France, had lived in Paris during his life, but for him to end up in France in exile and defeat, to die just weeks later, was a part of the whole tragedy of Spain.

'He was their greatest poet, you have to understand that, and he suffered so much personal loss that it comes through in his poetry. His brother became a fervent supporter of Franco, which was such a bitter blow, and he lost his wife, and his mistress, and everything he owned. When you read his poems they speak about every war and every separation and every destroyed life. Someone who has meant so much to his country is always worth studying.'

Madame Curelée seemed to be very proud to have the young intellectuals in her little hotel. Like all the Catalans Madeleine had met, she could be reserved but quickly caught the mood when passions were inflamed. Not only, she said, did she have the daughter of Luis Garriga staying with her, whom the whole village was now talking about, but also she had a scholar who had come to work with

Pablo Casals. As they sat together, she scurried about them, bringing a second cup of coffee, and then some tiny glasses of a local brandy. The mood in the room mellowed from passionate to relaxed, and Madeleine felt her own mood lifting as well.

An hour later, as they headed for bed, the young man lent her a volume of Machado's poems translated into French, and as she lay in bed waiting for sleep to come, reading the rather lyrical and often elaborate verse, her eyes lit on a line she remembered her mother quoting to her.

De mer en mer entre nous deux la guerre, plus profonde que la guerre – From sea to sea between us two is war, deeper than war.

Her mother's unhappiness, her father's death, their separation; it was all there in Machado's verse. His life and theirs were all part of the same history, which had been bigger than them all. She found the thought strangely comforting, and as Machado's verse revolved slowly round her tired brain she finally fell asleep, with her window open to the sound of the waves.

Chapter Eleven

The road to Amélie-les-Bains took them inland through the Roussillon plains to the foothills of the Pyrenees. Avenues of plane trees bordered the road between the villages on the way, and as they drove slowly along in Philippe's battered 2CV, he joked that the trees were there to show his old car where to go.

'Citroën began making these ten years ago,' he told Madeleine, 'to bring motorised transport to the peasants. I was one of the first to buy. But the old thing is showing her years a little now, and she creaks when we go round corners. She likes this straight bit, and hates those hills up ahead!'

He pointed out Canigou, French Catalonia's own little mountain standing distinct on the horizon from wherever you looked, its peak still tipped with snow.

'They say no man is a real Catalan who hasn't climbed

Canigou. So I've climbed it once a year for the last thirty years, and still no one thinks I'm a Catalan!'

They had set off early. Philippe had told her he wanted to pick someone up by eight o'clock in Céret, but he wouldn't tell her who it was. The sky above them was blue and clear, but the air was still fresh, and the early May sunshine had not yet touched the land, which was a dark, deep green all around them. An intense sense of expectation stilled Madeleine's tongue. She felt alert, aware, watchful almost, and was content to let Philippe chatter on as she sat beside him and watched the flat, cultivated fields and vineyards slip by.

Céret was a surprise after the narrow streets of Vermeilla and its brightly painted houses. Céret was a dream of yellow stone, with gently elegant streets leading into a centre of little squares and cool fountains. They passed the new Museum of Modern Art, which had been created just a few years before in the old town prison buildings. Picasso was a patron, and had gifted them numerous pieces of his work. Just five years earlier, she knew, he had given them a major series of painted pottery pieces. Paris might have its amazing art collections, but this place had a personal connection to Picasso, Matisse, Chagall and others, and she longed to visit the museum.

Now was not the moment, however. Philippe passed by the museum and turned into a narrower street. He stopped almost immediately in front of a shuttered shop front, with the legend *Objets d'Art Catalans* above it.

'We're here.' announced Philippe, and leapt out of his side of the car. Madeleine followed more slowly, and by the time she had waited for a car to squeeze past her, Philippe had already disappeared down a side passage. She hurried after him, and arrived to see the side door open, and a young man shaking hands with Philippe. Philippe waved to her impatiently.

'Come, come, Madeleine, and meet Jordi. Jordi, this is Luis Garriga's daughter, the girl I spoke to you about. Are you ready, Jordi? We should be on our way, no point in us coming inside. I can explain everything to Madeleine as we drive.'

Jordi held out his hand perfunctorily to Madeleine. He was a big, strongly built man of about thirty who might have been a rugby player, and the hand he extended was broad, with cracked, slightly discoloured nails. He was dressed in loose cotton trousers and a shirt which needed ironing, and his longish hair looked as though he only ever ran a finger or two through it, scorning scissors and hairbrush.

He seemed to find her evident bewilderment amusing, but didn't bother explaining. His tone was curt as he greeted her.

'Good morning, Mademoiselle. It seems we're in Philippe's hands. And yes, Philippe, we should go now. I can afford to keep the gallery closed on a quiet Monday morning, but I'll need to open this afternoon, and I don't have any help this week.'

Back in the 2CV, this time squashed into the rear seat, Madeleine craned her neck to hear as Philippe shot information at her over his shoulder.

'Jordi's father was shot alongside your father,' he yelled, looking briefly back at her and then at the road, narrowly

171

avoiding an oncoming car. 'There were only the two of them in the camp at the time, so the Germans didn't time their raid very well. Your father was killed outright, and Jordi's father was shot and captured, but survived. I wanted you to meet Jordi. I think it may help you.'

Madeleine's heart leapt. It hadn't occurred to her that she might meet the son of one of her father's comrades; that she might be able to talk to him. And his father had survived the war. Had he shared his experiences with Jordi, she wondered?

The back of his head gave her no clues. Jordi looked fixedly at the road ahead as though to make up for Philippe's inattention, and a long silence followed Philippe's words. Then Jordi spoke, still without turning his head, and his voice came back to Madeleine like a cold shower. The words were correct, but the tone was crushing.

'I gather my job this morning is to show you where your father died. I am prepared to do so. I am not sure whether it will help you, as Philippe thinks, but I can understand that you may think it important to go there.'

His whole demeanour was stony and unwelcoming, and Madeleine shrank further back in the rear seat. She sat in total silence as they continued their journey. She had come this morning with Philippe to visit her father's grave. That was one thing. But the idea of actually visiting the resistance camp with this man set her nerves on edge. She hadn't come prepared for the next step, and to go there with someone so overtly hostile made it a still harder step to take. And yet she wanted to learn: she had come here for that sole purpose.

Stomach knotted, she sat out the rest of the journey, half listening to Philippe and Jordi as they talked about some bullfight due to take place in Céret, and almost oblivious to the striking landscape emerging around them as they made their slow progress up to Amélie-les-Bains.

Amélie-les-Bains itself was a beautiful place, set in the hillside, a medieval spa town with dramatic views over the valley below. The River Tech ran beside the town, its shallow waters broad under a gracious bridge, preparing to drop into the valley of trees, and from wherever you looked you could see Canigou, standing guard on the horizon. To Madeleine's relief Jordi chose not to accompany her and Philippe to her father's grave. She and Philippe left him sitting at a café table next to the marketplace, where stalls were doing brisk trade, even on a Monday morning. He hadn't had breakfast, he told them, and would wait for them here.

As they left Jordi, and walked away through the bustle of the market, the tension which had constricted Madeleine's throat eased a little. Philippe walked at his usual brisk pace, his long, gangly legs ahead of Madeleine's by several yards. At a corner he turned, and seeing her set, pale face he stopped, and took her arm.

'This is all a bit too much for you all in one go, isn't it?' he asked. 'I should have told you that I had telephoned to Jordi. I'm not quite sure why I didn't; perhaps because I know that last step is going to be difficult for you, and yet I really think you should make it. If you don't want to go, just tell me, and we can cancel the whole thing.'

'No, no. I don't want to cancel. I want to see the place.'

Madeleine put her hand over Philippe's as it lay on her sleeve. 'You don't know the way there yourself, no?'

'No, I never knew. Luis didn't want to compromise me in any way. There were schoolteachers during the occupation whose pupils were threatened at gunpoint to make them divulge information. I lived too close, and too many people knew he visited me, he used to say. Why do you ask? Did you want me to go with you?' He paused, and studied Madeleine's face. 'Is it Jordi who worries you, then?'

She nodded, saying nothing.

'Yes, I see. He can be a bit intimidating, although not normally as much so as this morning. You know, Jordi's father was shot three times by the Germans that day. But more importantly, he was captured and taken to their cells in Perpignan, where he was tortured for three days to make him talk about his fellow Maquis and their operations. I don't know what he told them, but there were no arrests made as a result, so he must have put on a very good act. Once they had finished with him he was sent to the concentration camp at Rivesaltes, and if the occupation hadn't ended so soon afterwards I am sure he would have been shot.

'I knew him quite well after the war, but he would never talk about those days. He had a misshapen arm that no one ever mentioned, and he was always weak, and I know he had problems sleeping. But his biggest problem was with drink. After his wife died Jordi looked after him. He only died three or four years ago, and until then Jordi had done little else but take care of him. It isn't easy for Jordi to take you up there to where it all happened, but I believe it's good for him to go there too, otherwise I wouldn't have suggested it.'

Madeleine was silent, aghast. The lines from Machado came back to her, the war deeper yet than war. They were all, it seemed, part of a history that was bigger than themselves, and hers was only a small part. All those years that she had spent interred in the cold house in Forsham, Jordi had been struggling to support and take care of his damaged father. How old would he have been when his father was shot? Fifteen? Sixteen? Old enough to take on the burden but not old enough to do so without damage. No wonder if he didn't want to go back to the site with her. She looked up at Philippe.

'I think I have more to learn than I realised,' she said.

'You're doing just fine,' he reassured her. 'None of it is easy, for either of you.' He removed her hand gently from where it clung to his arm, and they went on hand in hand.

The cemetery was ornate, full of marble mausoleums reflecting the sunlight, framed by the cypress trees, but Luis's grave was very simple; a white stone cross on a square stone base. The inscription read only '*Luis Garriga, 1903–1944. Mort pour la France*'.

'He should really have been buried in the military cemetery,' murmured Philippe, as they stood together facing the headstone. 'But it was all I could do to have him buried at all at that time. I only put the headstone on after the war. And of course, Luis wasn't French, or in the army. It would all have been a bit complicated back then.'

Madeleine traced the inscription with her finger. 'I

prefer it like this. Papa wasn't a military man. He was a writer who was forced into action by two wars, one which destroyed his country, and one which destroyed him. He would have liked that he was buried simply by a few friends, as close as possible to Spain.'

'That's probably the best epitaph he could have, Madeleine, *ma petite*. I even queried whether I should really give him a cross, knowing how he felt about religion. But I did want him to be honoured like a real soldier, so I chose the same headstone as they all have.'

'He wouldn't have minded.' It was true, Madeleine thought. Luis was far too humorous to be bothered by a mere cross. Being close to Spain would have been far more important.

'How far are we here from the border with Spain?' she asked.

'As the crow flies? Maybe seven or eight kilometres. That's why *passeurs* like Enric worked from the Vallespir.'

'Enric?'

'Jordi's father. That's what he did during the war – helped people over the border to Spain. Your father worked with him for years. In fact, if I'm not mistaken, it was he who took you over from near Céret in November 1942.'

This second revelation took Madeleine's breath away once and for all, and she acquiesced dumbly when Philippe suggested they should move on.

Jordi was still sitting where they had left him by the market square, a cigarette in his hand, and a second or perhaps third cup of coffee in front of him. A few crumbs remained on a plate beside him, and Madeleine was relieved to see that he looked a little less forbidding. Indeed, as they approached he smiled, and signalled to the waiter.

'You must be needing a coffee,' he suggested, and Philippe nodded and sat down with obvious relief. Jordi took coffee too. Perhaps it was the caffeine which had lifted his mood, Madeleine mused. She wondered how long it had been since he last visited the site where the Maquis had lived. Surely he must have been back since the war? As she drank her *café crème* she hoped that Philippe was right, and that this visit would be helpful to Jordi, and not just an ordeal.

She was less tense as they drove out of the town, on a narrow road which snaked up into the hills above, and was able to appreciate better the spectacular view of Amélie-les-Bains and the river below. The hillsides were green with a forest of trees which hugged the road, but occasionally the road would open out, and new valleys would appear. It was very beautiful now, but it might not be quite so lovely in winter, she thought, and she wondered what sort of accommodation the men who lived out here in hiding had had.

They only had three kilometres or so to travel to where they would leave the car. Jordi signed to Philippe to draw over by a small lay-by, and then the roles were reversed.

'I'll leave you two to do this one on your own,' Philippe announced. 'I'll take a walk around here and wait for you. But take your time. There's no need to hurry.'

'We'll only need an hour, no more.' Jordi looked down at Madeleine's feet, and nodded approval at her flat walking shoes. 'It's not far,' he told her, 'but it's a rough track in places.'

It was not only rough, but a steep climb as well through endless trees, the ground carpeted with dead leaves which masked the track, which grew increasingly narrow as they climbed. Here there were no spectacular views and the track was not overlooked from anywhere. Madeleine trudged behind Jordi, who made no conversation, and just pushed ahead and left her to follow. After about twenty minutes he branched off the track, and led her along a very narrow path which was almost indistinguishable between the trees, and they then emerged onto a rough, uneven plateau, almost completely surrounded by a miniature red cliff of shale and earth, with trees perched uncertainly above, their roots poking through the shale, and presumably binding the cliff sides together. Here Jordi stopped, and turned to Madeleine.

'This is it. This was their camp,' he said baldly.

Madeleine looked round in amazement. 'But there's nothing here! I thought there would at least be some shelter, a stream for water, something? Where did they live?'

'Oh, there was a shed, quite a big one, which they built for themselves. And another small shed where they cooked. But there's no trace of them now. The wood has all been taken away to be used elsewhere. And they had water. You can't see it from here, but there's another path like the one we just came through, on the other side over there, which leads to a small stream which comes from a source further up the hill. It's often dry in the summer, despite the source, and they had to store water, but in winter they had fresh

178

supplies. But there weren't many men here, you know, not like the really big Maquis groups up by Thuir and Prades. They had caves there and old mineshafts they used to live in. Here they were much more out in the open, but they needed some people this side of Canigou, and this close to the border.'

'Like your father? Philippe tells me he was the *passeur* who guided me and my family over to Spain in November 1942. I remember him, I think. He seemed a really big man, at least to me then, a bit taller than my father, and he took us to a little cottage over the border. There was a man there who took us down in a cart with a donkey to join a train somewhere. I was only six, so I don't remember the details, but I remember being hidden under a tarpaulin in the cart.'

Jordi smiled his first genuine smile. 'That would be my father's cousin, Felip. The rest of the family lived near Jonquera, but Felip lived in the hills near his sheep. He loved helping my father after we had to leave Spain. He felt all the time that he was fighting the Germans that he was also fighting Franco. One Fascist was the same as another, he would say. At first, of course, my father was helping Spaniards to get into France and out of Franco's hands. It was only later that he started taking people in the other direction. Felip sheltered people going in both directions.'

'He gave us soup.' The memory came back to Madeleine suddenly. 'I was cold, and it was wonderful.'

'So you were six when you left France?' This was the first sign of curiosity Jordi had shown.

Madeleine sighed. 'Yes. We had to leave before the

Germans came, because my parents had both rather incriminated themselves through the work they were doing, and of course my mother was half English, which didn't help. We were supposed to return after the war was over, but then my father died, so we never came home.'

'You see here as home?'

'The only memory I have of family life is of here.'

'How ironic.' His voice had a bitter edge, but it didn't close her out. 'My only memory of real family life is from before the exodus, the *Retirada*, before we had to flee Spain. From when we arrived in France, life just became more and more complicated.'

Madeleine wanted to ask him about his father, but it was too soon. She stayed on less personal ground.

'Would you go back to Spain if you could?'

'Right now? To live under Franco? No. I don't think I could, and in any case Spaniards who left can't go back – they get arrested. I slip over the border sometimes to see my family, and they manage all right, but there are too many silences, and watching your neighbour, and gritting your teeth rather than fighting back. I don't think I could live like that. But one day! One day I'll be able to go back.'

Madeleine studied Jordi's rough face twisted in passionate defiance, his dishevelled clothes and unruly hair, and could see his point. She couldn't picture this belligerent man living quietly under an alien regime. He would make a good resistance fighter himself, but he would need action, not quiet, underground anti-Franco activity.

'So for now you're here,' she said as matter-of-factly as

possible. 'And you're running the gallery below where you live?'

'Yes. I make my living as a potter, making things that will sell to tourists.' Again his voice had a bitter edge. 'But when I can find time I'm a sculptor. We weren't allowed to go to school here, when I came to France, not at first anyway, and then came the war, so there wasn't much chance of any real schooling. I don't even write French well, so I'm not much good for anything else. But thankfully we had a neighbour who had a good business making ceramics after the war, and he gave me a job cleaning up and stuff, and then I found I had a talent. It's a nice soft place, Céret, for selling anything arty. People come all year round to the museum. So after a while I was able to afford the rent on the gallery, but I mostly sell other people's stuff. It sells better than mine.'

Madeleine felt almost uncomfortable in the face of Jordi's fierce intensity. He seemed to pin her to the rocks behind them with those unblinking brown eyes. Then he turned away abruptly.

'Is there anything more you want to know about this place?' he asked.

Madeleine looked around her. 'I don't know what to ask. I find it so strange to think of my father and yours living here for a year and half. It seems incredible.'

'They weren't here that long. At first your father was just in a safe house near Céret. My father worked from home in Céret too, until someone denounced him and he had to go into hiding. They had a couple of bases, I think, and kept moving them, but they ended up here about five months before the end. Just after the New Year, it was, in 1944.'

'And you were allowed to come up here?'

'Allowed?' Jordi laughed, with real humour. 'Oh no, I wouldn't say I was allowed! I came once with my father and I thought I was going to be shot!'

'What is that boy doing here?'

The Maquis' unit commander stood rigid in front of the door of the shed, his face contorted with anger. Jordi shivered in the freezing February air, and tried to make himself as small as possible behind his father.

Enric pointed to the sack of potatoes at his feet. 'He helped me to carry this up here.' His voice was unapologetic. 'He's of an age where he can be handy. I don't see why he shouldn't be. You've never complained yet about all the provisions he brings up here on his bike.'

'But he didn't bring them here! You brought them here. You met him on the road before, and you weren't stupid enough to bring him all the way to the camp.'

Other men emerged from the rough shed behind the commander, most of them surprisingly young, some dressed in makeshift combats, others in overalls, none of them dressed for the outdoors, having come outside in a hurry at the commander's words. There would be maybe eight or ten of them, Jordi thought, although he hardly dared to raise his eyes from the scrubby ground at his feet. As a group they could hardly have been more intimidating.

'The sack was too heavy to carry on my own. He brought fresh bread too, and some cheese. Have a look.'

182

Enric walked forward, leaving Jordi exposed on his own in the clearing. He didn't dare move, and fastened his eyes on his father's back.

'I don't care about the cheese, you damned fool! You could have left the stuff hidden down below and it could be collected later. Instead of which you've shown a child the way to the camp.'

'Except he's not a child,' Enric protested. 'He's only a year younger than young Montagnard here. If I didn't need him to watch out for his mother he'd be here with me full-time, doing proper guide work.'

'Well he's not here, is he!' the commander snarled. 'While he's living down there this camp can be of no interest to him.'

Enric didn't reply, and a silence hung between the two men. The men by the shed stood equally silent, expressionless but with watchful eyes. Then a figure pushed his way between them and moved forward. Astonished, Jordi recognised Luis, who used to visit them in Céret sometimes when his father still lived at home. So he was here too, with Enric! Jordi hadn't known – this was something his father hadn't told him. Luis was a Spaniard too, another Catalan, surely a friend? He had eaten with them many times. Now, Jordi knew, he would have been given some other name, since no one was supposed to know any of the Maquis' names. He looked Jordi straight in the eye without any apparent recognition.

'Do you remember how you came up here this afternoon, son?' His voice was gentler than the commander's. Jordi gulped, and took courage.

183

'No,' he lied. 'I was following my father, and all I could see was his back. The sack was heavy, and we had it over both our shoulders. I was right up close behind him. I didn't have any time to look around me.'

'Sure?'

'Yes, sir.'

'Then all we have to do is take you back down blindfolded, and there's no harm done.' Luis turned to the commander. 'Would that not work? We take the boy back down, and then we eat his bread, and next time he stays on the road where his father normally meets him.'

Enric was still standing in front of the commander, the cheese and bread in his hands. There was another silence, and no one moved, then the commander barked, 'Montagnard!'

'Yes?'

'Bring a scarf for a blindfold, and get that boy out of here. And boy!'

'Yes, sir?'

'You forget you ever came here, or even what your father's name is, right?'

'Yes, sir.'

'And boy!'

'Yes?'

'Thank you for the provisions. Tell your mother we know what it must cost her to send them to us, when there is so little food for anyone. Thank her for me.'

Jordi grinned at Madeleine. 'And do you know, he really meant it! He was genuinely grateful. And of course he wanted to be sure the supplies wouldn't dry up! But I was glad to get out of there that day, I can tell you!'

'I bet!' Madeleine returned the grin, feeling braver herself. It was a glimpse of her father, the merest glimpse, but a good one. 'So you only came that one time?'

'Just the once, until after the war.' Jordi's grin faded. 'Then I came back to see where the bastards destroyed my father.'

'So what happened, Jordi? How did the Germans find the camp?'

Jordi hunched his shoulder in a new gesture of exclusion.

'They were betrayed,' he said roughly. 'It happened all the time.'

He made a move back towards the gap in the cliff side.

'Come, we have to get back. Philippe is waiting for us, and I have a gallery to run.'

Very few words were exchanged on the way down the hill to the car. Philippe was waiting for them, smoking a Gauloise. He offered one to Jordi, who accepted it, and they stood for a moment smoking in a very male silence. Madeleine crossed to the other side of the road, and looked up at the hill. The entrance to the track was inconspicuous, and further up it, when you reached it, the smaller track leading to the camp itself was almost invisible in the trees. It would have been a thousand to one chance for the hideout to be discovered by the Germans by accident. So they had been betrayed, but by whom? A local, currying favour with the Nazis? Surely there were precious few German sympathisers by the summer of 1944, with the Allies on the verge of retaking France. Or had the resistance group been infiltrated? Did Jordi know? He had certainly not told her everything he knew.

As they climbed back into the car, Madeleine touched Jordi on the arm and asked, 'Will you show me your gallery?'

'If you want,' was the brief reply, but to her relief his voice was softer again.

The gallery was a tiny space crammed with artwork, paintings by a number of local artists on the walls, and on every available surface sculptures and hand-painted ceramics, most of which were Jordi's. His sculptures were of sullen peasants and labourers, an enraged, powerful bull and another injured, suffering beast, more anguished than angry. The ceramics were painted with images of labour and heat, and with bodies and lovers, sometimes touching, sometimes at gaze. His work was raw, hot, loaded with colour and completely untempered.

Jordi moved around opening shutters while Philippe and Madeleine wandered and touched. The work seemed to want to be touched. There was no attempt at cool displays or elegant presentation of the works, but the space was light and the colours glowed, and the pieces sat alongside each other in unfashioned harmony. Jordi referred to a new organic movement of art which Madeleine had never heard of, but she thought he didn't actually follow any movement, just his own basic instinct for beauty and anger.

There was a small room behind the gallery which Jordi used as a workshop. It was dusty, and rather too dark to be ideal for a working studio, but it was surprisingly ordered and well organised, with Jordi's materials catalogued on shelves along the walls. It was an intensely physical space which was obviously Jordi's whole world and possibly his refuge.

Philippe whispered to her that they should get lunch, but it didn't seem right to move Jordi from this space. She didn't know what or when he might eat, but she guessed it would be erratic and would completely follow his appetites. She didn't want to leave. There was too much that this young man had not yet shared with her. He had known her father. Surely he could speak about him? And she wanted to know more about Jordi.

As Philippe made moves to leave, she approached Jordi and planted herself in front of him.

'Thank you for showing me the camp today, Jordi. You must realise that I am really searching to understand everything that happened to my father and all that surrounded him, all the history I missed. I've come a long way to find out – practically run away from my family,' she laughed, with a new sense of freedom. 'Could you find the time to meet me again, do you think? To continue our discussion? Could you meet me once more during the short time I have here?'

Jordi contemplated her for a long moment, not unfriendly, just thinking, as if a major decision was involved.

'All right,' he replied at last. 'I'll meet you.'

Madeleine felt a wave of relief, then surprise as Jordi continued almost aggressively, 'But not in Vermeilla. Are you scared to go on a motorbike? No? Then I'll meet you at the entrance to the village tomorrow evening, after I close up here, and we'll go somewhere else. Somewhere where we can talk without ghosts. Give me an hour to come to you. I'll meet you at seven-thirty, is that OK?'

She nodded.

'Till tomorrow, then,' he said, and briefly shook her hand as though she was a stranger. She wondered why he would not come to meet her in Vermeilla. But the point had been won, and he was going to meet her. He hadn't closed the door on her, and he'd said they were going to talk.

'*A demain*,' Madeleine agreed, and the shop bell rang behind them as she and Philippe left the gallery.

CHAPTER TWELVE

It was considerably later than seven-thirty when Jordi met her the following evening, but Madeleine knew better than to complain. He pulled up at the junction outside Vermeilla on a small motorbike, and shouted above its rather rattly, clamorous engine for Madeleine to climb up behind him. The motorbike had once been black, but was now a well-worn grey colour, with rather more dust than paint. Madeleine pulled her full cotton skirt around her knees, and sat behind Jordi, putting her arms around him as he told her, and holding on tight despite her embarrassment as the bike throttled away over what seemed like an endless series of bumps in the road.

Jordi headed along the coast, heading south. The sun was setting on their right, behind the vines in the hillside, and to their left the Mediterranean soon came into view, deepening blue under a cloudless sky. They drove through

Collioure without stopping, much to Madeleine's regret, since she had already heard so much about this beautiful village, bigger and more artistically famous than Vermeilla, and she craned her head to see the medieval castle on her left, dominating and guarding the harbour, before they sped on and up another hill, losing sight of the sea for a while before it came back, a deeper blue than ever on their left, and they were again in the countryside. She wondered where they were going, but after a few more minutes they passed the entrance for Port Vendres, and drove down into the fishing port which Daniel had spoken of only a few days before.

Port Vendres was a bustling harbour, and Madeleine could see some of the modern fishing boats which Daniel had mentioned, berthed alongside the quay, and further along two bigger boats which looked as though they might be carrying cargo.

Jordi stopped halfway along the harbour, and parked the motorbike in front of a bar much busier than any in Vermeilla. Inside, fishermen and workmen were finishing glasses of pastis before heading home for dinner, and outside, tables facing the busy road and harbour were serving drinks and food. There didn't seem to be any tourists here, but a group of men in working clothes were eating fish soup, and a family was busy ordering, their noisy children in imminent danger, Madeleine thought, of running into the road.

Jordi waved Madeleine towards a table, and sat opposite her.

'I've always liked Port Vendres,' he announced, with

obvious satisfaction. 'It's a real sort of place, a working port, and full of people like me – migrants from all over, from the north, from Spain, people who don't go to tourist centres like Collioure or even Vermeilla. They want work, and they go to the big cities, but they have also come to Port Vendres. It's not so Catalan, perhaps, but it's not pretentious like Céret, and I like it. I come here sometimes and eat, just for a change.'

He seemed much happier this evening, freer than yesterday, and he sat with his face to the breeze and breathed in the air, stretching his legs by the side of the little table in a gesture of relaxation.

'It's a better place to talk, too, if that's what you want to do. Good neutral ground and everyone's too busy to be listening in.'

Was that an opening, Madeleine wondered? She was increasingly curious about this young man, and wanted to ask him questions, but was frightened of seeing his face close over again. The waiter brought a menu and offered drinks, and Jordi ordered pastis for both of them.

'The fish soup here is outstanding,' he said. 'Really pungent flavours, and a meal in itself. But don't let me dictate to you.'

'It sounds wonderful,' concurred Madeleine. 'It's something I haven't yet eaten locally.'

The food ordered, the waiter placed the two glasses of pastis before them, and Madeleine added a shot of water and watched it turn the milky colour which had always fascinated her. Gingerly she raised the glass and took a sip. It smelt of aniseed balls, and tasted worse, and she put the glass down hurriedly, her face screwed up in displeasure.

'To think I've watched people drinking this and wanted to taste it!' she exclaimed. 'I can see why they drink it in ports – it tastes like engine oil! Is this what you drink in Céret, or do you have something more civilised as an aperitif inland?'

Jordi laughed. 'Neither!' he answered. 'I don't really go out in Céret, except to go to party meetings.'

'Party?'

'The Communist party. I'm a member. It's quite common, you know, around here. We don't even have horns! The Communist party runs most things in Céret, and they don't turn away Spaniards like me. To me, the Communists are the only people who really speak up for ordinary people in France, and they're certainly the only party speaking up now, in the mess we're in. Have you heard about it? De Gaulle being imposed on us as head of state without elections, and all this talk of dissolving the republic. It's like Franco all over again. Those who crave power will always take advantage when democracy gets in a mess. You can say what you like about the Communists, and them being too tied to Moscow, but they wouldn't have allowed us to get into such a shambles, you can bet your life on that.'

He paused, and then gestured in the direction of his beloved Spain, a few kilometres down the road. 'And as for Spain, if the Communists had been able to control all the anarchists and other disorganised idiots back there, then the Republic wouldn't have failed, and we wouldn't have been living under Franco for the last twenty years.'

192

Madeleine thought of all she had heard about the Communist party in France. It was a mainstream elected party, she knew, unlike in England, and had been criticised by the Soviets for being too soft. She could imagine Jordi's embittered heart seeking out the discipline and comradeship offered by the Communists, the last group to stand up to Franco as an organised unit in 1938, just before the child Jordi had found himself on the cold road to exile in France.

'And do you hold any official position?' she asked.

'No, no! Far more humble. I leave official positions to my French comrades. It's just a way for me to feel involved, I suppose.'

His voice had a bitter edge. 'You really don't feel you belong here, do you?' Madeleine asked.

'No, I don't. It's hard to feel you belong. Great figures like Picasso and Casals get adopted by the French as VIPs, but even they long for home. Your father felt it too, although he was more a part of intellectual life in France. For the ordinary Spaniards like me this will never be home. Even my sister only partly succeeds in being French.'

'Your sister?'

'Yes, I have a younger sister. She married a chap from Perpignan and lives up there now, trying to be more French than the French, and not even speaking Catalan. She says it's a rough language, and her own children only speak French. She tries so hard it's almost sad.'

His voice was equally sad as he spoke. Madeleine put down her glass.

'I lost my own Catalan, you know,' she said. 'I always spoke Catalan with my father, and then when we had to leave I lost it. I hate it, being in Vermeilla, and hearing the language around me all the time, and not understanding. It makes me feel like a foreigner.'

Jordi looked at her with new attention. 'Yes, of course, you too are a displaced person. I keep forgetting. You sound just like any young lady from Paris. But you are a Garriga, after all, a Catalan.'

'A Catalan without a heritage. I know you feel like an outsider here, but at least you grew up knowing where you came from, and in touch with your family in Spain.'

Jordi grimaced. 'In a way, perhaps, but it's only really in recent years that I've been able to contact the family again, and I've only been able to smuggle myself over the border a couple of times. It's like I told you – those of us who left aren't welcome now in Spain, and we can be arrested, so the family seem very remote really, in a different world. And then my father . . .'

'Yes?'

'My father was a drunk.' The words were spat from Jordi's mouth in bitter challenge. 'Later in his life no one wanted to know him, and he shrank into himself. He would never have made any attempt then to reach his family. We even lost contact with Felip, and later heard that he had died. That's one of the reasons my sister wanted so much to leave home and forget all about us. It wasn't much of a house for her to grow up in. And she didn't really remember my father so much from his earlier years, when he was the greatest father anyone could have asked for.'

'He saved my mother, my brother and me.' Madeleine's words were a simple statement.

'And countless others,' Jordi's voice rose. 'And he never took a penny from anyone for helping them, when other *passeurs* were raking in money. He never lost his values, but he lost his strength. His moral strength, I mean. He hated feeling so weak, and he despised himself, and he took it out on my mother a lot. But she never stopped loving him. She used to tell us we should still be proud of him. And he was in such a lot of pain, a lot of the time.'

His tone pleaded with Madeleine. She wanted to reach out and touch him, but she didn't dare. How long had it been, she wondered, since anyone had shown him any affection? Probably not since the death of his mother.

Their soup arrived at this moment, and in the bustle of service Jordi recovered his poise enough to offer croutons and a bowl of spicy mayonnaise *rouille* to add to the soup, and to order a glass of house wine for each of them.

Madeleine tasted the soup appreciatively. It was stronger than any fish soup she had tasted before, and the *rouille* added a burst of heat and garlic. Amidst the sounds of the harbour at night, and the salt smell on the breeze, this bold, fragrant soup seemed to bring together all the tastes and smells of the Mediterranean.

Madeleine smiled at Jordi, and took up their conversation. 'How long ago did your mother die?' she asked him.

'Seven years ago. My sister left soon after. And then it was just me and my father. What about you? Your mother died too, didn't she?'

'Yes, just two months ago. That's what made me come

here. I suddenly wanted to find our roots, and so I came back to Vermeilla to find *Tonton* Philippe.'

'Philippe.' Jordi spoke the name reflectively. 'You know, Philippe was one of the people who stayed loyal to my father even after he lost most of his friends. My father respected him enormously. That's why—' he broke off abruptly.

'Why what?' asked Madeleine.

Jordi said nothing, and gazed intently into his wine glass. There was a silence, and then Madeleine repeated quietly, 'Why what, Jordi?'

He looked up at her, and let out a long sigh. Then he answered equally quietly.

'We kept it a secret for all these years, but I decided you had a right to know. You are Luis Garriga's daughter, and he died that day.'

He paused, and Madeleine waited, completely silent. Behind them the world seemed to have receded into the dark. They were utterly alone. She didn't dare move, for fear of breaking this moment when surely some momentous truth was going to be told. After some time Jordi continued.

'I don't know how much you know about that day. You've seen the camp. Well, by May 1944 there were eight or nine men living in the camp, but only your father and mine were there when the Germans came. They had been across to Spain overnight, and were sleeping, but the noise of the German arrival woke them, and they escaped out of the back of the shed and made for the other path which led from the far end of the clearing. That was always the plan if they were to be surprised in that way.

'They'd nearly made it when they were spotted, and the Germans fired, so they hid behind some rocks and fired back. From then on the end was always inevitable. There were far too many Germans and they couldn't retreat any further towards the path, so the goal was simply to take as many Germans as possible with them, and they didn't have enough ammunition to take that many. You know that your father was killed, but mine wasn't. The Germans shot him three times in the arm and chest, and he was taken out unconscious.

'When he woke up he was in a cell in Perpignan, and he told me he knew he was for it. To be captured was a guarantee of torture, and there were cases where people committed suicide rather than allow themselves to be interrogated by the Germans. But my father didn't have that possibility; he wasn't even able to move, because of his injuries. He told me they left him there for hours, which was deliberate of course, to leave him alone with his thoughts, and in pain, and without water, so that when they finally came for him his resolve would be weak. And he didn't know what had happened to Luis, so it was possible that he was in another cell, being interrogated at the same time.'

Madeleine shifted in her seat, and grasped her napkin tightly in both hands. Jordi paused and laid his hand over hers. His eyes never left her face.

'I'm sorry. None of this is easy to listen to. I won't go into what they did to my father. He didn't tell me himself, except when he was too drunk to know what he was saying. But what he did tell me, when he was finally released and fit to talk, was that the guards had confirmed that they had been betrayed. They had taunted him with it, telling him that it was a waste of time protecting the rest of his group, because they had no supporters, and had all been betrayed. And they told him who had done it.'

Madeleine knew that he was about to say the name of someone she knew, otherwise why did he have to tell her? Someone in Vermeilla, therefore. But who?

'Who, then, Jordi?' she whispered.

'It was that scoundrel of a barkeeper, Perrens. Jean-Pierre Perrens. He's the one who killed your father, Madeleine, and who destroyed mine. He ran a bar for the Germans, the collaborating swine. He must have thought he would curry favour, but why, when everyone was holding their breath hoping for liberation? Even collaborators were changing sides in May 1944. My father never understood why he did it, but he knew for sure it was him.'

Madeleine sat frozen, gazing intently at Jordi's face, as though his expression could explain things further. Jean-Pierre. Colette's husband. The little scene in Colette's apartment came back to her, and Jean-Pierre's frightened face asking where they had buried her father. It was believable that it should be him who had betrayed them, for reasons hidden in his twisted mind.

'You know, that makes sense,' she told Jordi. 'I met him on Saturday, and when he realised I was Luis's daughter he got very agitated, and kept asking where Papa was buried. He seemed to be frightened of something, maybe retribution. Colette explained that he felt very isolated during the occupation, being made to stay and work for the

Germans when most people in the village were evacuated.'
She fell silent, with that strange little scene replaying again
and again in her head.

'Do you think his wife Colette knew that he had
betrayed them?' she asked at last.

Jordi's hand was still covering her twisted fingers, but
now he removed it and took a final swig from his glass of
wine.

'I'd say she must have,' he replied, with grim decisiveness.
'You see, there is more to it than just Jean-Pierre Perrens.
The guards told my father it was Perrens' young son who
had led them to the camp.'

'What?' The word was startled out of Madeleine. She
stared at Jordi in absolute disbelief. 'You mean Daniel? But
that's not possible! He would have been nine or ten years
old at the time!'

'There were younger children than that who were used
to collaborate with the Germans, and to work for the
Maquis as well, if it comes to that. I don't suppose the boy
had much choice in the matter, but he did it, that I know.
He led the German troops all the way to the camp. So it's
a rather tall order to believe the mother was ignorant, isn't
it?'

Jordi's voice was almost matter-of-fact, but Madeleine
remained incredulous. He couldn't know what he was
saying. He didn't know these people. Had he ever met
them? She asked him, and he spat out that he had never
wanted to so much as see their faces. Did she know, he
asked her, what happened to filthy collaborators after
France had been liberated? About the summary executions,

the shaving of heads, the public beatings and humiliation of those who had done what Jean-Pierre and his son had done?

'But the Perrens family got off completely free,' he growled. 'My father wouldn't allow me to tell anyone, or use the information himself. So there they are, still living off that German café while my father rots in the ground. No, Madeleine, I didn't want to know them, and I have never been to Vermeilla since.'

Madeleine was still having trouble comprehending what Jordi had told her. She shook her head and focused on his last statement.

'Why?' she asked him. 'If Jean-Pierre Perrens betrayed them so badly, why did your father refuse to denounce him?'

'Because of Philippe, that's why. Like I told you, my father respected him. My father was released from prison in August 1944 by his own comrades. Did you know that this region is one of the few that was liberated by its own people? By the Maquis?' There was intense pride in his voice. 'But when my father was released he couldn't join in any of the celebrations. He was too ill after what they'd done to him, and then from being in that cesspit with no food or sanitation. It was a few weeks before he was strong enough to talk properly, and by then he'd heard how Philippe had buried your father, and now Philippe was back in Vermeilla, and more importantly, the Perrens woman had just had that second boy, and everyone knew the child was Philippe's. There was no way it could have been the husband's, that was clear enough. So my father said nothing. If he had denounced the family, he would probably have destroyed Philippe as well. So the bastards got away with it.'

Madeleine gripped her wine glass and said nothing. Philippe was Martin's father? It didn't come as a complete surprise. She remembered *Tante* Louise saying everyone knew Colette was his mistress, and Madame Curelée talking about the boys being Philippe's family. And she thought about Martin's education, his evident academic strength, the studies subsidised by Philippe. It all fell into place. All except for Daniel being involved. She thought of his gentle personality, his care of his mother, his smile and reticence. How could he have been involved in a nasty affair of collaboration and betrayal? And would Colette have allowed him to be? Was she involved too? Surely that was unthinkable. And what about Philippe? Did he know?

Their faces swam before her, of people she hadn't even known five days ago. But her father had known them, and trusted them. Surely, surely, surely. She felt sick, and cold, and thought she might faint.

It must have shown on her face, because Jordi took her arm and pulled her up from the table.

'Come,' he said. 'Let's pay and then we'll take a walk along the quayside. You look like death, and I feel like a criminal for telling you. But you were the only other person who had the right to know; the only person my father would have told, I mean. You had as much right as me. Not that you're probably thanking me right now,' he laughed grimly. 'I'm sorry, Madeleine, really I am. I know these people represented your past to you.'

They walked up and down the now quiet quayside for some time, and then stopped at another bar for coffee, and all the while Jordi talked to her about the port, its recent development, the new talk of a cargo terminal – anything, in fact, except the war, and betrayal, and the people in Vermeilla.

Madeleine tried not to think, and listened to Jordi's talk with half attention, listening to the sea. Machado's lines came back to her. The war is between us, a war deeper than war, she thought. I have to see these people tomorrow. Kind Daniel, overworked Colette with her tired eyes, cheeky young Martin who must surely know nothing, and Philippe. What about Philippe? Don't think. Not yet.

The walk and the coffee were successful medicines, and gradually she felt less sick, and merely terribly tired. Over a dead coffee cup she looked at Jordi and said, 'Could we go home now, do you think? Would you mind?'

He shook his head. 'Of course, we'll go right now. You've finished your coffee? Yes? Well your carriage awaits.'

As they mounted the little motorbike, which looked quite proud and shiny and black in the night light, Jordi told her to hold on tight.

'You're tired now, and it's cold. I don't want you to let go, and fall off the bike. You made it all the way to France, and we can't have you killed off now by your father's old comrade's son.'

His attempt at light-heartedness was touching. There was no sign now of the angry, embittered Jordi of some hours before. He was all concern, compunction even.

Madeleine held on tightly to his jacket and welcomed the cold air which rushed past them as the bike motored out of Port Vendres. It numbed the cheeks and froze her unjacketed arms, but her hands stayed warm in Jordi's jacket, tucked into his pockets. His back was solid and warm, and she tucked herself closer in.

Collioure came and went, with the lights from the magnificent castle reflected in the waters of the bay, and then they were at Vermeilla. Madeleine expected Jordi to drop her at the entrance to the village, but he swept down towards the quayside, and slowed down as they reached the market square.

'Where is your hotel?' he asked, and following her directions took her to the door of the Hotel Bon Repos.

'Very peaceful,' he commented, looking along the small quayside. 'Untouched, one would say. And it is, Madeleine,' he added, 'despite what people may have done. Don't lose sleep, will you? The war is beginning to be a long time ago, and people have the right to have remade their lives. In truth, the war now seems less important to me than what is happening in my own country. That's still happening, and still hurting my people.'

Madeleine stood by the motorbike and wondered what to say. The news he had just given her hurt as though it had happened yesterday. And she knew how bitter he still was really. But he was right that it was a long time ago, and she thought about all the people she had met in Vermeilla, all moving on – better than Jordi, she thought, since they were at home, in their own community, and not waiting for some lost past to become available again, as he was.

Jordi seemed a lonely figure, as he prepared to ride off on his own on the long journey back to Céret. Her hotel room seemed a little lonely too, and suddenly she felt a long way from Robert, and from *Tante* Louise, and Solange and Bernard. She had come home, she'd thought, but now it all felt very alien. She shivered.

'Jordi?' she said.

'Yes?'

'Thank you for telling me. It can't have been easy for you, raking up the past. But you're right that I needed to know.'

'Take care, Madeleine.' Jordi's voice was almost tender. 'Sleep and don't worry, and do whatever you think right. Trust your own judgement. We'll meet again soon, daughter of Luis. Come and see me, any time – you know where my little place is now. If you're worried, or even if you're not! Let me know how you get on, all right? And Madeleine?'

'Yes?'

'Be careful if you meet Perrens again. He's a rat, and rats will run from the big people and hide in corners, but if they are cornered . . .'

His hand came up and touched her cold cheek, and then he drove off, leaving Madeleine to make her solitary way into the hotel.

Chapter Thirteen

The night was long, with snatches of sleep bringing nightmares which jerked Madeleine awake again and again. In tortuous dreams her father stood exposed in that clearing, by a makeshift shed, while the German soldiers advanced towards him, and the ghost of Enric, standing to one side, hurled anger at him for sharing secret information which had led to their betrayal. 'You!' the young Enric kept repeating. 'This is your fault. You did this.'

And in other dreams she saw a small, slightly built boy pointing out a path to some soldiers and then scurrying away. Then Jean-Pierre's face swam in front of her, staring at her with the same intensity as when she had met him at the dinner table, gabbling about graves and revenge. Then she saw Colette, the day she had first met her, in the café, muttering 'Luis's daughter' as her whole body stiffened, then later smiling, seeming so welcoming.

It was testament to how much she had accepted Jordi's story that at no point did she think it might be wrong. There was a terrible logic to it, and in any case, where would German guards have got Jean-Pierre's name from if he had just sat quietly in his room above the bar waiting for the war to end, and had never made that fateful step towards collaboration?

As dawn broke, Madeleine dragged her body from the narrow bed, and sat by her window to watch the fishing boats return. She caught a glimpse of Daniel, hauling nets to lay them over the wall to dry, and then he was gone, home to sleep. She returned to bed herself and finally fell into a dreamless sleep, from which she woke unrefreshed at about eight-thirty, with sore eyes, aching limbs and skin that hurt to the touch all over her face.

'What do I do?' had been her endless question to herself through the long night. The darkness had brought no answers, only adding a sharp edge to her anguish. In the daylight things seemed no less bleak, but some hint of reason told her not to make things worse than they were.

In her long waking moments during the night she had tormented herself, asking again and again how it could be that Luis, who had avoided giving any information to Philippe, vulnerable in his position as his friend, could have revealed the whereabouts of his camp to, of all people, Jean-Pierre, whose home he visited clandestinely while German soldiers drank in the bar below? Surely this was the most obviously dangerous place to start talking?

Now, in the bright golden light of the Vermeilla morning, she remembered Jordi's story of visiting the camp, taken

206

there by his father. Who did they tell, she wondered, these men living wild in the hills? Who was considered safe? Enric had not seemed to blame her father, she noted, and nor did his son Jordi. There had been no mention of that act of unthinking betrayal. Or was Jordi merely keeping criticism to himself?

By the time Madeleine had washed and dressed it was too late for breakfast, but she had no appetite anyway. Half an hour later she was in the village post office, negotiating a call from the booth in the corner, hoping against hope not only to get through the French telephone system to England, but also to reach Robert at his accommodation in Oxford. She didn't stop to think that this was a time of day when he would be in lectures. She needed him so badly that surely he must be available.

A woman's voice answered the phone, mercifully very clear, and Madeleine asked for Robert.

'I'll see if I can find him,' the doubtful voice answered, and a long silence followed, probably while the woman went to knock on the door of his room. Madeleine had been through this process before of trying to contact Robert, and usually had to leave a message so that he could call back. Today her nails dug holes in her palm as she waited to be told he wasn't there.

'Hullo?' a man's voice questioned at last at the other end of the line. It was Robert, and Madeleine felt weak as she heard him.

'Robert, it's Madeleine,' she croaked.

'Madeleine? Are you all right?' His voice came from far away, but she could hear his concern. 'Where are you?'

'I'm in Vermeilla,' she replied. 'Don't worry, I'm fine. I just needed to speak to you, that's all.'

'You sound funny. Is everything OK?'

Madeleine wanted to laugh. Funny? It was such a bizarre word for how she was feeling right now. How could she begin to tell Robert about the last few days in a short phone call? The half-written letter to him was still lying in her hotel room, and Robert knew nothing about what had been happening here. And expensive seconds were ticking away.

'I've found Philippe,' she began, 'and Colette, and I've seen where Papa was killed, and I know what happened to him, and Robert, oh Robert, he was betrayed by his friends, here in Vermeilla, and I don't know what to do.'

'Woah, Madeleine! Calm down. You found Philippe, you say? Still in Vermeilla?'

'Yes, and Colette, like I told you, and all her family. They're all here, and they've been really good to me. But I think Colette's family betrayed Papa to the Germans.' She told Robert as briefly as possible the story Jordi had told her.

The simple fact of sharing the story made it more bearable. But Robert's reply shocked her nonetheless.

'You know, Madeleine,' he said, 'I think you may be getting too involved here. Nobody told us any of these people were angels, and you've only known them a few days, so you can't be too emotionally involved with them. If they did betray Papa I can see you want to know, and so do I, but will it change anything about the fact that he is gone?'

He sounded like all the people in Vermeilla, letting bygones be bygones, although from over there in England he was surely uninvolved as people here could never be, with their resentments and grudges buried rather than really forgotten. Madeleine thought of all the years stuck in Forsham with the grandparents, of her mother's pain and wasted life, of their denied heritage. It was not so easy just to let go as though it didn't really matter. She desperately wanted him to understand.

'He nearly made it, Robert! That's the point. He was killed when liberation was just around the corner, when collaborators were going into hiding and becoming patriots again. And why did he die? Not in some battle trying to free France, or on the road to Spain saving some Jew from final retribution, but because he spoke too freely to a man with a disordered brain, and because his friends weren't really his friends. It's so wrong! We could have had him back with us just a few months later. Our whole lives would have been different, and *Maman*'s life too – think of her!'

'Do you think most people in war die in clean, simple and glorious battle?' Robert asked, then continued quickly as Madeleine began to protest. 'I am not saying we have to accept this without trying to learn more, Lena. I'm only saying that when you do know, you can leave Vermeilla and make a life, and that these people you've met are not your family or even your friends. You don't have to feel loyalty to them, or so much anguish if they are traitors.'

'They were Papa's friends, and *Maman*'s!' Madeleine cried, thinking of Philippe's shining enthusiasm, and Colette's warmth.

'Was Colette's husband Papa's friend? Do we know that? We know Philippe was his close friend, but what have you heard to damage that? Nothing. In fact, from what you say, Jordi's father so respected Philippe that he didn't want to hurt him in any way. I'd say Philippe comes off scot-free in all of this. And what about Colette? Do you know for sure that she was part of this? You know, Lena, you should go to Philippe with this story, and ask him for the truth, since he at least isn't implicated at all.'

Madeleine digested his words through the crackle of the long-distance connection. 'And what if he doesn't know anything? Won't I just be causing him unnecessary grief, so long after the event, if he learns now that Colette's family betrayed Papa? His own family, even, if Martin is his son!'

She could almost hear Robert's mind turning over, as he considered the pros and cons. When he answered, for the first time his voice showed some anxiety.

'I don't think you have any choice, Lena, since obviously you don't feel you can just let this go without exploring it. I'd be happier if you would, if truth be told. I think this guy, Colette's husband, could be dangerous, and I can't see what you're going to gain by opening up old sores.'

Madeleine thought back to Colette's dining room, and how she had felt she was opening up sores by her very arrival. But Philippe had introduced her to Jordi, and seemed to think it was important for both of them that they talked and explored the past. She told Robert about this, and how Jordi had opened up as he told her his story. 'Would you leave it alone yourself, if you were here?' The question was a challenge.

'No.' His reply was slow in coming. 'No, I wouldn't. I wouldn't want anything to become public, after all this time, but I think I would talk to Philippe. Without asking him about his relationship with Colette, mind, Lena! You can't go prying into that!'

'I won't, I promise you.' Sounds on the line seemed to indicate that their time was up, and she rushed to finish. 'I'll call you again, Bobo, as soon as I know more. I need to tell someone, otherwise I feel too isolated here. It's a lot tougher than I expected!'

'Do you want me to come over?' His anxiety was evident despite his disembodied voice.

'No, don't be silly. You must have exams coming up. I'm fine, I promise you. And if it all gets too difficult I can always bolt to Paris, after all!'

'Make sure you call, then,' was the stern reply.

'I will, but we'd better quit now otherwise I'll never be able to afford it! And you can always call the hotel. Bernard has the number.'

'So he does, so he does indeed,' Robert reflected. 'All right, Lena, go off and beard your dragon, and don't have any more nightmares, big sister. I'll be thinking of you.'

'How did you know I'd had nightmares?'

Robert laughed, and kissed her down the line as the operator's voice intercepted their call.

'*Au revoir*, Robert,' Madeleine called, and then he was gone.

She stood for a moment in the little wooden booth, composing herself and drawing together her strength for the next move. Then she straightened her blouse, ran her hands through her loose hair, and stepped out into the post office. It had been empty when she began her call, but now there were two people at the counter, and a couple of elderly ladies sitting on a bench by the wall, unravelling village life, their woven shopping baskets held side by side on their laps, their legs covered by their long black skirts, heads shrouded in embroidered black scarves. They looked up as Madeleine emerged, and their conversation paused meaningfully. Everyone in Vermeilla knew who Madeleine was and why she had come here. She flushed as she thought about her conversation with Robert, her voice raised to be heard over the poor line, and was infinitely grateful that she'd been speaking in English. The thought that anyone might have understood her filled her with horror.

She gave the ladies a respectful nod and a '*Bonjour Mesdames*,' and whisked herself out of the post office as quickly as possible, pausing to breathe the warm morning air in the shade of the post office awning, taking her time and frankly reluctant to cross the street towards Philippe's house. Where would she find him, she wondered, at this hour? It was late for his morning coffee at the café, but there was no sign of him among the men playing boules in the square to her left. She could walk past the café and check for him there, and then try his apartment. If she found him in the café she would have to ask to go home with him. This was a conversation which had to be private.

If her stomach had been knotted that first day in Vermeilla, it was doubly so now as she approached the Café de Catalogne. There was no sign of Philippe inside,

212

but Colette was wiping tables by the window, and waved to Madeleine to enter.

'How are you today, my dear girl?' she asked as she kissed Madeleine on both cheeks. She was busy and natural, and warm and motherly, and Madeleine felt tortuous guilt for even suspecting her of something so evil as betraying her father. She quickly asked for Philippe, and Colette broke into speech before she had even finished the question.

'Ah, Philippe. Now I am worried about him. He was here yesterday evening complaining about a sore back, and I know how he suffers from that back, and yet will he go to the doctor? Not him! He says there's nothing anyone can do, and he just needs to lie down and rest it, but what I say is, no one knows what can be done to help them if they won't even ask. *Quelle tête de cochon* – pig head! But it's like that with men, *n'est-ce pas?* So today we haven't seen him and I don't doubt he is lying on his sofa, and he won't even have eaten anything. I mean to take him some food, but Marie didn't turn up today to work, and I am doing the tables on my own, as you can see. He'll have to wait until lunchtime, when the other staff come in.'

The flow of concern continued almost cheerfully, and Madeleine realised gratefully that with Philippe on her mind, Colette was not going to question her about the evening with Jordi, which had inspired some curiosity yesterday. It also gave her the opportunity she needed to see Philippe at home. She broke into the flow during a moment's pause, and suggested taking the food herself.

'I can go now,' she volunteered, 'and take him a late

213

breakfast, and make him some coffee. Does he have coffee in the house? And I'll see whether he feels like he may come out for lunch or if he prefers to stay at home and rest.'

'Now that,' Colette replied with pleasure, 'would be a real help, and would relieve my mind. Thank you, my dear! I'll put together a good breakfast for him. Have a coffee, and I'll be just a moment. You had a good breakfast yourself? You're sure? You'll take a small piece of tart with your coffee? No? You young girls don't eat at all these days.'

And Colette bustled off, returning some moments later with a bag of goodies which Madeleine was sure Philippe would never eat, plus coffee and milk and sugar 'in case he didn't have any in the apartment', and fifteen minutes later Madeleine was standing outside his apartment door, armed with her reason for visiting, and feeling marginally more confident than she had an hour ago.

Beckoned in by Philippe in a surprisingly hearty voice, she found him as Colette had predicted, dressed but on his sofa, a cushion behind his back, reading a book with a notebook by his side. He disclaimed any great pain, and laughed at the quantity of croissants and other delicacies sent by Colette, assuring Madeleine that he expected to be up and about by the afternoon. She made coffee for them both, and sat at the table opposite the sofa, wondering how on earth to open up the questions which seemed to be stuck between her stomach and her ribs. At last it was Philippe who came to the subject. Unlike Colette he had not forgotten her meeting with Jordi last night, and wanted to know how she had got on.

'You two needed some time to talk together,' he commented. 'I've often wondered how Jordi really feels about the war, and how much Enric shared with him. They were so very close at the end, having no one else, as it were.'

And so in the end it was easy.

'He had things he wanted to tell me,' Madeleine agreed. 'Things that his father told him, and that he has been keeping to himself ever since. I think it has been eating away at him, and since last night it has begun eating at me as well. Uncle Philippe, Jordi told me that it was Jean-Pierre Perrens who betrayed my father's camp, and sent the Germans there. I don't know what to think, but I needed to ask you.'

Philippe gazed into his coffee cup, as though seeing some long distant past, and then sighed.

'How did he learn that, I wonder? How did Enric know? I was sure no one knew outside the family.' His voice was weary, laden with memory which was quite clearly as painful as it was heavy.

'The Germans told him when he was being tortured. They taunted him with it to make him speak.'

'Oh.' His sigh was long and hung in the air. 'Poor Enric. He never said a word. Never in all these years.'

There was wonder in the words. Madeleine felt a huge reluctance to continue. She didn't want to step anywhere near Philippe's relationship with Colette. But she knew that having started there was more she needed to say.

'Jordi told me his father respected you, and didn't want to make trouble for Colette and her family, since they were friends of yours. So he didn't denounce Jean-Pierre. It's true, then, that he set the Germans on the camp?'

'Yes, *ma petite*, it's true. Sadly, it's true. Colette never forgave him, but he was already such a damaged person, withdrawing into his own world, and so she stayed with him, and ran the café, and raised the boys. There didn't seem to be anything else to do.'

'But why? Why, Uncle Philippe? What would make Jean-Pierre take such a terrible step? It seems such an incredible thing to do.'

'Who knows, my dear, what goes on in such a mind as Jean-Pierre's? You saw him the other day, and his outburst about your father. That, of course, was brought about by your presence, but it's clear he had all sorts of fears and paranoia associated with Luis.'

'And Colette knew?'

'Colette found out, Madeleine, and did everything she could to stop it. She sent a letter to me immediately to give to Luis, to warn him. But the Germans found the camp so quickly, before Luis came again to visit me. He was due to visit that very evening, I remember, and we should have been able to warn him in time.' His voice was anguished as he remembered. 'It was so terrible. How could the Germans have found the camp so quickly? I've never understood myself how Jean-Pierre could tell the Germans exactly where to go.'

The words burst from Madeleine before she could stop herself. 'But it was Daniel who showed them the way! Jordi told me it was Daniel. The Germans taunted his father with that as well, saying that even the child was part of the betrayal.'

'No!' Philippe's response whipped at her. 'No! You're wrong there! There is no way that Daniel was involved. No way, do you hear? Whatever any German bastards may have said!'

Daniel's face swam before Madeleine, with its gentle, genuine smile. He had taken her in like a sister, or maybe more. Could he have done so if he had been caught up in her father's death? And could Jean-Pierre have involved his own son without Colette knowing? And Daniel wasn't even living at home. Surely he couldn't have known anything about it. She rushed into speech again, her voice loaded with relief.

'Daniel was living with you at the time, wasn't he? So he was close to the camp. But he couldn't have known what his father had done, could he? He wasn't here in Vermeilla.'

Philippe's face closed over, and she felt him withdraw.

'He couldn't have known, surely?' she repeated.

Philippe took his time replying. 'Daniel was here in Vermeilla for the weekend just before your father died,' he said at last. 'He had been living with me and hadn't seen his mother for months, and suddenly there was a chance to come down here with a man we knew who had a pass to bring vegetables and fruits down from his farm to the coast, to the German bases in Vermeilla, Collioure and Port Vendres.'

He paused again, before continuing, his voice suddenly hesitant. 'It was Daniel who brought me the letter from Colette for your father. But he didn't know what was in the letter. I'd swear he didn't know anything, and certainly not how to find the camp. And he hated the Germans, like all the kids did then. They were all gung-ho, talking about liberation and how we were going to send the Germans packing. Daniel was even more excited than most.'

A silence hung between them, and Madeleine thought that Philippe was very far away, in Amélie-les-Bains fifteen years ago, surrounded by his schoolchildren, and taking that letter from Daniel, newly back from his visit home. There was nothing she could say. Nothing that he wasn't already wondering himself. She lifted their coffee cups and went to the sink to wash them, and still Philippe didn't move. She moved around the little kitchen area as quietly as possible, drying plates and cups and placing them in the same cupboard her mother had used all those years ago.

Behind her she felt rather than heard Philippe moving, straightening himself painfully against the back of the sofa, and as she turned he was shaking his head as if to wake himself up.

'We need to visit Colette,' he said. 'But not now, not when it's nearly lunchtime at the café, and not after lunch, when Daniel will be at the harbour sorting out nets. There's a lull in business at the café at around four, and Daniel will be there as well. That's when we need to go. Madalena, go to the café now and tell Colette I don't need lunch. I have the remains of her bread and some fine Pyrenean cheese. But tell her I'm feeling better, and will come to see her this afternoon. Will you, my dear?'

He held out his hand and she went to him, her face drawn and troubled. He stroked her cheek and gave a half smile.

218

'Daughter of Luis, don't worry now. We'll find the truth and the truth will help us all. Your coming here has unleashed a flood of information – unbelievable almost, when all these years we just got on with living and tried not to ask too many questions. But sometimes one individual, one simple person, can be a catalyst which prises open people's lives. And what you find out can't be controlled once the flood starts – it's stronger than us all. But it will be positive in the end. I believed that when I took you to meet Jordi. You needed to learn and he needed to talk, although he didn't know it. I don't know all the truth, but I believe we need it now.

'But we must never be bitter, whatever happened. Your father would not have been bitter. He understood human frailty and only real badness angered him. I put some of his writings in that envelope over there. I thought you might like to read them. It might help you to understand his life.'

Madeleine pounced on the envelope, and held it to her chest.

'They're only some old tracts and newspaper articles,' Philippe smiled.

'Maybe, but you have no idea what they mean to me! I've never read a word he wrote, or seen a single document that could give me even a glimpse of him.'

Philippe looked thoughtful. 'You mentioned that the other day, and you know, I find it very strange. How could Elise have kept nothing of Luis? It's hard to believe. Was there nothing even in the jewellery box?'

'The jewellery box?'

'Why yes. Didn't your mother keep the box? A silver one, with curved feet?'

Madeleine looked at him blankly. 'Yes, I have the box. But I don't know what you mean. It has her pearls in it, and some earrings, and a couple of rings.'

'But you checked the chamber underneath?'

He saw her bemusement, and started again. 'Your mother's jewellery box had a false bottom, and Elise and Luis kept their most secret documents in it – the stuff which would have betrayed them. I remember Luis challenging me to find it one day, because he wanted to be sure nobody else would ever discover it.'

Madeleine gripped the envelope between tight fingers. 'How does it open?'

'There's a seal on the bottom. I remember if you pressed that down, then at the same time you could twist one of the silver legs. And then you could lift off the bottom.' He paused. 'Where is the jewellery box now?'

'In my hotel room. Oh my God, excuse me Uncle Philippe, but I have to go.' She rose and moved towards the door, then came back and hugged him gingerly, trying not to put pressure on his sore back. 'Thank you,' she whispered, a tremble in her voice.

Philippe grinned. 'Glad to be of service. This may indeed be a day of revelations. You won't forget to meet me at four o'clock, at the café?'

'Oh no, I won't forget! There's no danger of that!'

Chapter Fourteen

Back in her hotel room, Madeleine picked up the jewellery box with shaking fingers, and turned it upside down. There was no line anywhere to indicate a flap, no sign at all that this bottom might open, but there was the seal, which stood out as a ridge around an engraved circle. Could it move? She pushed down hard on it, and nothing happened. But Philippe had been sure, so she worked around it with her nail, and when she pressed against the very edge it seemed to give very slightly, almost too little to notice. She held her finger in place, and with her other hand groped around the four silver feet with their ornamental claws. She held her breath when the third one moved a fraction, and then, quite easily, it twisted as she rotated her finger. It was uncanny, and she didn't dare shift her grip, but slowly she lifted, and as she did so the base of the jewellery box lifted away cleanly from the rest. So no wonder there were no

221

signs of a flap. This was an invisible join around the whole base of the box.

For a long moment she just gazed at the cavity she had exposed. Several faded pieces of paper nestled inside. With hands that shook, she leant forward and with infinite care lifted out the little sheets of paper, one after another. They clung to each other, nestled as they had been so tightly in the shallow space.

'My God!' she uttered in wonder to herself. On top there were three thin sheets, each a letter in an unfamiliar handwriting – the letters Philippe had spoken of, which Luis had written to Elise. So they made it to England after all.

She lifted them out carefully, and unfolded them along the fragile crease lines, terrified of tearing the cheap, brittle paper after all these years. Her father's words scrawled across the pages, in ink which had faded to a dirty brown already.

The first letter was dated March 1943, just four months after Elise and the children had left France. It was carefully reticent about what Luis was doing or how he was living. It could have been a letter from any French civilian to his wife. Madeleine read with a mixture of hunger and diffidence, suddenly timid in the face of this strange script, all Spanish loops and swirls, of a man whose handwriting she had never seen.

I believe that you got home safely, and I hope it hasn't been too hard, my love. I think about you and the children without cease. It's like taking a drink of water,

or my morning coffee – something I do instinctively,
and which is part of living my life. You are always
there, and I see you in every mirror. Hold Robert for
me, and my lovely Madalena, and tell them both we'll
soon be together again. The news we get from the
radio is mixed, but Montgomery seems to be making
progress in North Africa, so maybe we really will be
relieved from across the Mediterranean. Meanwhile I
know you are all safe, and just knowing it keeps me
positive. And always your smile lives in my soul.

Madeleine read the letter several times, rushing at first and
then slowing down, finding the feel of her father. She didn't
want to put it down, and found herself simply gazing at the
text, the image of Luis in his safe house floating elusively
before her. Eventually she laid it carefully to one side, and
lifted the second flimsy sheet.

This letter was different. It was dated November 1943,
a full year after they had left, and Luis seemed to have
fallen into a deep trough. The Allies were making inroads,
he wrote, but it was all taking so long. When would it all
end?

I know I shouldn't write like this. We need to stay
strong, and believe me, my darling Elise, for the most
part I do, but the act of writing to you makes me weak.
I am in a dark tunnel, and at the end I can see your face,
and I am reaching out to touch you, but you are so far
away. Can you feel my touch? Dream of me tonight,
and I will hold you, and all the rest will fade away.

It felt like an intrusion to be reading these words intended only for her mother. And the dark tunnel had never come to an end for either of them. He had never again touched her mother's face. Madeleine brushed her hand across her eyes, and picked up the last of the letters.

The third letter had been written in May 1944, and Madeleine realised with a jolt that it was dated less than a month before Luis had died. Luis was buoyant again, with the Allied invasion of France expected imminently.

We are going to be liberated, he wrote, and I too am feeling more liberated than I have for a very long time. By the time you get this letter hopefully this whole region will be free of Germans. And before too long you will all come home. Elise, my love, I know now that I can live by your memory alone until I see you again. You are close by me again now, but there was a while when you were desperately hard to find. What did Voltaire say about folly and the first law of nature? My reading is rusty but you will understand. I have leant on you to climb out of my furrow – leant on the boundless clemency and strength that I know to be in you, and the constancy you have for us both. You are so beautiful and so much more than I deserve. Believe me that I am yours, Elise, and I will always be yours, and soon we will be together again.

The letter went on to ask about her and Robert, but Madeleine had eyes only for that paragraph. By the time Elise had got this letter, possibly Roussillon had been liberated, but also Luis was dead. So much hope for the future seemed to be mixed up with so much anguish for how he had been feeling. What was the quote from Voltaire? It lurked somewhere in her consciousness, but she couldn't bring it to the fore. Something about the folly of despair? She would need Philippe's library to answer the question.

She looked again at the jewellery box which had held these letters secret all these years. There were more papers in it, and when she lifted the first of them she realised that they were Philippe's letters, in his spidery writing. She put the letter abruptly back in the box. I'll read this later, she told herself, but for now she couldn't bear to read the news of Luis's death. She was dazed and amazed by her father living. She had only just rediscovered him. *Please don't kill him off yet*, she pleaded dumbly at the little pile of paper.

She placed the heavy silver bottom back on the jewellery box, but didn't lock it in place, almost in fear that she might not be able to open it again. For a long time she sat gazing at the wall, not moving, and then a protest in her stomach reminded her that it was lunchtime, and she hadn't eaten yet today.

There was a picnic waiting for her downstairs.

'The oven is broken,' wailed Mme Curelée, 'and all our other guests have left this morning. I wondered whether you might like to eat a picnic on the beach since the weather is so beautiful? Or I can serve you the same food in the dining room if you prefer? But it will all be cold, alas.'

To be outside in the sun, with a sea breeze! Madeleine embraced the idea like a deliverance, and within minutes had put on her simplest cotton dress and was walking along the beach to the very end, away from the village, carrying the sheaf of Luis's newspaper articles and tracts to read over lunch.

At this end of the beach there were no boats or bathers, since a scattering of rocks broke the water in the shallows and made swimming unsafe. The same rocks formed almost a wall at the rear of the beach, and continued from the end of the beach in a jumble around the coast to the next bay, on the way to Collioure. Madeleine spread a blanket on the rough mix of sand and pebbles, and lay down in the heat of the midday sun, letting its rays seep into her skin and ease her tired nerves. Bread, chicken, a soft goat's cheese and a cherry tart had been packed in Mme Curelée's picnic basket, as well as a small flask of red wine, and in the warmth of the sun and the wine Madeleine succumbed to her tiredness and dropped into a soothing sleep. It was no more than a doze, really, but one peopled by dream-like figures. She dreamt of her father as a young boy, in some village in Spain, bare foot and laughing in the street. He looked like Robert as a boy, but tougher and browner, and at one point in the dream he went inside a narrow door into what she knew was his home, and she was sure she was going to see his family, but then she woke up.

She lay disconnected for a while, gazing at a small cloud working its solitary way across the sky, then she shook herself mentally, and stood up and went across to the big, round boulders which fringed the end of the beach, where a little stream trickled down through the rocks to the sea. She washed her face and hands and drank a little of the water, which was fresh and not too warm. Then she spread her father's articles around her. Later this afternoon, she thought, they're going to remind me my father is dead, all these people who knew him when I didn't, but for now I have him to myself.

From the intimacy of reading his letters to the woman he loved, it was a different experience meeting Luis the writer – her father as a public figure. Philippe had put together some of Luis's most passionate pre-war writings, sophisticated, complex pieces arguing the case for France to finance the Spanish Republican army, calling it the key defence against Fascism. Mussolini and Hitler were funding Franco, it seemed, but France had chosen a policy of 'non-interference', like lots of European countries. Luis argued that there could be no 'neutrality' in this war – to try to be neutral was to advance Fascism in Europe. He praised the thousands of Frenchmen who travelled to Spain to fight against Franco. The souls of the Frenchmen who died, he argued, would call out from the grave to reproach their government, which could have stood with them. It was the soul of her father which Madeleine saw, etched in his writings about Spain. He must have hated not joining the fight himself in Spain. His longing came through in every word he wrote.

These passionate pieces contrasted with some very simple World War Two tracts which Philippe had included in the bundle. The Civil War was lost, and Spain was beyond saving for now, but there was still a fight to be won here in France, and Luis's efforts had moved to wartime resistance. The tracts were single propaganda sheets urging people to keep faith, giving the frequencies for Radio London, telling them the Allies were winning the war, and that Maréchal Pétain's promises of a good life under the Germans were already being terribly betrayed. The tracts were in plain language, crudely printed, and must be the same as tracts appearing all over France, Madeleine thought. They revealed nothing about Luis himself, except for the risk he took in producing them.

Next to these, and very different again, were the newspaper articles Luis had written during the war – his carefully maintained 'cover', written for a Perpignan newspaper which was firmly under Vichy control. These articles talked about the best way to grow vegetables, how to help children to learn discipline, how to follow simple German rules, and how to reduce fuel consumption in your home. These were Madeleine's favourite pieces, so tongue-in-cheek as they were. They were so innocuous as to be laughable, but she wondered how they could have fooled any Vichy official, given Luis's public record of radicalism before the war.

Most of these articles had been cut out from the newspaper, but in two cases the rest of the page had been left intact, and these full pages made interesting reading. A Perpignan man had been caught stealing and sentenced to two years detention – he would undoubtedly have joined the forced labour being sent to Germany, Madeleine thought. The River Têt had flooded again, damaging some close-lying farms. The local mayor had spoken at a school prize-giving, and had awarded a special prize for 'public service'. It all seemed quite safe and parochial, except for a small piece reminding readers to be alert for the activities of Jews and Communists, and to report any Jews still working in forbidden professions. 'We cannot be too much on guard,' the article said. 'All around us there are Jews and Bolshevists plotting to bring down our beloved France.'

She lost herself so much in Luis's working world that it came as a huge shock when she found one final sheet, typed on the most basic imaginable machine, presumably from his resistance hideout. 'Freedom is coming,' it declared. 'The Allied invasion is imminent, and we will liberate our beloved Roussillon from the German oppression. It will be over this summer, and they will flee our land and leave us free again. Hold faith and watch for ways to help us. Every man and woman will have their chance to serve France.'

Suddenly the world of the Perpignan press receded, and the paragraph full of hope and redemption he had written to Elise swam before her eyes. Here he was again just before his own end, and reading the tract all Madeleine could see in her mind was the camp and the German rifles advancing towards the shed. The impudent, eager, radical Luis, who had been so alive, was dead after all.

She put the paper down sadly, checked her watch and realised it was gone half past three. It was time to go to the next confrontation, and God knew what it would bring. Slotting the sheets of typed paper back into the envelope, she rose quickly, suppressing emotion, and walked back along the beach. In a last gesture towards her previous mood, she took off her sandals to walk in the shallows, digging up the tiny pebbles with her toes.

She returned to the hotel to change, and sat by her window for a moment before setting off for the café, looking out at the bay, raw nerves taking over as she listened to the cackle of the seagulls. Philippe believed that the allegations against Daniel could not be true. She had so much faith in Philippe, and she desperately wanted him to be right. But jagged nerves sharpened their edges nevertheless against her stomach wall.

I don't want to go, she thought to herself, then, *Or is it that I don't want to know? God help me, can't I live for just a while in the world where my father is alive, and writing and working and hoping?*

But she had asked for this meeting, for these answers. She was the catalyst and the ferreter of news. There was no point in giving in to weakness now. Philippe would be waiting for her.

CHAPTER FIFTEEN

Philippe was at the café when she arrived, painstakingly assuring Colette that his back was better, and that he had eaten a decent lunch. He was standing as straight as possible at the bar drinking a tiny coffee when he spotted Madeleine. He gestured to her to come forward, and immediately broke through Colette's anxious questions.

'Colette,' he cut in. 'Can you tell me where Daniel is? Upstairs? Well, Madeleine here has been doing some research into Luis's death, and there are a couple of things we need to ask him. I'd like you to come with us too, if you can. Can you leave the bar now?'

As Colette nodded in bewilderment, he called to the barman that Madame was going up to her apartment for a while, and led her ahead of Madeleine up the steep stairs. Philippe in command! Without him Madeleine knew she would never be climbing these stairs.

He was equally decisive when they reached the apartment. They found Daniel cleaning his shoes in the homeliest possible fashion. Madeleine was intensely relieved that there was no sign of his father. She was not sure how she would have faced Jean-Pierre Perrens right now.

Daniel rose to greet them, kissing Madeleine on both cheeks, and Philippe asked after the fishing before suggesting they should all sit down.

Confronted with two bewildered faces, he launched straight into speech.

'Daniel and Colette. In the last few days Madeleine has been learning a lot about her father's death. I took her to his grave, but I also introduced her to the son of the man who was with him when the Germans attacked him. This young man Jordi took her to the camp where Luis was living, where he was shot. And he told her some things which his father had said. Madeleine, I think you should tell again now what you heard from Jordi.'

All eyes turned to Madeleine. Colette was gripping one hand in another. Daniel's face was unreadable. Madeleine's stomach was churning now, and she wished she could sound one fraction as assured as Philippe.

'It's true,' she began, 'that Jordi was able to tell me some things. You see, his father was captured by the Germans that day and tortured, and they taunted him with information about who had betrayed them.'

She looked towards Colette, in desperate apology. 'They told him that Monsieur Perrens was the man who had denounced the camp to the Germans.' She was relieved that her voice didn't seem to be trembling. Colette reached for her son's hand, and cast an anxious eye towards the hallway, as though her husband might appear at any moment.

Madeleine continued. '*Tonton* Philippe has told me that you found out, and tried to warn my father. That you sent him a letter, but it didn't reach him. He told me . . .' Now her voice was trembling after all. 'He told me that Daniel carried the letter up to him at Amélie-les-Bains.'

Colette held Daniel's hand as if frightened to lose him. She tried to speak, and failed, then looked over at Philippe, who nodded.

'Just tell her, Colette,' he said, almost tenderly. 'She knows anyway, and she just needs you to confirm it's true.'

Colette held his gaze for a moment, then looked musingly at her son's hand in hers. 'I am so sorry, Madeleine.' she spoke in a whisper. 'I've lived for many years now with the shame of what my husband did, and the anguish of knowing I didn't manage to warn Luis in time.' Colette looked at her son. 'I think Daniel has understood over the years what his father did. He has said some revealing things sometimes, hasn't he, my son?'

Daniel looked down at the floor and answered in a mumble. 'Yes, *Maman*, I have understood.'

Madeleine didn't know how to continue. But there was only one way to the truth, and that was to speak.

'But that's the main point of what I wanted to say,' she blurted. 'You see, the Germans who tortured Jordi's father told him one other thing. They said that Monsieur Perrens denounced the camp, and then his son showed them the way to it.'

There was silence. Daniel looked up, startled, and Madeleine felt a huge wave of relief. This is news to him, she thought. He didn't do it.

Colette made to speak but Philippe stopped her.

'No one is saying Daniel did anything wrong, Colette, if he did what his father told him to at the age of nine. But there was a clear assertion from German guards who had no reason to know of Daniel's existence. For myself I can't imagine that Daniel would have known the way to the camp, but I'd like to hear Daniel tell us what happened without anyone speaking for him.'

Daniel still looked as startled as before, his eyes now fixed on Philippe. He said nothing, and the silence stretched between them.

'Just tell us, Daniel, what you did that day. You came up to Amélie-les-Bains with the letter. You had a lift with Paul the market gardener, didn't you?'

'Yes.' Then more silence.

'So tell us.' Philippe's voice was insistent.

Daniel looked at him helplessly. '*Tonton*, I came up with Monsieur Paul, as you said. And I came to the house – your house, *mon oncle* – before lunchtime. You were at the school.' He seemed to be struggling with himself, and then with a deep exhalation of breath he continued.

'I wanted to take the letter to *Tonton* Luis, and I thought I knew where the camp was, but I was wrong. I got lost and never found it.'

'But why did you want to take the letter to Luis?'

Colette broke in. 'It was addressed to Philippe, not to Luis! You didn't even know it was for Luis!'

There was another long silence, too long, while Daniel's eyes were fixed on his mother, and then he spat words at her, words that sounded as if they were being wrenched from him. Words that fell between him and Colette with a meaning all to themselves as he withdrew his hand from hers.

'I knew it was for him. I heard you and Papa arguing that weekend. I knew everything, *Maman*! Everything, do you hear? I knew what was in the letter. Not just that Papa had betrayed him, but the rest as well. I heard you . . .'

Colette looked aghast. 'My son!'

'Yes, but not your only son, *Maman*.' The words exploded from him. 'I had heard what Papa said, but I could hardly believe it. I wanted to see *Tonton* Luis myself and ask him if it was true. I used to hear you, you know, you and Luis, in the front bedroom, talking as if you didn't want anyone to know. I didn't know what you were doing, but I knew somehow that I mustn't go inside. But I didn't really understand how that could have made you pregnant.'

The word 'pregnant' was torn from him, and Colette just sat, her face set in horror. Madeleine felt slightly sick, and held the arm of her chair to steady herself. Philippe sat quietly, watching them all, a look on his face which might, incongruously, have been one of peace.

A skim of tears filled Daniel's eyes as he continued. 'I heard him as well, telling you that he was going to be moving to a new camp on the road above Amélie-les-Bains, and that if ever you needed to reach him you could find the camp up that track, and to look out for a turning on the right. So I went up there and looked, but I must have missed it. It was all just trees. I was looking for ages, and seemed to climb halfway up the mountain, and then I was scared, and I knew *Tonton* Philippe would be finishing school, and that I ought to get back. So I gave up, and just went back to Amélie-les-Bains and gave the letter to you, Uncle. You never knew that I had come up from Vermeilla in the morning, not the afternoon. But I never found him. I never found him, I tell you! And I didn't lead any Germans to his camp!'

Madeleine could see the young child, deeply disturbed, with all of his simple faiths shaken to the core, combing a mountain path in the heat of a June day, becoming more and more distressed as he floundered, lost and alone, gripping that all-important letter in his sweaty young hand. And the letter? It warned of Jean-Pierre's betrayal, but did it also tell Luis that he had made Colette pregnant? Colette his mistress? Suddenly, the real meaning of that quote from Voltaire came back to her, ringing out clear as a bell from her schooldays. It was not despair, but the weakness and pathetic errors of man he was writing about, and the first law of nature he was calling upon was that man should forgive and understand, because we were all weak together. Was that what Luis was writing, an admission to Elise of his affair with Colette? Was that his weakness?

Colette's face told the truth. She looked bleak and inexpressibly tired, and frightened. She looked at Daniel, who had his eyes fixed on the floor, and then at Madeleine, whose eyes were fixed on her. She raised her hand as if to ward off Madeleine's gaze, and then finally she spoke.

'What my son is saying is true, Madeleine. The reason why Jean-Pierre denounced your father is because he discovered I was pregnant, and he knew very well that it wasn't him who was the father. He was unable, Jean-Pierre, to be a real husband after the accident. It was a lonely life, on my own running the bar, keeping everything going. And for your father . . . for Luis life was also very lonely, with his wife and children so far away. It was just for comfort, you know. Just for comfort. He used to talk to me of Elise, and I knew how much he loved her. He came down sometimes to Vermeilla to scout for information. He maybe came once every three or four months, no more. And sometimes we would snatch some time together.'

She looked again at her son, who wouldn't meet her eye. 'Don't blame me, Daniel,' she beseeched. 'We hardly ever met, and I could number our actual encounters on the fingers of one hand. The last time he came was in February that year. I was pregnant already, but I didn't know it. Soon after that I knew, of course, but there was no way I could tell Luis. I could maybe have sent a letter to Philippe to pass to him, but I just couldn't. It seemed such a dreadful thing to do to him. I knew that at some time he would come back down to Vermeilla and then I would have to tell him. And I knew that at some time I would have to tell Jean-Pierre. But in the meantime I just carried on as if nothing had happened, and sometimes I could forget that I was pregnant and going to have a child who was not my husband's. It was only three or four months of pretending, but it seemed longer.

'And then came that weekend, when Jean-Pierre confronted me. I was six months pregnant by then, and women in the village could see clearly that I was expecting. There was some muttering, but not much. After all, no one else knew for sure that my husband and I couldn't . . . that he couldn't father a child. It was easy enough just to behave like any other pregnant woman and brazen things out. But not with Jean-Pierre. When he found out he simply exploded. He frightened me. For years he'd just been depressed and withdrawn and fearful, but there was something desperate about him when he realised that the whispers in the village were true. I suppose it confirmed everything that was worst in his life. He was impotent, I was running our lives and playing the man's role, and finally now he was a *cocu*, a cuckold, and his wife had been deceiving him with a man who was a hero, a real man, and worse, that I was going to bring that man's child into the world!

'It was so terrible that that was the weekend that Daniel came to see us. I hadn't seen you for months, my son, and I was so happy to know you were coming, but that whole weekend turned into a nightmare. I kept you downstairs as much as I could, "helping" me in the bar, but then he came down too, and started acting like the life and soul of the party with the customers. Customers!' she spat. 'They were all Nazi scum, but he buried himself with them and after a while it dawned on me what he was doing. It hadn't occurred to me that he could be so bitter as to turn traitor just to get his revenge on Luis. *Mon Dieu*, I was so frantic. That's when you must have heard, my son, because that night I could not keep quiet. I hoped you were sleeping, but I had to find out what he'd done. And he was so pleased with himself! Triumphant, even. As though he'd proved now who was the real man, who had the real power. I never hated him more.'

Colette's voice petered out, and she sat still. Only her hands kept moving, twisting round and round, crushing a customer's bill she had brought up the stairs without thinking, and she cast another glance towards her husband's room down the corridor.

Philippe reached out and touched both her and Daniel, and then spoke almost meditatively to Daniel, who hadn't lifted his eyes from the floor.

'When you told us you were scared up there on the hill, when you were looking for Luis, was it just because you got lost, Daniel, or was there some other reason?'

'Some other reason?'

'Yes. Did you see something? Or hear something that frightened you? You know, you were up there on the afternoon when Luis was shot – when the German militia came. I think they saw you. They would be local militia from Amélie-les-Bains – they would know who you were. I think they used that to bait poor Enric in his jail.'

'I didn't see any Germans!' Daniel's denial was emphatic, inflamed.

'But did you hear anything? Did you hear any shots?'

'Shots? You mean the hunters?'

'There wouldn't have been any hunters, Daniel. Not at that time of year, and not during the occupation.'

Daniel was thinking hard. Colette too was alert. The

miseries were forgotten as Daniel tried to bring that afternoon back to his mind.

'There were shots,' he agreed. 'I didn't know what they were for or where they were coming from. They seemed to be coming from a long way off, kind of muffled. I suppose that was the effect of the trees. It's funny – I'd forgotten. Completely forgotten. But now I remember I was frightened, a bit. I didn't feel safe, so I decided to head back. My God, don't tell me I heard Luis being killed?'

'I think so, Daniel, and I think that it's a very good thing that you missed the turning to Luis's camp. You didn't know that the Germans were already on their way, close behind you. If you had found the camp, I think you too could have been killed.'

'Or my arrival could have put Luis on his guard!' Daniel's voice was bitter. 'If only I'd had enough sense to find the way. How could they find their way so easily, when I missed that track even though I was looking for it?'

'Because Jean-Pierre told them, that's why.' Colette was still twisting her hands around the tiny ball of paper. 'You overheard Luis telling me that the camp was up that path from the road. Well, he didn't tell Jean-Pierre. All he did was describe the clearing where the camp was, surrounded by earth walls, and how they'd had trouble getting wood up the little sidetrack through the trees. He didn't say how to get there! It was at dinner here one evening. But Jean-Pierre knew it! Imagine, some bare old clearing that no one even thought about, but my husband had to know it, from the days when he used to go hunting, before his accident. He didn't even say so to Luis, though I don't know why. He kept it for later and crowed to me that he knew where the Maquis camp was. He said there were three or four possible clearings, but that there was one in particular which fitted the bill exactly. The way he spoke worried me, but at the time I didn't have any reason to think he would ever use the knowledge.'

Philippe reached over again and placed his hand on her shoulder. 'I think Luis always made him feel inferior,' he said. 'I don't suppose he knew what was happening between you two, but he could see how friendly you were. At the time he would just have liked knowing something that Luis didn't want him to know.'

Madeleine hadn't spoken since she first blurted out the Germans' accusations against Daniel. She watched them all like actors on a stage. She thought they had forgotten she was there, caught up in their own scene of disclosure and discovery. There was an explanation for everything, it seemed. Jean-Pierre was less wicked than pitiful and tortured, Daniel was an innocent caught up in an adult tragedy, Colette was a lonely woman who had found herself pregnant.

Which left Luis. Luis who had taken easy comfort in France while his wife stood up for him against all the forces of her disapproving parents, and nurtured her children's love for him far away in England, and hoped and planned for their reunion. Luis who had spoken frivolously about his camp and betrayed his fellow Maquis. Luis who had never known that he had another son. Another son! The so-called hero who had died leaving his wife to shrivel away in England, his children to grow up struggling for his memory, and his best friend to raise his remaining Catalan child as closely as he could in his image. The hero who was responsible for all the raw unhappiness being exposed before her.

All at once Madeleine felt sick, physically sick. She desperately wanted to leave, to be on her own. But she couldn't leave, could she? She had started this. Philippe had called the meeting, knowing a lot of what she was going to hear, but she had pushed and pushed for answers. At least, she thought, I can get some air. She rose to her feet, muttered 'Excuse me' and stepped out onto the balcony. There she stood with her hands glued to the railings, taking deep gulps of air, looking down into the narrow gap between the houses, down to the cobbles below where normal people were moving around doing ordinary things.

Nobody followed her. She could hear her head pounding, her pulse beating a rock and roll rhythm, and above her eyes a nerve kept twitching. The May evening felt cold in the deep shade of the alleyway. Cold. How could she be so cold? She ran her hands up and down her arms, and then a shawl was thrown around her shoulders. She didn't turn. She didn't want to see anyone, to engage with anyone. She might have to be part of their tears and emotion if she did.

'I called him Martin.' It was Colette's voice. 'I made a bargain with my husband that I would stay with him and not tell what he had done if he would accept Martin as his son. I didn't dare call him after Luis. I had to call him Martin, because it was Jean-Pierre's father's name. It was the only thing I could do to throw the wool in front of people's eyes and persuade them the child was really Jean-Pierre's.

But it didn't matter what his name was – to me he was Luis, and when I sang to him I saw your father.'

Madeleine didn't move. She wanted to close her ears. She gripped the railing so hard it hurt her fingers, and willed this woman to disappear. But Colette kept talking.

'I loved your father, Madeleine, but he didn't love me. He loved Elise with so much passion that I ached with jealousy. It was a passion such as I have never known. But they shared something I could never share with him either. Your mother was cultured, sensitive, educated. They had conversations I didn't understand, and he said things about her which made no sense to me, although I remember every word he said – that she was floral, that she could smell people, intuit them, and that she had always known who he was, and where he lived in his head. He called it "affinity".'

There was a doggedness in Colette's voice, as though she had waited a long time to say these things, and now was determined to finish. It came out almost mechanically, expressionless, addressing Madeleine's rigid back as though she was in a court room.

'I was happy afterwards that Luis never got my letter. How complicated it would have been for him to learn he was to have a son. You see our relationship just wasn't like that. I wasn't his mistress. We were just friends who went to bed together because we were lonely, because there were so many gaps in our lives. Two weak people who brought about a tragedy. Because it was us. We did it. Not my husband, or Daniel, or anyone else.'

'Whose tragedy?' Madeleine spoke at last.

'A lot of people. We always knew here that the greatest tragedy was your mother's. That is why Philippe wrote to her again and again, trying to make contact. He loved your mother, you know, but he loved your father even more. And that was Philippe's tragedy. I've watched him since the war. If he could have worn your father's shirts he would have.'

'Jordi's father was tortured for days.' Madeleine muttered. 'He died an alcoholic.'

'Another one, then, whom we damaged. There's a long list. Don't think I don't feel it,' Colette sighed. 'And there are all the children. You and your brother, and Jordi, and now my Daniel it seems. It was a high price to pay. But what you have to understand is that we weren't bad, Madeleine. Your father saved so many people, helped so many, fed so many, freed so many. And I was just weak enough to love him.'

Chapter Sixteen

Two hours later Madeleine was sitting in the passenger seat of Philippe's little car as it drew into the centre of Collioure. The walls of the medieval castle loomed to her right, and to the left was a sort of man-made gully which led down to the shore, and which Philippe told her was designed to take floodwaters away to the sea. Beyond it was the old town, with a network of streets similar to but larger than Vermeilla.

Philippe led Madeleine down by the side of the gully to the quayside, holding her hand and almost dragging her along with him as his long legs strode forward, heedless of his sore back. He had pressed for this trip, back in Colette's apartment, as Madeleine stood shaking and insisting she wanted to leave.

'You haven't come this far to go and hide in your hotel room,' he told her. 'You'll eat with me tonight, and we'll see what we talk about. We'll go to Collioure and eat anchovies, as simple as you like.'

The idea of food made her feel sick again, but she had acquiesced passively in all Philippe's plans, and stood now on Collioure's quayside, trying to focus on the outstanding beauty of the place. To her left was the bell tower immortalised on canvas by Matisse and so many other artists. To her right the bay swept round in a wide curve, encompassing two beaches, and two distinct parts of the little town on either side of the castle. It was Vermeilla made more dramatic and spectacular, with the same colours and charm but an added touch of elegance.

Philippe led her to a restaurant terrace and pulled out a chair for her with a view across the bay. He ordered drinks and she found herself drinking a glass of something sparkly which might have been champagne. It slid down surprisingly easily, and the light, chilled liquid soothed her aching throat and seemed to settle her stomach.

Philippe raised his glass across the table. 'To your very good health, *ma petite*, and to all the good days to come,' he said.

Madeleine took another long sip of the bubbly, and felt it trickle down her throat. That trickle was like cool silver balm, but her hand was shaking, so she put the glass down.

'I don't see the good days to come, *Tonton* Philippe' she replied. 'But if we must drink, let's drink to you. Whatever you did, you did with the best intentions, and you never stop trying to help.'

'And how do you feel now about your father?'

The cold, hard lump twisted again, deep inside

Madeleine's stomach. She wanted to shout *How could he, how could he?* but instead she replied with a question of her own.

'Did you know, during those months before he died, that Papa was having an affair with Colette?'

'No, Madalena. Remember that I didn't come down to Vermeilla for well over a year. I was out on a limb in Amélie-les-Bains, and the only news I had of home was what Luis brought me. Luis himself only came to the coast a handful of times between the end of 1942 and when he died – a handful of times in more than eighteen months. I think to call his relationship with Colette an affair is an exaggeration.'

'So when did you find out?'

'When I read the letter, on the evening of Luis's death. When they brought me his body I knew that something in the letter had gone badly wrong, so I opened it and read it.'

'And what did you think?'

'So many questions! To be honest, Madeleine, I was too stunned and desolate to think too much. What I didn't do was judge. It would have been a presumption to judge, when so much unhappiness and trouble was involved.'

Something erupted in Madeleine, an anger which burnt her throat, her face, her eyes. She almost spat at Philippe. 'I might have known you would defend everyone! Whatever anyone does, you're always going to find an excuse for them. Didn't it occur to you that two people's philandering had put a whole team of Maquis in danger? Had caused the arrest of Enric, with all the inevitable consequences?'

'People were under enormous pressure, Madeleine.'

'But *people* didn't do it! My father did!'

'Yes, but not many people lived life with as much passion as your father. It was his strength, and also maybe his weakness.' Philippe spread his hands almost in supplication as he continued. 'You want your heroes perfect? Well in that case you should stick to novels. Your father wasn't perfect, but he was still extraordinary, and you need to accept that to be able to get his memory back in focus.'

Madeleine thought of Colette's words, 'Two weak people who brought about a tragedy'. But Colette wasn't a weak person – far from it. She'd had moments of weakness, but picturing her in her café, forced to serve the occupying forces, all her neighbours gone, with a damaged husband upstairs, and her son many kilometres away, Madeleine could imagine what a delight and comfort Luis's rare visits must have been. She was like a beast of burden, Colette, passively enduring, quietly bearing more than her fair share. But Luis? Where was his excuse?

Bitter bile rose in her throat, and she gazed out to the darkening waters of the bay, inhaling deeply and fighting back tears she didn't want to shed. She was aware of Philippe beside her, waiting for her response, but there was nothing to say, was there? What did he want of her? That she should forgive everything, smile and pretend everything was fine?

'My mother had to live with this too, you know,' she threw at him, and when he looked at her in surprise, she felt almost jubilant for a moment. But it didn't last.

'He wrote to her,' she said, her voice flat as a pancake. 'I found the letters in the jewellery box, just as you thought. His last letter told her he'd been through a dark tunnel, and pretty much admitted he'd been unfaithful. He was happy again because liberation was in sight, and said he'd found her again. He said she would understand!'

'And so she would!' was Philippe's almost inevitable reply.

She was too exhausted to try to justify herself, to fight Philippe's determined assault in defence of her father. He hadn't seen her mother after the war, the destroyed ghost of Elise. But there was no point in replying. She wanted to be on her own, but he wouldn't let her rest. Couldn't he see how tired she was?

She spoke more to satisfy him than anything else. 'If I accept what you say, where does that leave us? Where do we go from here?'

'Well, you can walk away, of course, and go back to your old life,' answered Philippe immediately, as if he had hoped for this question.

'Or?'

'Or you help me support Colette now as she decides what to tell Martin. And you help me with Daniel. I couldn't get him to speak this afternoon about his own feelings. You've just discovered a shocking truth as an adult young woman, but Daniel has been carrying the same knowledge as a secret since he was nine years old – heavy baggage for a sensitive child. And now it's all out, and he can talk, if he will. I'm hoping he may talk to you more easily than to me.'

Daniel and Martin. Martin and Daniel. A half-brother

and his half-brother. Her brain quite simply reeled.

'I want Robert to come!' she wailed. 'I'll do what I can, but I want my brother here. My real brother.'

'Tomorrow, Madalena, we will talk to the world, but right now we will eat, and you will eat and feel better, and we will drink more wine, and celebrate being here, alive. Look, the moon is already out over there, across the bay! Drink Madalena, and love life, just like your father did.'

He ordered a plate of anchovies, and a little dish of tiny fried fish, and Madeleine did as she was told, and drank wine and ate, and deliberately dulled her mind, and didn't speak, and watched the lights of Collioure brighten as the dark descended over the bay and shrouded the castle in a strange kind of intimate mystery. It wasn't a remote castle, but a part of the town, a mass of golden stone which matched the stone of the church, the bell tower, the harbour walls. They connected, embraced, and encircled the safe harbour they had been built to protect.

The castle had been the German headquarters during the war, and countless prisoners had been kept there. She'd heard that as the occupation ended and the Germans prepared to flee, they considered torching the castle and killing all the prisoners from pure vengefulness.

It was also where the French authorities had kept the fleeing Spanish militia at the end of the Civil War – all the men who were considered the most dangerous. And from here they had released a troop for a day to act as guard of honour for Machado's funeral.

Later, as they returned to the car, she found her voice, and asked Philippe where the cemetery was.

'Just up the road,' he answered, 'But it will be closed now for the night. Why?'

'I met a young couple working on Antonio Machado's new grave there,' she explained. 'And they gave me some of his poetry to read. He seemed to write about everything that we've been talking about – war, and separation, and the sense of loss, and the struggle to make a life through it all.'

Philippe almost bounced in excitement, and stopped dead in the street, his huge, ungainly feet planted squarely in front of her and blocking her way forward.

'Two quotations!' he exclaimed. 'I'll give you two quotations, and then I'll tell you a little story. Antonio Machado wrote, *"My philosophy is fundamentally sad, but I myself am not a sad man."* He lived some hard defeats, but the quotation I love the best of his is this one. *"Wanderer, your footsteps are the road, and nothing more; wanderer, there is no road, the road is made by walking. By walking one makes the road, and upon glancing behind one sees the path that never will be trod again."* It's not a message of easy reassurance, but neither is it a message of despair. We create our future. It is not ordained. We have to keep on going, and look ahead, and know what is behind us but not try to go back there.

'And my little story? Your father knew Machado. He'd met him in Paris, many years before. Machado was much older, but Luis admired him hugely, and loved his company. And when Machado arrived in Collioure, so sick, fleeing from Franco, Luis came to see him, and he brought Elise. He said he wanted her to feel him, to know the man and not just the words. They found him wasted, desperately ill and hardly speaking, but your mother came away saying he had a "being", an essence and reality, and that this filled the room.

'And that, Madeleine, is the essence of your mother and father's relationship. Their reality exists beyond anything else that happened. And there we end all discussion for tonight. And tomorrow we talk to the world, and you talk to Robert, and we put one foot in front of the other and make a road.'

I don't want to talk to the world, thought Madeleine. I only want to talk to Robert. Oh, how I want to talk to him. He seemed to think I was exaggerating the importance of what Jordi told me, but it's worse, so much worse than even Jordi could have suspected. It was funny, really, that all her life Madeleine had thought of Robert as the little brother who needed to be protected, the boy young for his years who seemed so vulnerable, but since their mother's death he had become her confederate, the cornerstone of her sense of family. She could see more clearly how well Robert had coped with their reality as a child. How he had kept his own inner self while making a compact with their grandfather, and won his support and affection without once becoming his puppet. Grandfather needed Robert more than Robert needed him, and she had no doubt that if Grandfather cut off funds for his studies Robert would calmly follow a different course and build a new future. He knew how to make the sun shine, she thought, as she never would.

Right now, here in this deceptively beautiful, serene

corner of France, Madeleine felt terribly alone. Philippe, Colette, Daniel – they had their own tragedies, but what she had learnt today was hers alone to deal with. But if Robert was here then they would be two people together facing this new, desolate landscape. Would Robert know how to turn this situation in Vermeilla into something positive? There was a good chance, she thought, that he would know better than her.

The next morning found Madeleine back at the post office, sitting in the same little cubicle as the day before, but this time the voice at the other end told her to wait and disappeared for ages before returning to say that Mr Garriga was not in his room. The wave of disappointment which washed through Madeleine was almost more than she could bear. She fought back new tears, and left a message, which the voice, a porter she thought, assured her would be left in Robert's pigeonhole. She thought hard about her message, but finished merely by asking him to call her at the Hotel Bon Repos. There was no point even beginning to explain what had happened, not in a scribbled message in a pigeonhole.

Leaving the post office she was at a loss what to do. She could see Philippe playing boules with a group of men in the square, their sleeves rolled up and their overall jackets laid on the bench behind them. He would be busy all morning, and in any case, they had agreed to meet during the afternoon to plan the 'next move', as Philippe insisted on calling it. Were they moving forward, or simply swimming to save themselves from sinking?

Philippe had finished off the Machado quotation last night as they drove home in the car. '*Wanderer there is no road. Only wakes upon the sea.*' They'd been driving back along the coast road, and the moon was lighting up the water with such brilliance that it reflected onto the sands. Madeleine had responded by commenting how wonderful it would be right now to be in a boat running for the open sea, rather than trying to forge some kind of way ahead without any road. Papa, she thought, you have taken away my past, and I can't see my way into the future. How could you, how could you?

Right now, standing lost outside the post office, with Robert a million miles away, Madeleine wanted to move, to walk, to empty her head and fill her lungs. She was tempted to walk along the coastal path towards Collioure, which she had heard was often a crumbled cliff path, but with magnificent views. But then on impulse she turned her steps up towards the vineyards, and climbed the hill with a ferocity which set her panting, finishing up by Daniel's little field of vines, sitting quiet and deserted in the morning sun, as peaceful and timeless as they had been the previous Sunday, when the world still stood upright and dreams were still intact.

There was no wind today, just the slightest hint of breeze, and the sun was hot. What time of year, she wondered, had Luis and Colette begun their affair? In the cold of winter under blankets, or in the heat of the summer, naked to the world? She hoped he had waited until summer, and had at least missed them for a few months. She had an image of a younger Colette, with her grave good looks and without the deep, tired lines which underscored her eyes. Luis was in front of her, standing by the table, that same dining table, listening to her intently.

'They're bringing more troops in all the time now,' Colette was telling him. 'There's hardly a house not requisitioned for something. You'll never get to their headquarters, of course, in the castle in Collioure, but you could do worse than to target old Henri's house. It's the biggest in Vermeilla, and there must be ten men sleeping there, but the word is they use it as an office as well, and there are papers there.'

'Are there any movements on the beach?'

'Only the fishing. That continues, of course, and they send a German soldier out with them night and day to watch what they're up to. There's a small German launch tied up on the quay but it doesn't seem to move much. I heard there was some small ship anchored in the bay at Collioure last weekend, and of course they're all over the harbour in Port Vendres.'

Luis nodded. 'I'll go along to Collioure tonight after dark,' he said. A frown crossed his face. 'What about you, are they leaving you alone?'

'It depends what you mean. The bar is full of them, of course, especially in the evenings, and they can get a bit lewd. They don't have much respect for French women, so I stay upstairs if I can when they start getting drunk. Luc runs the bar for me then, and tries to keep his ears open. During the day they're no bother, except for always wanting foods we can't get. They bring me stuff to cook for them – I've got a rabbit stew downstairs. You'll have some, of course, and I'll give you a whole rabbit to take back with you.'

'Don't, Colette! Don't put yourself in danger.'

'Oh, I'm not in any danger. Apart from my virtue, that is!'

'And where is Jean-Pierre while this is going on?'

Colette frowned, and gave an instinctive look over her shoulder, although for once she knew he was not at home. 'You know, Luis, Jean-Pierre is getting stranger and stranger. He hardly goes downstairs at all at the moment, and he mutters to himself. He's scared, I think, and feels helpless. It's so bad for Daniel to see him like this.'

Her face was full of pain and worry, and Luis reached out a hand and stroked her cheek. His voice was very soft as he answered her.

'The sooner you get that boy away from here and back to school with other children the better. He could come with me tomorrow, even, and I'd take him to Philippe, if you'd let me.'

'I know I should.' Her voice quivered. 'It's just he's all I've got.'

'I know, Colette, I know.' Luis kept his hand against her cheek.

'It's worse for you, Luis, up there alone, with all your family gone.'

Colette's hand stole up to touch his. Their eyes held, and Colette gave a tiny gasp, her lips parting in surprise. Luis leant forward and kissed her.

'Luis, we shouldn't.'

'I know.' But he kissed her again. 'Where's Daniel?'

'There was a truck going to Perpignan. Daniel went with his father to take him to the chiropodist. It's the first time Jean-Pierre's been outside the village for years, I think.'

'Well he couldn't have timed it better.'

Was that how it had happened, Madeleine wondered? A rare moment alone, an intimate look, and then the succumbing? She thought of the front guest bedroom in Colette's apartment, and shook her head to try to banish the couple she saw there. Elise seemed so far away. All she could see was Colette, with Luis's hands entwined in her hair. And Daniel on the other side of the door.

Chapter Seventeen

She returned to the village in something of a daze, and realised she'd sat longer than she'd thought among the vines. Philippe and the boules team had finished their game, and gone home to eat, and Madeleine came awake and headed straight for the hotel, thinking Robert was maybe trying to get hold of her. But it wasn't Robert who had been looking for her. Standing outside the Hotel Bon Repos, placidly smoking a small cigar and watching Vermeilla life making its way to lunch, was Bernard. He'd come, he told her, with his most charming smile, to see what she'd been doing to this harmless little place. Robert had sent him, of course, more worried than he liked to admit by their conversation yesterday. Call us, Bernard and Solange had said, and Robert had taken them at their word.

'Have you been starting a new war, my dear?' asked

Bernard. And then, reading her tense face and bruised eyes, 'Lunch first, and then you can tell me.'

He wasn't Robert, not her Robert whom she wanted so badly, but Bernard was as rotund and reassuring as ever, and in his elegant presence the events of the last few days seemed somehow much less dramatic. Over a lunch on the quayside she told him her story as simply as she could, and watched as his eyes widened when she came to Luis's affair.

'Well,' he said as she came to an end, 'who could ever have believed that? Maybe Solange was right thinking you should never have come down here on your own. You've had a lot to contend with all alone here, haven't you? And have you seen this new half-brother at all, since all these revelations?'

'No. No, I haven't seen him yet. I don't want to see him! But I suppose I must some time. I don't even know what Colette plans to tell him. He has been the only one here living completely carefree, not knowing anything. I need to see Daniel as well. He's the one who worries me. He's so good to everyone and too quiet, much too quiet, and I still can't believe I actually accused him of betraying the camp.'

'Should you really be worrying about all the others in this story, do you think? I'd rather have expected you to be more worried about yourself just now. I have to say, you've taken a very mature role, coping with all this on your own, and even on behalf of the rest of them.'

Madeleine gave a rather threadbare laugh. 'Do you think so? If the truth be told I feel so knocked over I can't think straight. And anyway, I haven't been completely alone. I've had Philippe, and for him I think I qualify as family. Did I

259

tell you, he still lives in the same apartment that Robert and I lived in as children here? Which reminds me! Oh, hell! I tried to call Robert this morning, but he wasn't there, so I left a message for him to call the hotel. I was hoping he would call at lunchtime, but seeing you made me forget, and now I may have missed his call. He doesn't even know about Colette and Papa – about Martin.'

'Well, there's a delight still in store for him,' Bernard murmured ironically. 'But don't worry about his call. We agreed yesterday when he phoned me that he would call Solange this evening in Paris. Phone calls to here seem to be difficult. And he was worried enough on the telephone to talk of coming down here himself this weekend, after getting through some examination he has today. Just decide how much you want to tell Solange, and we'll call her later this afternoon and give her instructions to get Robert moving. I think, like you, that this story now needs his presence.'

Madeleine eased back in her chair, deliberately relaxing the tightened muscles around her neck, and sipped her coffee. Bernard had arrived from Paris, wafting with him the magic of a world where people had telephones at home, and called each other with ease, and planned journeys from England to France without batting an eyelid. She could leave everything in his hands, it seemed, and he would have thought of everything. How his urbane persona would deal with her new world in Vermeilla was a question she left for later.

She needn't have worried, she realised when Philippe almost fell over them outside the post office later that afternoon. Philippe's big head bobbed up and down energetically as he shook Bernard's hand, his thick mane of hair flapping above the Parisian's neatly trimmed, thinning coiffure and speckled moustache. Philippe must have been fifteen years older than Bernard, but you wouldn't have known it. He swept them along in his wake, and if Madeleine had wondered how she was going to approach the Café de Catalogne again, she found herself outside its doors before she had even had time to think where they were heading. She faltered at the door, and let the two men go ahead of her. She wanted to see Daniel, but the thought of seeing Martin appalled her. She followed slowly behind Bernard, her heart pounding.

There was no sign of Colette or Martin in the bar, but Daniel was at the counter, talking to his friend of the other day, Eric the newly-wed fisherman. Philippe was ahead of her, already talking, and waving forward Bernard. Daniel, she saw, had frozen at their entrance. In the flurry of introductions of 'our friend from Paris', Daniel's silence went unnoticed. He watched Madeleine from deep inside a set, unfathomable face, and she wondered how you could ever hope to be forgiven for throwing accusations of abetting a slaughter at a young man as sensitive as Daniel.

She waited while Bernard greeted both young men with his usual smooth complaisance, and then Philippe drew him off to a table, calling for coffee and his usual afternoon slice of whatever patisserie Colette had baked that day.

The two men settled down to talk, two confident men from very different worlds, linked perhaps by their intellect. Madeleine heard Philippe mention chess, and knew a board would appear within minutes. It would provide them both with the means to get to know each other in the most comfortable way possible.

Which left her, standing at the bar, comfort far from her mind, wondering what to say to the young man who was watching them all with remote eyes and an almost supernatural stillness. Eric broke the silence, greeting Madeleine with a flirtatious grin, and holding her hand for rather longer than necessary.

'Well, Mademoiselle, all these days and we didn't meet again. But today is my lucky day, it seems. What have you been doing with yourself in our little hidden, uneventful village, where nothing happens from one end of the week to the next?'

Uneventful was not a word which Madeleine would have chosen herself to describe her time in Vermeilla, but Eric was not to know. She smiled at him, but freed her hand and held it out to Daniel, who seemed to become aware of it gradually, and then took it in a non-committal grasp. Madeleine squeezed, and didn't let go, and answered Eric.

'I've been incredibly well looked after, thanks. I feel as though I have found a family here, and Daniel has been wonderful, showing me around, taking care of me.'

Listen to me, Daniel, she was thinking. *Look at me!*

Eric dug his friend in the stomach with his elbow. Daniel still stood withdrawn, like a tortoise in its thick shell, eyes watching from just inside.

'Lucky dog, you,' chuckled Eric. 'That's the advantage of owning a bar, Mademoiselle. It's a natural meeting place, and you're king of your own dungheap. So he's been showing you around, huh? Where? Around the village? Oh, his vineyard? All very fine, but has he taken you out for a ride at sea? That's what you need, is a nice boat trip. Hey, Daniel, you should take out my launch. That's the way to make romance blossom!'

There was a silence, during which Eric watched his friend with a growing frown.

'You're not normally this quiet, my friend. Have you swallowed your tongue? It must be serious, then,' he joked again, more puzzled this time.

The moment of supreme awkwardness stretched on. Madeleine waited for the earth to open up and suck her in, but nothing happened. All she wanted was to speak to Daniel, but as they stood there the chances of him talking to her were becoming more and more remote.

Then, surprisingly, Daniel gave a brisk nod of his head, as though he had come to a sudden decision. He nodded at Eric, and said, 'All right, then, I'll take your boat! If you want me to take Madeleine to sea, it might as well be today, when there's no wind, and I can be sure she won't be seasick.'

His voice was hard as he spoke, and sounded so unlike the gentle Daniel that Madeleine wanted to cry. She hadn't really shed any tears yet, but right now she wanted to. Tears for the lost memories, the lost certainties, and tears for Daniel, who had lived with those memories and certainties since the age of nine.

She rushed to fill an awkward gap as Eric stared at Daniel now in blatant surprise.

'I would love to go out for a boat trip,' she declared, and

realised it was true. She had spent so much time these last twenty-four hours in intense discussions, sitting around tables and in people's sitting rooms, that she longed for action, to be outdoors and doing. And especially away from this café. She kept looking at the door, or towards the stairs, expecting Martin to appear, or Colette, or, stupidly, and terrifyingly, Jean-Pierre Perrens. She could handle being with Daniel. The others she wasn't ready for yet.

'Shall we go now?' she asked. 'It might be a good idea to go now, while there's still time before the light goes.' She looked into Daniel's closed face. 'Don't you think? Daniel?'

Daniel looked up briefly and then nodded. 'Do you want a hat?' he asked, inconsequentially, and she shook her head.

'OK then, let's go,' he muttered, and turned abruptly to leave.

Philippe and Bernard were deep in their chess game, and Bernard merely nodded when she told him where she was going. Philippe, though, gave a small, satisfied smile.

'Have fun,' he said, as he watched Bernard move his rook.

Bernard looked up then. 'Are you going now?' he asked. 'And coming back here? Then I'll wait for you here. This,' he gestured at the chessboard, 'may take some time.'

Eric left the bar with them, and the two young men stood back to let Madeleine pass first through the café doorway, which was open to the warmth of the May afternoon. Madeleine emerged into the street just as Martin came around the corner, his school bag over his shoulder, bursting with untidy bits of paper. Madeleine's chest pounded on sight of him, and she recoiled involuntarily and stepped back onto Eric's foot. She apologised, and hoped that her embarrassment at squashing his toes would be cover for her blazing cheeks.

She was trapped between the two men behind and the young boy in front of her. Her brother. It was useless to call him her half-brother. Blood was blood, and Luis's son was inevitably her brother.

Martin greeted her gaily, as he might any family friend. She looked into his face, and he smiled the smile which was different from Daniel's. Was it like Luis's, she wondered? Her memory wasn't good enough to tell her, and she conjured up Robert's face to try to help her. Robert had such a brilliant smile, one which lit his eyes and dimpled one cheek more than the other, and this boy's smile was indeed familiar. Martin was his mother's son, but alongside Robert she suspected that he would be similar enough in looks to be quite troubling.

'Are you going out?' he asked, and then, when he heard where they were going. 'Shall I come too? It will be lovely out there today.'

He looked guilelessly at Daniel, but Daniel, who normally had so much time for him, shook his head in strong denial.

'You have homework to do,' he said.

'I don't ever remember that stopping you going to sea after school,' protested Martin.

'Much you remember! I left school when you had barely started! Anyway, that's why I'm a fisherman and you're going to be a doctor, remember?'

'But it's such a lovely day!' Martin wheedled, as Madeleine had heard him coax his mother. But Daniel was already walking off.

'Tell *Maman* I'll be back long before dinner,' he instructed, and Madeleine followed gratefully as he strode away from the café. She realised she hadn't even spoken one word to Martin. She just wanted to escape, and as Daniel headed at a brisk pace towards the sea she allowed herself to be sucked along in his wake.

At the next corner Eric left them. 'I'll leave you with this strange fellow,' he smiled at Madeleine. 'Perhaps you can improve his mood today. And as for you, lump head, mind how you treat my launch.'

Daniel laughed spontaneously, almost his natural laugh. 'Says the man with the poorest kept fishing boat in the fleet!' he taunted, and dodged as Eric lunged for him.

His laugh followed Eric down the side road to his home, but then petered out, and as he looked at Madeleine he simply waved his hand towards the quayside, and then led the way wordlessly to Eric's small wooden launch. Unlike the shallow fishing boats which were hauled up the beach, the launch floated alongside the small jetty. It was about fifteen feet in length, with a half cabin housing a professional-looking wheel and set of dials. Three fishing rods were tied to the side of the tiny cabin, but on this vessel there was no smell of fish, and the white paintwork gleamed in the late-afternoon sunshine. If Eric was known for his poorly kept fishing boat, he had a different attitude towards his pleasure launch, it seemed.

It wasn't until they had negotiated their way out of the

harbour and were beyond the sea wall that Daniel spoke at last. Dumbstruck by the sheer beauty of Vermeilla from the water, by the rush of ozone and the fresh kiss of the breeze as the boat gathered speed, Madeleine was gazing towards the horizon trying to decide where the deep blue of the Mediterranean met the sky, when Daniel's voice hit her, raised above the noise of the engine, as though goaded by the very sight of her.

'Do you find it romantic? That's what you thought you were coming to find, wasn't it, when you came down here from Paris? A romantic little village on the edge of the Mediterranean. The village your mother no doubt described to you, full of charming rustics. Well, now you know what we're really like. Murderers and adulterers. Ugly cowards. The sunshine and the sea and the beaches are just cover, to please the tourists, and our guests from Paris.'

His voice was angry, but what came through to Madeleine was a deep misery and disillusionment. She fixed on the only part of his tirade that seemed worth answering.

'My mother never described Vermeilla as rustic. In fact she never described it at all. We never had any access to her memories of here after she heard that my father had died. I may have romanticised it, I suppose, like little girls do. I needed it, you see. I clung on to my memories.'

She forgot to raise her voice above the engine noise, and Daniel craned forward trying to hear her, and then, in exasperation, switched off the engine. The sudden silence was overwhelming, and neither spoke, until Daniel finally replied.

'But your mother was like that man from Paris, full of fancy words and soft handshakes. Like you too, really, I suppose, only you seemed different.'

'You remember my mother?'

'Oh yes, I remember her. Not well, not like I remember your father. She left too early. But he stayed. Oh yes, he stayed.'

Luis and Colette in the front bedroom, Luis's hands entwined in her hair. And Daniel on the other side of the door.

She looked at Daniel. 'When I arrived in Vermeilla you seemed not to know who I was. In the café Philippe introduced me to you as Luis's daughter, and you acted as though that meant nothing to you.'

Daniel didn't answer. Now he too seemed to be studying the horizon.

'Did you notice my mother that morning?' he asked. 'She was so shocked by your arrival. I think I knew then that everything would soon be over. It was a relief, really, although I don't think I realised it would come so quickly. How long have you been here? A week? Less? Poor *Maman*, after all these years of pretending nothing had ever happened!'

'Philippe talked about one person being a catalyst which prises open people's lives. But he also said we needed the truth. Do you think we needed the truth, Daniel? Would it have been better if I hadn't come? If people had remained in ignorance?'

He shook his head in irritation. 'Who was in ignorance? My father knew what he had done, and about my mother.

So did Philippe, and so did I. The only thing was that none of us ever admitted it. The only one in real ignorance was Martin.'

Madeleine thought about the young Daniel playing his lonely part in this silent conspiracy.

'The adults all knew about each other's part, but none of them thought that you knew anything about it.'

Daniel's eyes were fixed on the horizon again. Madeleine tried to find the words to take them forward.

'How did you cope, Daniel, all those years ago? Didn't you want to tell your mother?'

'No!' The word was torn from him. 'I never wanted to tell her! I knew what my father was like. I knew how hard her life was. When I learnt that she was pregnant I just wanted to get to Luis, and make sure he looked after her. She was always so alone. Then when Luis was killed I knew it would have to be me who looked after her. It was my fault for not finding Luis. I should have told him and then she would have been all right. And if she wanted to say the baby was my father's, then that was fine by me. She wanted me to believe it. She wanted life to be normal, don't you understand? And it was my job to help her.'

Daniel's voice had risen again, and Madeleine longed to soothe him, but there wasn't anything she could say. She thought of the Daniel she had known since her arrival, so gentle, always smiling, always thinking of others – the brother who stayed at home and helped provide for his family. Maybe this new anger would help him to begin thinking about himself, to become someone different. Now that he had admitted to Colette that he knew, the

269

responsibility shifted to her, surely? Where did it come from anyway, this strange sense of responsibility among the young for the things that adults do?

'I used to think it was my fault, too,' she managed to say, 'when my grandfather was foul to my mother. My brother could always charm him out of his bad moods, but I couldn't, and I used to stand by and watch as he took it out on my mother, and feel hopeless and stupid. I always felt I needed to make it up to my mother, and I guess that's how you felt too, really. It's strange how children are.'

Daniel looked clear at her this time. 'What happened to you, after we killed your father?'

'You didn't kill my father!'

But she told him, the whole story of her pathetic childhood, what happened to her mother, the petty tyranny of her grandfather, the memories and the longing for 'home'.

'It was a privileged life, really,' she finished up. 'Upper class and all the things you were accusing me of. It's all true, and compared with most people I haven't had anything to complain of. It was just very narrow and it wasn't really "our" life, if you understand what I mean. But millions of women lost their husbands in the war, and not all of them reacted like my mother. She just didn't pick herself up again, and my brother and myself have spent a long time trying to understand that.'

'Maybe she felt guilt too,' Daniel mused. 'You say her brothers had both been killed, and she was seen as a failure. She probably felt responsible for her father's unhappiness.'

'Yes. Yes, you're probably right. I remember when the

news came through about my Uncle John dying. He was killed in action in Italy in the spring of 1944, and when I think about it, it was only a very few months before we heard about Papa being killed. Nobody really knew what had happened to Papa, and what he had been doing, but Uncle John was in the real war, I suppose, as far as my grandfather looked at these things, and he was covered in glory. They never stopped talking about him, and yet my father's death was never spoken of. Poor *Maman*. The French were just people the Brits had saved as far as my grandfather was concerned, and had nothing to be proud of. And as for the Spanish, they were unmentionable! I don't know what my grandmother must have thought, but when I think about it, she never spoke French all the time I was growing up. Never once spoke her mother tongue. And she made a shrine of Uncle John's bedroom at Forsham.'

She looked up at Daniel and realised that she'd been speaking purely to herself. How much could any of this mean to him, born and raised here, on these shores, part of this sunshine, and this endless sea?

But Daniel was watching her with close attention, his face alight with interest. 'And if your father hadn't died?' he asked.

As she looked at him, she realised with a shock that it would not have been enough. For her life to have been the way she had always dreamt of, not only would Luis Garriga have needed to have survived the war, but Martin needed never to have been born. At the point of visualising her mother returning to Vermeilla after the war, with Colette and her baby *in situ*, Madeleine's imagination ceased to function. The fairy tale didn't exist, the dream was a bubble which had burst long ago, long before that afternoon in the hills of the Vallespir.

'If my father had lived, he had a child here to care for. He was no longer really my father,' she said bitterly.

'Wasn't he? You know, I used to hate him. I blamed him and I blamed myself. But listening to you just now, I was thinking, the only real blame lies with the war. It's what the war did to you, to your grandfather, to your mother, to me and my family. It smashed up lives and left people to live with the consequences.'

Madeleine contemplated this. Machado's words came back to her. *From sea to sea between us is war, deeper than war.*

Would it go away for people one day, she wondered, this legacy of war? Daniel was right. It was too big, and too callous, and individuals within it were twisted and turned and thrown about like so much flotsam. She glanced again at Daniel.

'Is that what we're doing, then, living with the consequences?'

Daniel laughed. 'Each in our own way, I suppose that's what we're doing.'

He seemed genuinely, if rather morbidly, amused, and perhaps the very craziness of their situation was reason enough for laughter. Or was it merely hysteria? Madeleine was glad to see him looser at any rate, and felt some of her own tension releasing.

'I'll tell you what, Madeleine,' Daniel continued, still with the same humour. 'If we accept that we're in a situation we didn't cause and couldn't have done anything to stop, then the best thing we can do is get on with whatever's left. I say we should get the engine going again and go towards Collioure to a prime little fishing area where we might catch some sea bream. It won't actually solve anything if we catch any, but it will give my mother some pleasure, at least. What do you say?'

They spent a magical, forgetful two hours fishing for bream, returning with not a lot to show for their endeavours, but for Madeleine, the experience was a revelation. Drenched in sun, sweating as she cast and cast again and learnt to send her line skidding through the air before it sank under the water, her hair askew and her dress covered in smears of the stinking bait they found in a bucket, she let Daniel hold her arms and show her how to reel in a fish, and then hit it over the head like him without a second's compunction.

As dusk fell they turned back for Vermeilla, aware that they were going to be late for dinner, whoever they were each supposed to be eating it with. Four small fish lay in the bottom of a black bucket, and Daniel was telling her tall stories of fish he'd caught in the past.

'You'll have to take me out again, in that case,' Madeleine laughed. 'To prove you're the fisherman you say you are. Any brother of mine has to be able to live up to his bragging!'

Daniel's smile faded, and he snapped, 'I'm not your brother, Madeleine.'

She looked a query. Hers had been a light-hearted remark, and they'd joked more than once this afternoon

273

about their shared half-brother. But Daniel had turned away, and was tidying the rods with one hand while he held the wheel with another.

'I'm sorry, Daniel,' she said. 'I didn't mean to touch on a raw nerve. It's just that I've had such a good afternoon. As good if not better than I could have had with my own brother. We are kind of family, you know. What do you think you are, my half-brother once removed? Or my step half-brother?'

Her teasing tone made no impact. He kept his back to her, and busied himself in the corner tying cords around the rods.

'Daniel?' Madeleine questioned, slightly alarmed.

'It's all right,' he mouthed, so that she had to struggle to hear him. 'You can be whatever you like, Madeleine. Just whatever you like.'

His meaning was suddenly unmistakable, and Madeleine drew back into the far corner, jolted by an intense consternation which left her with nothing to say. So Daniel had that kind of interest in her! And she hadn't seen it. How could she have been so naive? And yet she'd been aware of an attraction towards him, earlier in the week. What had happened to make it seem so impossible now? It dawned on her with a jolt that it was Jordi who had changed things. She had a sudden vision of him, angry, challenging, disquieting. Daniel didn't disquiet her. Oh God, she thought, where will all the complications end?

She was relieved to see Bernard waiting for them on the quayside. He was on his own, sauntering along looking into the fishing barques, and came towards where they berthed to take a rope from Daniel.

'Well, I may have said I'd wait for you at the café,' he said, 'but even I couldn't make a chess game last that long! Where have you been? Fishing? Any good booty?'

He handed Madeleine ashore and raised an eyebrow in query. She smiled at him.

'It's been amazing, Uncle Bernard,' she reassured him. 'We didn't catch much, but I think that was my fault. I wasn't that good, but it was excellent fun.'

Daniel had finished tying up the launch and jumped ashore. He seemed to have recovered his assurance, and greeted Bernard calmly.

'She's actually pretty talented,' he told Bernard. 'We'll go out again another day, if you'd like to come with us, sir?'

Bernard took Madeleine's arm, and prepared to saunter off towards the hotel, further along the quay. It was quite funny, thought Madeleine, but also vaguely irritating to have a gentleman like Bernard treating her again like a young lady needing protection, after all she'd been through on her own.

Bernard thanked Daniel on her behalf, of all things, and went to move away. She freed her arm and moved back to Daniel.

'Thank you, Daniel,' she said, touching his hand. 'I've had a great afternoon. And you helped me a lot. Thank you for your friendship.'

He looked her straight in the face again at last.

'Don't thank me, Madeleine, and I won't thank you.

We'll just get on with making the best of things, all right? That's all there seems to be left.'

There was bitterness again in his voice, but Madeleine chose not to notice it.

'It's a deal, and we'll go fishing again one day and see if I can do better. I'm sorry I didn't catch anything worthwhile.'

He looked down into the bucket at the four fish. 'It's not so bad!' he countered. 'My father will have some good fish for his lunch tomorrow. Will we see you tomorrow?'

'Maybe. I'm waiting for news from home, from Robert. I'm hoping he's going to come over here.'

Daniel made an unfathomable gesture. 'You certainly have reinforcements,' he remarked. 'I'll look forward to meeting your brother.'

My other brother, she was tempted to say, wanting suddenly to laugh, and then to cry.

'Goodnight, Daniel. Better fishing tonight,' was all she said. And then she turned to safe, comfortable Bernard, and Daniel disappeared up the street with his catch in his hand.

Chapter Eighteen

It seemed Bernard had made himself quite at home at the Café de Catalogne. He had talked politics and the state of the country with Philippe, and then they had ventured into talking about the past. Philippe had asked for *Tante* Louise, remembering her visit to Vermeilla, and remembering also the daughter Solange as a Parisian beauty who had terrified the Vermeilla men with her chic ways. Bernard, who loved his wife, had quite naturally found Philippe highly intelligent, and forgave him for winning at chess.

Bernard had also met Colette, and young Martin. Of Colette he was less flattering, calling her 'basic' and 'mediocre', and 'one of those women who age really badly'.

'Colette is beautiful,' Madeleine found herself protesting. 'If we worked like she does we'd look tired too.'

And Martin? The boy was well enough, obviously bright, Bernard commented, but just a boy, after all. Seen through Bernard's childless, middle-aged eyes, Madeleine suspected all young people below the age of adulthood must seem like a foreign species.

Philippe, though, had talked at length about Martin, and how it was time for him to know about his real father. Philippe argued that with Jean-Pierre Perrens becoming more and more unstable, he was capable of blurting something out at any time, and the young boy was too bright not to pick up on any small snippets he overheard.

'Did Philippe talk about Daniel as well?' Madeleine asked.

'To say that he needs to move on – that he's been repressing his own needs all this time, and now needs help to find out who he really is. The only one Philippe doesn't seem to be worried about is you, my dear! He says you have solid feet!'

'How very nice of him.' Madeleine's voice was subdued.

'But it all leaves me feeling rather uneasy, in truth. More than uneasy. There seems to me to be so much repression and unfinished business here that I can't somehow share Philippe's optimism for everyone's future. And I can't see, either, where you are going to fit in here, Madeleine. You're not exactly going to move in with the "family" are you? It's all terribly incestuous, if you'll forgive me saying so.'

Madeleine found herself nodding. 'I know. We keep taking those unknown steps down an unknown road, but it feels to me as if the road is blocked here in Vermeilla. I don't know what we're all going to do, or where on earth I'm going. It's such a mess, and so many people are hurting, and there's still more misery to come, I'm sure.

'But I'll tell you one thing,' she said more aggressively,

'the road won't lead me back to Forsham! I've escaped from there and I'm never going back.'

Robert phoned the hotel that evening. Standing in the hotel reception, mercifully empty, Madeleine's voice broke as she told him about their father, and he went very quiet on the other end of the line.

'I'm in London right now. I headed up here after the exam this afternoon, and I'm staying with Cousin Cicely, before heading off tomorrow morning,' he finally told her. 'Solange and I agreed that I get an early train from London to Paris, and she is arranging a ticket for me on the first possible train south. I suppose I'll have to stop off somewhere on the way, and I'll get to you sometime on Saturday. If you speak to Solange tomorrow evening she'll be able to tell you where I am.'

A Robert who casually travelled up to London and stayed overnight with his fashionable cousin, before jumping on a train for Paris. Things were certainly changing. The static world of Forsham before their mother's death now seemed like a lifetime away.

'We'll be waiting for you,' Madeleine said. 'I'm so glad you're coming.'

'Yeah, well maybe by the time I reach you I'll have understood what you've just told me. I just want to thump someone. Tell me, who do I thump?'

'No one, Robert. Sadly there's no one left to thump. No one fit to thump, anyway.'

Madeleine felt incredibly depressed. No one to blame, no one to thump. Just an unholy mess and a taste of ashes in the mouth.

Robert's voice came back, sounding a long way away. 'And how about you, Madeleine? Are you all right?' he wanted to know.

'Bearing up,' was all she could say. 'But hurry up and get here.'

'On my way,' he assured her, and sounded more positive.

Bernard then phoned Solange, and Madeleine escaped onto the quayside to breathe the mellowed evening air, in time to watch the fishermen pushing their boats down the beach, heading out to sea. Daniel would be there, and she hoped the night of physical labour would help soothe the wound they had reopened in his soul.

'What's for tomorrow?' Bernard asked her later. 'Do you have any plan of campaign?'

'There's nothing to campaign about. Nothing we can do, is there? I want to wait for Robert before I see any of them again.'

'So what would you like to do tomorrow? Go for a drive? Philippe has offered me his car.'

Suddenly a road opened up in front of Madeleine, and she knew what she wanted to do. She wanted to see Jordi. A surge of pleasure went through her at the idea of seeing him, in his chaotic studio, surrounded by his bulls and his angry, sensual figures. He felt like an ally, a comrade-in-arms, far from the compromised life of Vermeilla. In Jordi's life there was not much compromise.

Would Bernard take her? It seemed he would, with a smile on his face that made her think she must be very transparent.

'If you take me, then Jordi will bring me back on his motorcycle,' she said, hoping it was true.

'Or I can come back for you. The day will be yours, child, and you can just phone when you want and I will be here for your call.'

So the following day saw her driving out with Bernard, on the same road through the plane trees, leading them from one little Roussillon village to another, on the way to Céret and the Pyrenees beyond. The day was sunny for now, but there was a strong wind whipping up the sea which apparently promised rain. The locals were happy. It had been an exceptionally dry spring, it seemed, and the ground needed the rain. Mme Curelée paid lip service to the needs of the vineyards at the same time as she bemoaned what rain might do to custom at the hotel over the weekend.

But for now it wasn't raining, and the cool, rather humid breeze was welcome in the car. Canigou, the Catalans' very own, friendly mountain, stood before them all on its own, still peaked with snow and seeming to float on the misty blue of the horizon, the blue of the foothills, the Vallespir. Early fruits, as yet unripened, packed the peach trees which stretched to either side of the car as it made its slow way past the farms and gardens of the Roussillon plains, past Le Boulou and on towards Céret. The journey seemed longer than four days before, when Madeleine had headed up to the Vallespir with Philippe, thinking only that she was going to see her father's grave. She had known nothing then about all the betrayals which had burst upon her in the last few days. She had been on such an innocent quest, and it seemed incredible that so short a time could have changed her life so much.

Today's seemingly interminable journey at last reached its end as they drove between the yellow stone buildings of Céret, and past the Musée d'Art Moderne. Bernard wouldn't come inside Jordi's gallery, insisting that he would just park outside the museum for fifteen minutes, so that if Madeleine found it wasn't a good time to call she could come away quietly and he would be there. The soul of discretion! Had Philippe told him about Jordi's edgy character, she wondered?

But at the point of going into the gallery she felt all of Bernard's qualms and more. What was she doing? This was the man who had held the world at bay for years. Why should he want to see her? But he had told her to come. Told her he would be there. She opened the door and went inside.

A little bell above the door brought Jordi from the rear of the shop. He froze when he saw her, and then made a sudden move forward.

'Madeleine.'

The single word burst from him, and then he stopped, physically, in the middle of the shop floor, surrounded by his ceramics and sculptures. A silence followed, and Madeleine thought, I haven't got any words, I don't know what to say, I don't have any experience of this. And as she looked at him, the thought came to her, comforting and reassuring, that neither did he. They were two young people who had never before ventured down these paths, and they would have to invent the words as they went, taking steps down Machado's unknown road.

'You said to come,' she ventured at last.

He smiled at last, and a smile which lit his deep brown eyes. 'Come in. I'm glad you're here.'

He led her into the back room, where a huge, half-painted vase stood waiting for him on the work table. A woman's face emerged from a dark background, her hair tossed back as though by a storm, and her eyes blazing with what might have been anger or passion. She was beautiful, but crudely finished, with hard edges, and Madeleine wondered whether Jordi planned to soften her. Probably not, she thought, wishing she knew more about art, and could identify the genre he was following. All she could do was sense it, and it hit her with a force that surprised her that this woman was in love but not happy. There was a loneliness and a hunger in the image which disturbed her.

'You were working. I'm sorry.'

'I'm not. It's all right. You can stand by the vase and it will help me paint. You have the same lines in your face. She could be you, you know.'

Madeleine looked at the impassioned face and felt small and inadequate.

'I've never felt like that. I don't even know how. I'm just ordinary.'

'We're all ordinary. But we are Catalans. Look at her face, and see those bones. She's a Catalan too. And she knows how to yearn, how to dream.'

'I've never known how to dream. I was brought up English, remember. I don't even speak any Catalan.'

283

Madeleine was surprised at the bitter intensity in her own voice. What was she doing, speaking like this to a man she'd met four days ago?

But Jordi answered as though it was normal, picking up her words, responding instantly with a challenge.

'You can learn Catalan. Anyone can who wants to. And you can learn to live by feel, to stretch out and breathe the world. You've got that capacity in you, if you let yourself grow.'

'You make me sound like a stunted tree!'

'No. You're not stunted, you're just half grown. When Philippe asked me to show you the camp the other day, I thought you were some English girl coming her to feed her curiosity – to gape, if you like. But there was such a sense of longing about you, like you were looking for your life, for someone to be. Like you were just half a person.'

Half a person. It sounded so inadequate. She repeated it mechanically, and Jordi's voice softened as he continued.

'Oh, there's plenty to you, Madeleine, I'm not trying to belittle you. There's a part of you that feels so grounded I want to grab hold of it to keep me steady. It's more like you're a tree with great roots but you need feeding to grow. You've got your roots, but you've been deprived of knowing them.'

'So I am a stunted tree, after all!'

'No, you're a tree learning to grow. It's me that's the stunted tree.'

Madeleine shook her head, and traced her finger slowly around the face on the vase.

'You're not stunted, Jordi.' She hesitated, then

continued, straining to bring back words she had heard and which touched her memory. '*Tu ets molt gran, amic meu.*' My friend, you are truly big.

Jordi laughed, a shout of pure delight. 'A Catalan after all!' he crowed. The smile in his eyes caught her own, he reached out to her, and she placed her hand in his.

As his fingers closed around hers, the front door of the shop opened and seconds later they heard the ringing of the bell and an exchange of voices.

'*Merde!*' cursed Jordi, and went through to the shop. Madeleine stood breathless, holding the edge of the work table with one hand. She was still there when Jordi returned a few moments later.

'These people want to browse,' he told her. 'We can leave them for a moment. And then when they've finished I'm going to shut up shop and have a holiday. I want to show you Céret. But I'll tell you what you should do meantime – go to the Musée d'Art Moderne, and as soon as I get through here I'll come and join you there. If you haven't seen it you should do, and it's often better seen and felt on your own.'

Madeleine smiled, and found some words. 'I'll see if I can learn to live by feel, then, and meanwhile you'd better make a sale here if you're going to take the rest of the day off!'

She touched her cheek to his in what could have been a sisterly gesture, and left the shop by the back door.

The museum was busy with tourists, couples from all over France strolling through its simple white rooms. Madeleine slipped through them, just looking, not stopping yet to read about any of the artists. Learn to live by feel – well, so she would. She recognised Picasso and Matisse, but others she didn't know, and a lot of what she saw she didn't understand. But she knew she was seeing a special grouping of paintings, and knew that many of the artists had lived here at the same time in Céret, calling each other together in artistic alliance. A portrait by the Catalan artist Manolo caught her eye, and a rich avenue of trees by a Hungarian painter, but she finally came to a halt in front of a painting so crude that it almost seemed to have been painted by a child. A village street, figures with guns, and a dead body spreadeagled in the centre – barbarous because it was intimate, not the battlefields of large-scale warfare, but the close-up massacre of life. She didn't like the painting, or even admire it, but it held her attention, and she couldn't move on. She sat on a bench some paces away while couples passed by in front of her, and Jordi found her there, a knot of creases on her forehead, her hands clasped almost impatiently on her lap.

He sat beside her. 'Chagall,' he said, looking to see what had caught her imagination. 'A Russian painter. He was Jewish, and had to flee France to escape the Germans during the war. He loved his village life, though it has been rather badly shaken up in this picture, don't you think?'

'It isn't even realistic,' Madeleine responded.

'No. But is that the point? Picasso once said that when Matisse died, Chagall would be the only painter left who understood what colour was. Does it disturb you?'

'I don't know. It made me stop. I thought it could have been my father.'

286

'Shot in his village? I suppose he was, in a way, but that's not for now, Madeleine. Come with me, and I'll show you Picasso's ceramics.'

There was a whole series of painted ceramic ware by Picasso, all depicting bullfights. Was this what Jordi had followed, in choosing to paint bulls so often on his pottery? But Picasso's bulls were analytical compared with Jordi's hot, animalistic images.

'You paint bulls too,' she murmured.

'They're part of life here,' was his simple reply. 'And they have balls.'

His crudity shocked her for a moment, then she checked herself. What Jordi expressed was always visual, she thought, and always powerful. What would he say about her new-found brother, she wondered, and suddenly wanted to tell him.

People were leaving the museum, heading for lunch, and Jordi and Madeleine made their way with them, out into the sunshine, where the fresh breeze had reached even inside the narrow streets of Céret. They ate at a little table on a pavement in a central square, gracious with old stone buildings, grouped around an ancient fountain with nine jets of water. Jordi told her how the lion's head on the fountain had been set facing Spain, but that when France had annexed this part of Catalonia they had turned the head round to face north.

'It got turned back again later on the sly,' he told her. 'This is a town with strong Catalan emotions!' As they ate she told him what had happened since he left her in Vermeilla. His brow contracted more and more as she told

287

him, and instead of being reassured she felt increasingly anxious as she watched his reaction.

'So let me get this straight,' he said at last. 'No one has yet told this boy that his father is not his father, and that he has acquired two siblings overnight, and no one has told the father either, that the story is blown. And you haven't even seen the mother since, so you don't know how she is reacting mentally.'

'My Uncle Bernard has seen her. He didn't get much of an impression, though – I think he wrote her off as simply stupid.'

'Stupid or not stupid, she must be going through all kinds of hell right now wondering what to do, and how to manage what still has to come, and in particular how to manage the boy's anger when the time comes.'

'He adores his mother,' Madeleine said inconsequentially.

'But will he adore her when he finds out how he was conceived? And what about the father? From what I can see, there's going to be a lot more trouble before this is all over. You've opened up Pandora's box, Madeleine, and we don't know what may come out.'

The concern which edged his voice struck harsh on Madeleine's jangled nerves. 'Philippe told me I was a catalyst, but he believed it was overall a good thing.'

'He certainly thinks positive, your Philippe! My own experience is just a bit different, that's all. I don't mean to alarm you, Madeleine, just take care, that's all. I'd like to say I cared what happens to all the rest of them, but most of them can go rot in hell for all I care, especially that traitor Perrens. But as for you, Madalena, they've done

288

enough to my little growing tree, and if they touch one single hair on your head . . .'

His voice was fierce, and he broke off, shaking his head. Madeleine was moved, but laughed as well.

'Trees don't have hairs, señor, and I truly think you're overstating the danger. I think we're in for a lot more unpleasantness, for sure, but I don't think anyone will get hurt. Monsieur Perrens isn't capable, and Martin is just a boy.

'No,' she continued, with a sigh, 'I think the violence was all played out up there in the camp, in 1944. Has it occurred to you, Jordi, that if my father hadn't slept with another man's wife, and spoken so loosely about the camp, then the Germans would never have found it, and your father would have survived the war unharmed. And then your life could have been so different too.'

'Oh, I can see that, all right, but you know, everyone in the war made human mistakes. My father was attacked for taking me up to the camp that time, remember? But others did the same, or almost the same, especially in 1944, when ordinary people could smell their freedom and were right behind the resistance. The Maquis began using ordinary people to help them in lots of ways. There was always risk, and always criticism, but all your father did was to talk about the clearing in general terms. He wasn't to know Perrens could identify it.'

'He didn't have to sleep with his wife, though.'

'No, he didn't have to sleep with his wife, but my point is that it was a human error, not anything malicious. And he paid for it with his own life. Perrens, on the other hand,

289

was an informer, a wilful traitor. If he'd wanted to get back at your father there were many ways to do so, but he chose the most underhand, despicable way possible.'

He looked across at Madeleine with his usual directness. 'Will you come walk with me, Madeleine? Can I show you my town, and maybe take you to stand on the Devil's Bridge?'

Madeleine felt a bubble of pleasure burst inside her. He was offering her the chance to forget the past and the future for a while, and to share with him this moment in the present. She held her breath for a second then found the courage to speak as directly as he.

'I would love to walk with you, Jordi,' she said, an uncontainable smile warming her cheeks. 'I seem to be discovering for once in my life how strong it makes you feel to have a friend, so take me to see this devil of yours.'

CHAPTER NINETEEN

It was a very special afternoon. Jordi led her through the streets of Céret, taking her hand at one point to lead her through a small gap, and then forgetting to let go again. They roamed past statues by Manolo, one image of Catalan womanhood, and another outside the bullfighting arena which depicted a slim, elegant toreador and supposedly paid homage to all the bullfighters of the world. Madeleine had a problem with this, and was glad to leave the arena behind them, but Jordi laughed at her, and told her she wouldn't be a true Catalan until she had witnessed her first bullfight.

'I'll just have to stay French, then,' she retorted, laughing as Jordi bowed ceremoniously to the toreador as if about to take to the ring. And then they moved on, further out of the town, towards the Devil's Bridge and the open countryside. They passed fields of cherry trees, some already picked clean, others laden with fruit, and Jordi told her about the forthcoming Cherry Festival, for which Céret was famous.

'You'll see the Sardane danced again,' he said, 'which hasn't been danced since Franco came to power. It's still banned in Spain, you know, because the authorities think it is used to send secret signals between rebels.'

It was hard to worry about the troubles of the Catalans this afternoon, when Jordi spoke of her joining him for the festival in just a couple of weeks' time, and took for granted that she would be with him. And he too, this afternoon, had forgotten the burdens which so often seemed to saddle his life, and was alive with energy.

The Devil's Bridge was a fantastic medieval arch spanning the River Tech, joining the town to the fields beyond. There was a local legend about a pact with the devil, and a missing stone the devil had removed from the bridge, but the really magical thing about this bridge, Madeleine thought, was the view. To the south was Céret itself, and beyond it was Spain, and the path through the mountains that Madeleine had followed herself as a tiny refugee. To the east was the coast, too distant to see, with the plains of Roussillon in between, and to the west was the Vallespir, the wooded valley which climbed into the Pyrenees, the length of the Tech river. Céret, Jordi told her, was the capital of the Vallespir, and above it were the middle and high Vallespir, lush hunting ground and home to the Maquis in wartime.

They stood together on the high arched bridge, contemplating the river, which stretched away on both sides, shallow after a long spell without rain, bumping serenely over the rocks which jumbled the river bed, and untouched by the wind which whistled around the top of the pointed arch. It was a warm wind, not the cold mountain wind, the Tramontane, but it freshened the air nevertheless after days of unseasonal hot days. Perhaps imagining a chill in the air, Jordi stood behind Madeleine and placed his hands on her bare shoulders.

'Look,' he said, pointing her towards the east, in the direction of the sea. 'Look how dark the sky is over there – the rain has already reached the coast. It'll be raining in Vermeilla right now. It'll be here, too, before tonight.'

Madeleine looked up at the sky above them, still the same azure blue, just peppered with clouds. It was hard to imagine rain, after this week of unbroken sunshine in the deep latitudes of the south.

Turning her head she caught Jordi looking at her, and blushed. 'Then it's lucky I came inland to see you, isn't it,' she stammered, and stopped as his head came down and he kissed her.

For a moment Madeleine didn't move. *I've met this man three times*, she thought, then, *What would Grandmother say?* And then she turned to face him fully, and hooked her arms around his neck as she brought his lips to hers again.

She couldn't remember much later of what they said that afternoon, or where they went. They roamed through the cherry trees, and Jordi plucked fruit to feed to her, his fingers staining red and ruining her clothes as he held her again and again. He seemed to shed a weight that day, and was like a boy, teasing her, climbing onto high branches to look for better fruit, laughing at her as they forded the river, jumping from islet to islet, drenching their clothes in water. Her sandals would be beyond repair, Madeleine thought, but her bare legs dried in minutes in the sunshine.

All her past life, all their joint past struggles, were forgotten that afternoon. Madeleine felt as though she had grown wings, and every challenge Jordi laid down for her she leapt to meet, her hand in his, and her windblown face turning constantly towards his.

By the time they regained the stone-lined streets of Céret the sky had covered over, and it was growing dark. A spot of rain hit Madeleine as they turned into Jordi's little alleyway, and he looked up with some concern.

'We're in for a downpour, and I have to take you back on the motorbike. You'll be soaked.'

'So will you, *mon ami*, and you have to do the journey twice!'

'It would be madness to do the journey right now. We'd be driving straight into the storm. My suggestion would be that you stay here for a while, and we can have dinner before you go back, and wait for a break in the rain. What do you think? Do we drown you now or try not to drown you later?'

'Later!' Madeleine voted without hesitation, returning his long, slow smile. 'But I'll have to call the hotel, so that Uncle Bernard doesn't worry.'

They went to a nearby café, and while Jordi negotiated for use of the phone the owner brought Madeleine a glass of sweet wine similar to the Banyuls of the coast. She waited for Jordi, and they drank together, clinking glasses.

'*Salut i pau*,' he toasted her in Catalan. Health and peace.

'We especially need the peace!' she joked, and went off to make her call.

At the Hotel Bon Repos the phone was answered almost immediately, and Mme Curelée's voice came through very indistinct across the crackly line. You could almost hear the rain on the phone lines, thought Madeleine. She asked for Bernard, and had to shout to make herself heard.

'He isn't here, Mademoiselle,' came the reply. 'Philippe Lemont came looking for him a couple of hours ago, saying the young boy Perrens had gone missing, and they both went off together.'

'Missing? Martin? Where has he gone?'

'Nobody knew, it seemed, but why they are worrying when a young lad takes some time for mischief is a mystery to me.'

Madeleine felt a sharp stab of worry. 'What is the weather like there, Mme Curelée? Is it still raining?'

'Raining! We have such a storm as I haven't seen for years. The quayside is ankle-deep in water, Mademoiselle, and you need to take care coming to the hotel. We have sandbags in front of the door to stop the water coming in.'

Madeleine could hear the harassed tone in Mme Curelée's voice even through the distorted phone line. She said goodbye and hung up, and returned to the table, where Jordi had already caught the worry on her face.

'Martin has disappeared,' she told him. 'Something has happened. You were right, Jordi.'

'What information could you get?' He didn't waste time with exclamations or surprise.

'Nothing more. Mme Curelée obviously thinks there is nothing to worry about, and that he must be off on some boy's adventure, but she doesn't know the background, and she's more worried about the rain and the floods.'

'You want to get back.' It was a statement, not a question.

Fifteen minutes later they were on the road, Jordi's only waterproof jacket in thick leather wrapped firmly around Madeleine, despite her protestations. It took well over an hour to make the journey, often through rain which made the road almost impassable and cut visibility down to a yard or two in front of them. Madeleine hung on to Jordi, and tried not to think of what might have happened in Vermeilla. Rain poured down her face and plastered her hair to her head under her scarf, her skirts created a puddle of water which froze the thighs, and her bare calves almost lost feeling in the stormy winds.

Eventually they rode into the outskirts of Vermeilla, and the street lights made their progress easier. Jordi shouted to ask where they were going, and Madeleine directed him to the Café de Catalogne. Jordi nodded and said nothing, and suddenly Madeleine was reminded of Jordi's vow never to come to Vermeilla. And here she was directing him to the home of the very people who had ruined his father's life.

But only at the café could they learn what had happened, and as they drew up outside Jordi didn't hesitate to follow Madeleine towards the café door. As she looked into his face, though, she saw none of the carefree Jordi of this afternoon.

296

He had the burdened look which she had earlier seen disappear, but perhaps, she hoped, not quite the hard-edged look of earlier in the week. As she scanned his face he gave her a quick smile, and squeezed her hand.

'We'd better find out what's been happening,' he said briefly, and she led the way inside.

The warmth of the café hit them as they stepped through the door. It was deserted, except for the barman, and, at a table far to the rear, Bernard and Philippe, deep in discussion with a local policeman. As Madeleine and Jordi approached, the policeman picked up what looked like a map from the table and headed past them towards the door, pulling his rain cape over his head as he did so.

He gave them a curious look as he passed them, and Madeleine realised they must make a strange sight, two completely drenched people dripping water from every part of their bodies and clothing. If her face looked like Jordi's, then they were both white and strained from cold and the stress of the journey. Philippe and Bernard were looking at them both with astonishment.

'*Bonsoir, mes oncles*,' Madeleine rushed into speech. 'Uncle Bernard, this is Jordi, who brought me back on his motorbike. We got,' she said, gesturing helplessly to their clothes, 'a bit wet. But when I called the hotel Mme Curelée told me Martin had gone missing, so I thought I'd better get right back.'

The two men were still gazing at them blankly, but finally Philippe pulled himself together and got up to greet Jordi, and called to the barman to bring coffee and brandy, and towels. They rubbed the worst of the wet from their hair and clothes, dried their faces, and wrapped the towels around themselves to ease the shivers which set in as soon as they began to react to the warmth of the café.

'You need to get changed into dry gear,' declared Bernard. 'But you probably want to know what's happened here before you go.' Madeleine nodded, and sat down to drink her coffee. Jordi sat in a chair in the background and watched, nursing his hot coffee cup in his hands.

'Where's Colette?' asked Philippe, and Bernard gestured towards the stairs.

'Upstairs. She's preparing food for the search party. She won't come down just now.'

Philippe nodded. Madeleine was shocked by his appearance. His bony, boyish face was tightly drawn and he seemed suddenly older, furrowed, and his very movements were hesitant as he began to speak, his hands held open almost in supplication.

'Colette told Martin today,' he explained. 'I've been urging her to tell him the truth, because it seemed to me that above all we needed to avoid him learning it by chance, from some dropped word or by overhearing a conversation. Think how awful that would have been!

'But I think now I was wrong. It should have waited until Colette was calmer, and had got over this week a bit and made her peace with Daniel. Too much haste, that's always been my weakness, and not enough thought.'

His voice raised briefly in self-anger, and then he looked towards the stairs and checked himself. Madeleine kept her voice gentle as she questioned.

'So what happened?'

'Well, she told him. She tells me it was incredibly difficult, and he wanted to know all about his real father, and how he had died, and why he had died, and Colette said she just couldn't tell him the whole truth about Jean-Pierre, and was controlling how much information she gave out. But she was crying, and Martin's voice was raised, and they made too much noise, and Jean-Pierre came through to the sitting room. He doesn't move about much on his own, you know, so nobody ever expects him to appear. But today he did, just at the wrong moment, and he started yelling at Martin, saying he was nothing but a common bastard, and his mother was a whore, and that his "father" had just got what was coming to him, and Martin had been lucky to have house room all these years, and more to that effect. Colette couldn't tell me everything – she was shaking like a leaf when I spoke to her. Anyway, Martin screamed back, saying he hated him, and had always hated him, and called him despicable, and a murderer, and when Colette appealed to him he told her he hated her too, and left, ran out of the room and away, and no one has seen him since.'

'How long ago did it happen?'

'About three o'clock. He came home early from school because a teacher was ill, and it was a quiet moment here in the café, which is why Colette decided to talk to him. What time is it now? Eight o'clock? So five hours ago.'

'But wouldn't he have gone to a friend's house?'

Philippe shook his head in desperation. 'We've checked everywhere. Daniel thought he might have gone up to the vineyard, to his shed, but he's not there or in

299

any of the other sheds up there. And we checked the school. But of course he could have taken the bus to almost anywhere. It's the bad weather which is worrying people, including Henri, the policeman you saw just now. Now that it's dark and some hours have gone by, a good few people in the village have become involved. They just know that a teenager had an argument with his parents, but they're worried nonetheless, and since the fishermen won't be out this evening we have a good-sized squad looking for him.'

Bernard nodded, and added, 'Philippe and I have been given the unofficial role of coordinators, so we get to stay in the dry. What's worrying us most is that it had barely begun to rain when he ran off, and he only had on his school shorts and shirt. So we're really hoping he's taken shelter somewhere.'

'Yes.' The voice was Jordi's, coming from the shadows, and Bernard looked at him in surprise, as though he'd forgotten he was there.

'Yes,' said Jordi. 'You only have to look at the state of Madeleine and me after an hour or so on the motorbike. If he hasn't found shelter he'll be in real danger. Poor kid, we need to find him quickly. So tell us, where are your team looking, and where is left to cover?'

Philippe looked at him in amazement. 'There's no need for you to go looking, Jordi! No point either – you don't even know what Martin looks like.'

'No, I don't, but Madeleine does.'

'You can't mean to take a girl out on a search like this? In this weather?'

'Madeleine isn't a girl, she's a woman. You'll come with me, won't you, *ma belle*?'

Madeleine nodded vehemently. 'We just need to change clothes first, that's all, and we need some oilskins. And you need to tell us where to look. But my worry is that he doesn't want to be found. If he's hiding somewhere, how on earth is anyone going to find him unless he comes out voluntarily?'

'That would be all right, Madeleine.' Jordi was incisive. 'It actually doesn't matter if everyone is out there looking for nothing, provided the boy is safe somewhere. That's the best case scenario for all of us.'

There was a silence. Madeleine stood up abruptly. 'Come on, then, let's get looking. You'll tell us where to go, Uncle Philippe?'

Philippe nodded. 'Get changed, and then I suggest you cover the whole beach area again as far as the coast path. It's been done, but some time ago, and now the search has moved away up into the hills and further along the coast path. I've been worried that Martin might be hiding in the rocks almost anywhere behind the beach further along, and in the dark no one would find him if he kept well hidden. But now the teams have moved on, there's just a chance he may not be hiding so intently.'

Bernard looked at Jordi's muscular frame, and then down at his own rather rounded figure, and gestured towards Philippe.

'You'd be better borrowing clothes from Philippe than from me,' he said ruefully. 'Although to my mind Philippe is too tall, and his trousers will hang off you.'

'No,' Philippe shook his head. 'That's no good. What we need is Daniel's clothes. He's a bit taller and thinner, but his fishing overalls are loose and would do you very well, Jordi. Come with me and we'll ask Colette.'

He made towards the stairs, and then turned back to see that Jordi hadn't moved. He was still sitting in his chair against the wall, looking straight at Philippe without speaking, and his whole body said no. Philippe looked nonplussed, and Madeleine thought, they don't understand what this means for Jordi, even to have come into this café. He can't go upstairs, where Jean-Pierre lives. Doesn't Philippe see that? She moved from where she was standing towards Philippe, until she was positioned almost protectively in front of Jordi.

'Why don't you get the clothes, Uncle Philippe, and then Jordi can change at the hotel, in Uncle Bernard's room?'

Philippe nodded, still perplexed, but too preoccupied to question. He disappeared up the stairs and came back some minutes later with a clean set of overalls, and some fresh underwear which he passed surreptitiously to Jordi as though afraid Madeleine might see them. He also had two sets of oilskin jackets and trousers.

'These will fall off you, Madeleine, but you can always tie the trousers around the waist. It's better than getting wet again, like before.'

Bernard came with them to the hotel, leaving Philippe to man the café in case of news. Madeleine rubbed her body roughly with a dry towel, and threw new clothes on, covering herself afterwards with the smelly oilskins, and then hurried downstairs again to find Bernard and

Jordi already waiting for her in the hallway.

'Very elegant, my dear,' murmured Bernard with a smile. Madeleine grinned back.

'Catalan fashions, my uncle,' she answered.

Jordi laughed. 'Right, let's go.' They went out into the unabated storm, leaving Bernard to make a hurried dash back to the café.

The night closed around them, and the rain drove into their eyes from the dark, angry waters of the harbour.

'We go all the way along to the left to start,' Madeleine shouted to make herself heard, and they began a cold, fruitless search, along the village seafront, from the end of the sea wall, with nothing but open sea beyond, where huge breakers crashed over the wall and poured over their oilskins, and Jordi held Madeleine to stop her slipping. There was nowhere to hide here, with nothing but the sea wall and the stone-flagged quayside all around, and the quayside stretching before them in front of the village streets seemed equally fruitless, but as the beach opened up on their left, Jordi roamed it back and forth, almost to the seafront and back, and again, and again, covering the bare sand, although nothing could possibly be there, surely. Then the fishing boats loomed ahead, drawn up as high as possible on the beach, away from the waves, and tied firmly to avoid any danger of them being swept away. They searched the boats, the nets, the boxes of equipment. Their night sight had improved, but there was no sign of a living form.

They moved on, holding hands for spurious warmth, and headed along the beach away from the village, to where the tourists would swim, and where Madeleine had lain only two days before, eating lunch in the sunshine at the very end, by the rocks and the tiny stream. There were rocks behind them all along the beach, and here was where Philippe had thought Martin might hide. It seemed unlikely to Madeleine. Surely a boy wanting to run from hurt would head much further from home, but the other searchers would be covering other areas, and Philippe wanted them here. They could only make a small contribution, especially as neither of them knew the area.

So they searched. The gaps between the rocks were large enough for a young boy to push through, and there were obviously holes behind where he could huddle. They pushed into each hole as far as they could, Madeleine first, as the slimmer of the two, flashing her torch into the darkest corners, with Jordi supporting her from behind. They called non-stop for Martin as well, but there was nothing there, nothing even this black night could hide.

They turned their attention to the area above the rocks, Jordi clambering up, and then reaching down to help Madeleine to follow him. Up here was a broad ledge with scrubby bushes, and behind that a sheer rock face that no one could have climbed. They raked through the bushes, making their way cautiously along the rocks in the lashing rain towards the end of the beach. Ahead the ledge opened up, and they came to the path which led up from the beach to join the coastal path to Collioure.

'Not that way,' Madeleine said, pointing up to the right. 'That's the path, and the search party are already along there. We have to stick to the beach.'

Jordi nodded, and wiped drops of rain off her frozen nose.

'You all right?' His voice was impossibly tender in the circumstances, and Madeleine leant upwards for a kiss.

'Doing just fine,' she reassured him. 'Let's keep going.'

He took her hand again, and they headed down the path back to the beach. There were a few more rocks behind the beach which were quickly covered, and then they were at the end. Ahead was the little outlet of water, barely a stream two days ago, surrounded by rocks, where Madeleine had washed her face and hands. Tonight it was a raging torrent of white water, bursting through and over the rocks towards the sea. It was impossible to get closer than several yards away.

There certainly won't be anything here, Madeleine thought, but Jordi had taken a step further up the beach, away from the sea, to where there was a bigger lump of rock which stood proud of the cascading water. He leapt for a point halfway up the rock where a piece jutting out gave him a foothold. Madeleine watched and held her breath as he climbed up, and stood on the top of the rock, with the wind almost taking his feet away, and the rock slippery beneath him. He scanned the jumble of rocks beyond the torrent, and pulled the torch from his pocket to flash it across the water.

He scrambled back down the rock, and exclaimed urgently.

'There's something there. Something white, on the rocks, way past the water, but I have no idea how you would get to it.'

'Martin?'

'I don't know, Madeleine, but it could be. It isn't moving.'

Madeleine felt her blood run cold.

'What can we do?' she said.

'We need help. There must be some way to get to those rocks, but we may need ropes, and we definitely need someone who knows the terrain.'

'Let's go,' Madeleine said. And then, 'Do you think he's alive, Jordi?'

'I don't know. I just don't know. But he could be, and as long as that's the case, we can hope.'

Hope. Take back the news and hope. *Wanderer, your footsteps are the road*. Let him be alive, prayed Madeleine, and we'll make a way forward. I promise you, Martin, we'll make a way forward.

She reached for Jordi, and together they ran back along the beach towards the village.

CHAPTER TWENTY

They could see Philippe and Bernard at the door of the café when they turned into the street. They were talking to three figures in heavy waterproofs, although the rain seemed finally to be easing off. Jordi had set a pace which Madeleine could barely keep up with, and her breath was coming in gasps by the time they reached the group. Everyone's eyes were on them, and before they had stopped running Jordi had started to speak.

The men listened intently as he told his story, and then Philippe demanded, 'Just a shape, you say, on the rocks?'

'Yes, a white shape. I couldn't say for sure it was a boy, but it's the right size. It was too far away for the torch to pick anything out, so all I could see was the blob of something pale against the black rock.'

The oldest of the men spoke up. Madeleine recognised him as Serge, the man who had first spoken to her about her father, on her first day in the village. Was it only six days ago? Since then Madeleine had learnt that Serge was the owner of the most successful fishing boat in the village, and a spokesman for the whole fleet.

'We were on the path earlier on, in daylight,' he said. 'You can see down to those rocks when you get to the top of the cliff, and we didn't see anything.'

'But surely that's good news?' urged one of his companions. 'If that shape was just some netting or something, it would have been there all day. Only a human could have come there after we passed.'

'Can you get onto the rocks without crossing the water?' Jordi asked.

It seemed you could, by a track down from the path. The rocks were used by villagers as a spot to catch fish from, and only the children ever went across the stream, Philippe told them. Their more sensible elders had created a way down through the bushes from the top path.

'Is it somewhere Martin would have headed for?' Madeleine asked, recovering her breath.

'Possibly. He's not as keen on fishing as some of the boys, but he dabbles, and it's certainly somewhere he might go today if he wanted to be quiet.'

'Or wanted things a bit wild!' Serge added with some scepticism. 'By the time we came down from the path the light was fading, and the sea was already pretty wild, and it had been raining for some time. He wouldn't have got across the stream, that's for sure.'

The group had started moving by this time, back in the direction of the beach. Philippe and Bernard caught up with them, having fetched coats and hats, and they headed at a half walk, half run for the track which ran above the beach. At the end they met the path, where Madeleine and Jordi had been earlier, but instead of turning left towards the beach, this time they turned up the hill to their right. Almost immediately they saw moving lights and heard voices coming towards them, and within a few moments four figures emerged from the night ahead. It was the other group which Philippe had spoken about, which had been searching the path one last time. Daniel was among them, and Eric, Madeleine saw. They looked wet and grim, but at the sight of Philippe and the others Daniel's tight face brightened. He surged forward.

'What are you doing here? Do you have any news?' His voice drilled the air, caught between hope and misgiving.

'This young man thinks he saw something on the rocks, past the stream,' Serge muttered.

Daniel looked an enquiry towards Jordi. 'On the rocks? What did you see?'

'Just a shape, that's all. Something pale which didn't move. But it was the right size.'

Anxiety made Daniel belligerent. 'How on earth did you see anything of the sort? Who are you, anyway?'

Madeleine spoke up. 'He's with me, Daniel. We were doing our own search along the beach. Philippe asked us to. And of course there was no way to cross the stream, so Jordi climbed up on to the rocks this side of it just to have a look. We think what he saw needs to be investigated, that's all.'

'Investigated?' Daniel gave Jordi a puzzled look, then

turned to Serge. 'Are you going down the track? Do you have enough torches? It'll be hellishly slippery – we'll need ropes.'

The 'we' was almost a challenge, but Serge didn't blink. He nodded, and said, 'Yes, we'll need ropes, and maybe five or six men, to be sure we can bring him out, if we find him.'

Eric stepped forward. 'Me, then, as well as Daniel. I must have lost more fish off those rocks than anyone in the village!'

He put his arm around Daniel, who responded with a tense smile. The whole group moved back along the path, which climbed steeply up towards the cliffs between Vermeilla and Collioure. It was inky black, and Madeleine held onto Jordi and followed his torch. Within less than a hundred yards they stopped by a narrow gap in the undergrowth to the left. Serge pulled a haversack from his back and pulled out three thick blankets, and, underneath them, some lengths of rope. The blankets went back into the bag, and then six of the men set off down the path, roped together with plenty of slack between them.

The rest of the party waited. Philippe moved across to stand by Madeleine and Jordi, Bernard by his side.

'They've got a bit of a climb to get down there,' he explained, 'and it's just a dirt track, so it will be slippery, as Daniel said. You've seen how quickly we climbed, coming up the path to here. But the track is the only way through the undergrowth. Further up the cliff path you get wonderful views over the sea, but just at this bit there's some pretty dense vegetation, and a tangle of brambles which is impassable. You get glimpses through sometimes, and you can scramble down to the rocks in places by daytime, but mostly, of course, people use this little track down, which is fine when it's dry, or they cross the stream. It's normally just a trickle.'

'I know. I had lunch on the beach just by the stream on Wednesday.'

'Well, if we move back along the path, we'll be getting closer and closer to the level of the rocks, and we can keep in contact with the men by shouting to them. Thank God the rain has stopped, and that wind has calmed down a bit. We may even make our voices heard.'

It seemed like hours before they could actually hear the men on the rocks below, exchanging advice – 'Watch this bit, it's treacherous; step here; give me your hand' – and then, at last – 'There it is! There's definitely something there!'

The group on the path followed as closely as they could, and as they neared the beach they were only a few yards above the rocks themselves. They could hold a conversation with the men below.

It was Daniel who called out, 'It's definitely him. Look, he's wearing his shorts and school shirt. He must be frozen, poor mite.'

Serge reached him first, and went silent while those behind him hurled questions. Madeleine could imagine him hunched over the body, reaching for the boy's pulse, feeling his cold wrist, checking for warm breath on frozen cheeks.

'He's alive!' came the cry at last. 'But he's very cold,

and his pulse is weak.' Another pause and then, 'I can't feel any broken bones. We'll wrap him as warm as we can and bring him back up the path. It's going to take a while, though. We want to keep his body as immobile as possible. Somebody go and call an ambulance. Tell them we need a stretcher at the top of the track.'

The group on the path sprang to life, and two men set off at a run for the village. The rest had nothing to do but wait, and Jordi wrapped warm arms around Madeleine from behind, and spoke into her ear.

'He'll be all right, Madeleine. He's young and fit, and he'll recover fast. He must have slipped and knocked himself out, but he hasn't been there all afternoon, we know that.'

Madeleine brought her hands up to cover his, and caught Bernard watching them. He exchanged a glance with Philippe, and Madeleine shot them both a smile of pure elation. Her world had been changed today, and something in her had been completed. Her new brother was going to live, and there was no more anger or tension left, only relief and a deep happiness.

Half an hour or so later the men emerged from the track, moving gingerly, with two men going before, lighting the path for the others, holding tight to the ropes in case anyone should slip with the blanketed bundle. They laid Martin delicately down on the broader coastal path, and Philippe immediately knelt down beside him and felt his pulse, then chafed his hands.

'He's so cold,' he muttered. He took the scarf from around his neck and wrapped it around Martin's head, rubbing his hair gently through the soft wool. No one spoke, but Daniel knelt beside Philippe and held his brother's hands between his own. The unconscious boy's face seemed desperately pale, even in the dark night, and when torchlight occasionally touched him it gave him shadows and furrows far beyond his years, and yet he looked almost absurdly young.

It seemed an age before the ambulance men arrived, men who were obviously well known to everyone except Madeleine and Jordi. They wrapped Martin in new, dry blankets and checked the body, nodding satisfaction as they moved from legs to torso to arms. Then they lifted him easily onto a stretcher, and fastened straps around him to hold him steady.

'He'll be fine,' one of them told Daniel, patting him on the shoulder. 'A night in hospital and tomorrow he'll be nagging us to leave. But he must have hit his head, and he may have some concussion, so we'll have to keep him under close observation. And we need to get some heat into him as soon as possible. He's suffering from slight hypothermia.'

'I'll come with you,' Philippe said. 'If he wakes he should have one of us with him.'

'And me!' Daniel's voice was urgent. 'I'm going with my brother.'

He looked across at Madeleine, who was still holding Jordi's hand. '*My* brother!' he said, defiantly, holding her gaze.

'You don't want to go and tell your mother?' Philippe asked.

'I'll do that,' Madeleine said hurriedly, with her eyes still on Daniel. 'I'll tell her everything's fine.' She had a vision of Colette in her apartment, all alone with her worry, alone as she had been most of her life, and had a sudden desperate desire to bring some comfort to her.

'Don't let her come to the hospital tonight,' the ambulance man instructed. 'The boy won't wake for a while, and he'll look a whole lot better tomorrow than he does now. Just tell her everything's going to be fine.'

'Tell her I'll come back for her first thing in the morning,' Philippe added, and the whole party moved off towards the village, the ambulance party turning off before the main village onto the nearest access road, where the ambulance was waiting. There was a lot of jocular backslapping among the remaining men, as they headed off to their warm homes, and then, as they reached the end of Colette's street, there were just Jordi, Madeleine and Bernard left.

'Do you want me to come with you?' Bernard asked.

'No thank you, Uncle. Not unless you want to. You're not even wearing oilskins, and you're shivering. I think you should go and change, and see if Mme Curelée still has any supper left for you.'

Bernard grinned. 'Well, I seem to be leaving you in safe hands! You'd better come back to the hotel afterwards, young man, and we'll get you a room.'

'No thanks, sir. I'll be fine. Philippe has offered me a bed, so I'll stay tonight at his place and get away at first light to open my gallery.'

'But you'll come back tomorrow to meet Robert?' Madeleine's voice was urgent.

Jordi smiled. 'Yes, *carinyo*, I'll come back tomorrow. This is a play I want to see the end of!'

'You seem to be one of the principal actors,' Bernard commented with his usual irony, and then he was gone, heading for warmth and a glass of Mme Curelée's best wine.

The café was in darkness as they approached, but the door wasn't locked, and they stepped inside into the warmth, and then looked at each other, wondering what to do next. Why was the café closed so early? It was perhaps not surprising that there were no customers, but the café had been open as a base for the search parties, and Philippe had said Colette was preparing soup for them. The silence and the darkness stood between them and the stairs at the rear of the long room, and there was no light filtering down the stairs, so presumably the door to the upstairs flat was closed.

Philippe and Bernard had left the café without telling Colette where they were going. Had she gone looking for them? Jordi shot Madeleine a look of enquiry, waiting for her lead.

'Colette must be upstairs,' she said, trying to sound confident. 'Do you want to come up with me?'

She made some tentative steps forward into the café, but Jordi's voiced stopped her.

'Wait,' he said urgently, and brushed past her. He moved towards the stairs, and then bent to the floor. For a moment Madeleine couldn't see why, but then she saw he was leaning over a human shape. Martin came to mind, but this wasn't Martin. She moved to join him, and looked down at the huddled wreck of Jean-Pierre Perrens, lying at the bottom of the staircase.

'What's happened?' she asked.

'He's dead. His neck's broken.' Jordi's reply was carefully neutral. 'Is this Perrens?'

'Yes, it's him.' Madeleine couldn't take her eyes off Jean-Pierre's body, the crippled legs tucked almost shamefully beneath him, and his head twisted at an odd angle from his neck. He looked small and strangely inhuman, as though this bag of broken bones could never have been a man, could never have taken vindictive revenge on his wife's lover, or later on his wife's child. It occurred to Madeleine that she had only met this man once, on the day of his outburst over lunch. He had figured large in her life for several days, and she had dreaded seeing him again. But there was nothing he could say or do to her now. Nothing he could say or do to anyone.

The silence around them was absolute. Not even any sound of rain now penetrated the café. Madeleine and Jordi stood together hypnotised, eyes fixed on Jean-Pierre Perrens.

'What do you think happened?' Madeleine asked.

'Well either he fell or he was pushed,' was Jordi's typically uncompromising reply. 'You said he didn't move around much on his own?'

'No, he was semi-crippled.' Madeleine's voice sounded loud to her in the quiet of the café. She was glad of the dark. It made the body seem less real, less substantial.

She couldn't have said what made her look up, but after a moment she lifted her eyes to glance up the narrow stairs, towards the apartment, and as she did so she caught sight of Colette, sitting on a step halfway up, half hidden in the gloom, looking down on them without moving.

'Colette?' Madeleine's voice came out in a whisper.

Colette didn't answer. She moved her eyes to meet Madeleine's, but nothing else moved, and her stillness was uncanny. Madeleine looked to Jordi, but he didn't move either. The silence hung in the air, and then Madeleine moved up the stairs. She sat on the step below Colette, and repeated her name.

'Colette? Are you all right?'

Colette fixed her eyes almost painfully on her, and eventually she spoke.

'He wasn't a man. He was my husband but he wasn't a man.'

Her voice was flat, expressionless, and she spoke as though it didn't matter, as though she was telling a casual story.

'Do you know how he became crippled? He got into a fight on the railways, on a train, with one of his workmates. They were fighting over some woman, some *salope* who worked in the office. She was the other man's girlfriend and Jean-Pierre had been sleeping with her. The other man threw him from the train. Nobody ever told the truth about it, and Jean-Pierre didn't want to press charges, but that's what happened. My husband, crippled because he had screwed another woman. And yet that same man, that *connard*, my husband, made me pay for the rest of my life for what I did with Luis. I lived with that, but what he did today I could not forgive.'

317

Madeleine let the meaning of the words sink in. Colette's eyes strayed away, back to the body lying grotesquely at the bottom of the stairs. Madeleine followed her gaze, struck by how steep these stairs were. Colette didn't even seem to notice Jordi, standing beside Jean-Pierre. He seemed a long way away to Madeleine, in a deep hole far beneath them.

How long had Colette been sitting there, she wondered? And what had she done?

'Colette, did you . . . ?' she began, and then stopped as Jordi moved, and she saw him shake his head with a quick frown. He spoke then, directly to Colette.

'He fell, Colette, didn't he? Was he trying to go after Martin? He shouldn't have tried to come down the stairs on his own, not with his legs being so weak. It must have been terrible for you to find him like this.'

Colette looked at Jordi for the first time, without curiosity. She didn't answer, and Jordi's voice became more insistent as he came up the stairs towards them.

'We'll go up to the apartment now,' he said, taking her hand and urging her upwards. 'Come, Colette, there is nothing you can do for your husband now. Let's go upstairs.'

Madeleine put her arm around Colette. 'We found Martin,' she told her. 'He's going to be all right.'

Colette looked up urgently. 'Martin? You found him?'

'The men brought him up from the rocks beyond the beach. We think he fell and banged his head. They've taken him off to hospital, but they say he'll be fine.'

'You're sure? He's all right?'

'Yes, yes, he's fine, and Philippe and Daniel have both gone with him to the hospital. So now, why don't you do as Jordi says, and come upstairs with us.'

Colette's hand closed around Madeleine's, and she looked pleadingly into her face. 'He said he hated me. He ran away . . . so unhappy.'

'He loves you, Colette.' Madeleine rose, easing Colette upwards, and between them she and Jordi coaxed her up to the apartment, and into a chair. Jordi disappeared downstairs again and reappeared a few minutes later with a glass of brandy from the bar.

'Drink this, Colette, and listen to me. I have to go and bring the police here. We have to report your husband's death. But you have to be clear on what happened. He fell down the stairs, remember, trying to go after Martin. He was worried. You didn't see him, remember? You didn't know what he was doing.'

'Going after Martin,' Colette repeated, as though the words were in a different language.

'Jean-Pierre fell down the stairs. You had just found him when Madeleine and I came in to tell you the good news.'

'Martin . . .'

'Yes.' Jordi's voice was infinitely patient. 'Martin is safe and well. But your husband didn't know that, and he wanted to look for him, didn't he?'

Colette took sips of the brandy and nodded.

'Don't say anything unless they ask you, Colette,' Jordi said, 'and it'll all be fine, you'll see.' He looked across at Madeleine, who was standing silent by the table. 'Stay with her, Madeleine, and don't let her go back out onto the stairs. I'll go for the police. Is there a local policeman? Where does he live?'

'Just in the next street, I think. A house with a green door. But Jordi—'

'Come with me to the door,' Jordi said, and took her by the hand, then, once out of sight of Colette, 'are you all right?'

Madeleine was trembling slightly. 'Yes, it's just the body, and Colette, and everything. Did she push him, Jordi?'

'Oh yes, I'd say so for sure, but she mustn't say a word. Don't let her admit it, Madeleine. She has to keep the truth to herself, even with us, otherwise she'll never see this through.'

Madeleine shivered. 'Yes, I see that. I'll tell her about Martin, and not talk about Jean-Pierre at all. But don't be long, will you?'

Jordi shook his head briefly and opened the door. 'As quick as I can, don't worry.'

The next hour passed like a strange dream from which Madeleine was sure they would all suddenly wake up. She repeated Jordi's story to Colette again and again until he arrived back with the policeman, but in truth the story was barely needed. The poor local policeman was the same man who had been in the café earlier, during the search for Martin. He was an old friend of Colette's, a local in the bar, and he was so shocked by the sight of Jean-Pierre's body that he did nothing but exclaim and commiserate with Colette, never dreaming that anything more than a terrible accident had occurred.

Colette just sat in dazed silence, drinking a cup of hot,

sweet tea which Madeleine had prepared, while people came and went. The policeman sent for the local doctor, who prescribed her a sedative and urged her to sleep.

'My son . . .' was all Colette said, to which the doctor replied breezily that he'd heard all about Martin being found safe and well, and that if she slept now she would be able to see him in the morning.

As the doctor prepared to leave, Colette clung to his arm for a moment. 'My husband . . .' she began, and Madeleine, standing by her side, held her breath for a painful moment.

'Don't think too much about poor Jean-Pierre, Colette,' the doctor said gently, with his hand on her shoulder. 'He didn't have much of a life recently, did he, and he wouldn't have known what was happening when he fell. It would all have been over in a second. He would just be happy to know your son is safe. You have two fine sons, my dear, and Jean-Pierre was very proud of them both. Now, let the young lady put you to bed, and I'll come to see you tomorrow.'

Jordi and Madeleine stayed in the apartment until Colette was in bed, and the sedative had finally closed her eyes. Everyone else had gone, and the silence had again descended on the café as they crept back down the stairs. The lights were on in the café and the body was no longer there. It was almost possible to believe that nothing had happened. They turned out the lights and pulled the door to behind them, and stood in the street, breathing the night air, wondering what time it was. Madeleine had no idea how long they had been in the apartment, but the night, now calm, seemed incredibly beautiful.

'Will you walk me home, Madalena, to show me where I am staying?' Jordi asked.

'Follow me,' she replied, taking his hand.

As they stood in the street outside the little building, Madeleine leant into Jordi's shoulder, and he drew her close.

'We got through that all right,' he said. 'Thank God. Whatever that poor woman did, she doesn't deserve to be punished any more.'

Madeleine reached up and ran her fingers through his long, unruly hair, and he caught her hand and brought it to his lips. He looked tired, and suddenly Madeleine felt a terrible weariness dragging at her whole body, and a bleakness she couldn't find the words to express.

'No one needs to punish her, Jordi. She'll punish herself. She's been blaming herself ever since the war, and now she has to live with this all on her own. She'll be even lonelier than ever.'

'Welcome to the world of secrets, *carinyo*.' The words were hard, but Jordi's tone was matter-of-fact. 'But she's managed fine, for all that, you know, raising two sons who love her, keeping them all going, keeping her respectability here in Vermeilla. And now she won't have that husband as a millstone round her neck, and they can all be free.'

He bent and kissed her. 'We're part of the secret, Madeleine, but the boys will never know, and Martin can even believe that Perrens was sorry and coming after him. It's not such a bad ending.'

'No.' She sighed. 'What a day! Do you know that this morning I didn't even know you! Not properly, that is.'

'Oh, we knew each other. We just hadn't realised it, that's all. When I met you, you had a bruised look which made me feel I wasn't alone, but you had something more too. You had hope. You came along to give me hope, *ma belle*, and to set me free too.'

'Me? Jordi, please, I am just nothing. I've always been just nothing, all my childhood, all my life. Here in Vermeilla I've caused nothing but trouble, coming in like a silly little innocent, full of questions and idealistic notions about my father. I can't see how I can have given anyone hope. You made a life, like Colette, a brave life from tough beginnings, but I've never done anything except live in my grandparents' house and concoct ridiculous dreams around my father.'

'Hush!' Jordi laid his fingers on her mouth, and kissed her forehead. 'You have a quality you don't even know yourself. Innocence is a gift, not a crime.' He shook his head as though trying to work something out. 'I've never been much of a person for words, Madeleine. I've been better with my hands. But somehow with you it's easy to speak, and because you're so open I can be too.'

Madeleine looked at him in wonder. Was she so open? It was a challenge merely to keep up with his own candour, or so it seemed to her. She still felt inadequate, but maybe this was something she had to live with. What she didn't feel was alone in her incompleteness. She met his eyes and the need in them shook her. She reached for him at the same time as he pulled her to him. He kissed her with the desperation of a man released from captivity, and she felt all the emotion of the day, all the emotion of too many years, translated into a physical hunger which pulled her tighter and tighter to him as his big artist's hands held her close.

Who am I? This isn't me, she thought, then, *Yes it is. I am all of this*, and a vision of Luis came before her, laughing and reaching out, not for the compensatory love which Luis had shown Colette, the soothing oblivions of war, but for the real passion which had lit up his life, she was sure now – the all-consuming embrace of Elise. I am my mother and my father, she thought, but more. I am more than any of them here, now, and maybe I can be free.

CHAPTER TWENTY-ONE

The sun showed its face timidly at first on Saturday morning in Vermeilla, but the wind had shifted and the Tramontane was rising, swirling in from the Vallespir and cleaning up the skies, pushing the clouds back out to sea. By lunchtime, as Bernard and Madeleine stood waiting for the arrival of the train from Toulouse which should be carrying Robert, the skies above were a perfect blue, and it would have been hard to believe in yesterday's wild, pummelling rain. The brisk wind cooled the temperatures, and reminded Madeleine of her first morning in Vermeilla, just seven days ago, when she had woken to the same Tramontane, stirring the harbour waters in front of her hotel window. The weather since had changed and developed as rapidly as had everything else in this momentous week. And now the weather had come full circle, repeating the work of nature and laughing at the mere events of man.

The evidence of yesterday's storm was still all around them. The storm drains which carried rainwater to the sea were still pouring grey torrents into the bay, there were slimy mud swirls on the quayside left by the drying floodwaters, a falling branch had damaged the mayor's car, and outside every building the women were cleaning steps and sweeping up debris. And drama had come to the Perrens family, with their son in hospital after slipping on the rainswept fishing rocks, and that poor soul of a father of his killed trying to come down the stairs in his distress.

The village was buzzing with the news, and had they had less to do in cleaning up there might have been still more talk. But the women still found time to cook and take food to the café for Colette, and to light candles in the church for the soul of the father and the health of the son.

Philippe had come to see Madeleine at breakfast time, just as she was giving Bernard a carefully edited, official account of the night's events. The hotel was empty save for them, and Philippe had closed the dining room door behind him when he came into the room. Martin, he told them, was doing fine. He had been seriously cold, and it would be some time before his embattled body recovered fully, but there was no lasting damage. As for his mind, it was harder to fathom. The boy remembered nothing about his fall. He had come to the rocks, as Madeleine had thought, looking for solitude and the wild spray of the sea, but he didn't know what time it had been, and no one knew how long he had been there, except that he hadn't been lying there when the searchers had followed the cliff path earlier in the afternoon. He hadn't said much, Philippe told them, and no one wanted to ply him with questions when his mind was foggy and concussed.

He didn't know either that his 'father' Jean-Pierre Perrens was dead. Philippe had learnt as soon as he came back to Vermeilla this morning. Daniel hadn't come with him, refusing to leave Martin, and so he didn't know either. But Philippe had seen Colette.

What she had told him Madeleine couldn't fathom. Philippe's questions seemed quite normal, but his eyes fixed her with what she thought was an overly searching gaze. But this, she realised, might just be her own guilty imagination playing tricks on her. In the late hours of last night she and Jordi had agreed that even Bernard and Philippe should not be told the truth, unless Colette chose to tell Philippe. It was her secret to tell, not theirs, and their whole concern was to set the idea of a tragic accident so firmly in everyone's mind that no one asked Colette any questions she might struggle to answer. They weren't out of the woods yet, they knew, since Colette's state of mind was so disturbed, but she had the habit of silence, and it was silence they needed now.

Philippe might well know already what had really happened on the café stairs last night, but in front of Bernard he wouldn't, she knew, say anything. Colette, he told her when she asked him, was still groggy from the sedative, and clearly in a state of shock, but her main concern was to see her son, and he would be taking her to the hospital later in the morning, when Martin was more likely to be awake.

327

'He looks good,' he told them, 'and it will do her good to see him.'

'And us? Should we see him?' Madeleine wanted to know.

'When his mind is stronger, then yes, it will be very important for you to see him. Robert arrives today, yes? Well the café won't be opening today, but you should bring him to visit me later at the apartment. I don't suppose he remembers where he started out his life. Come round and I'll have some Banyuls to offer you, and then tomorrow maybe we can go to see Martin.'

So here they were, waiting for the train, and it seemed incredible that it was only just over a week since she had waved Robert goodbye at the Gard du Nord. Neither of them could have imagined that he would be back in France so soon, and under such circumstances. But this was his story too, and she longed to see him.

As the train drew in she reminded herself that there was no guarantee he would be on it. This was the first possible train he could be on, assuming everything on his journey had gone completely smoothly. She scanned the small trickle of passengers as they left the train, and for a moment didn't see Robert, until Bernard tapped her arm and pointed with a smile. It was a couple, the young man on the platform helping a lady from the train, taking her case and then holding out a hand to help her down. The lady was Solange, and Madeleine thought simply, *Of course*. It seemed so inevitable.

'Well, Bernard,' Solange commented, as she kissed him and Madeleine, 'I hope you have been useful to this poor child.'

'It has all been most instructive,' was his rather cryptic reply, but he put his arm around Madeleine as he continued. 'This "poor child", as you call her, has been through more than you know, but she has proved herself a pretty strong force. And good,' he added dryly, 'at recruiting allies.'

Robert just stood looking around him, and said ultimately to Madeleine, 'I don't remember anything, Lena. Will you show me?'

They walked that afternoon all over Vermeilla, through the cobbled streets to watch the men playing boules, along the beach to where the usual trickling stream was still a swift flowing waterfall, then back to the harbour wall to gaze over the impossibly blue waters of the Mediterranean. Robert was quiet at times, and especially when Madeleine told him about the events of the previous night. She didn't hide the truth from him about Jean-Pierre Perrens. He was the only person she would tell, but he needed to know everything she knew. And she told him about Jordi, since he had so much to share in the week's stories, the lives stripped bare. It was Robert's life too. He didn't question her about Jordi, except once, when he simply asked, 'Will I like him, Lena?'

'I hope so, Bobo,' was her answer. 'It's important.'

At dusk they went to visit Philippe, all together, Bernard and Solange, Madeleine and Robert. For Solange it was a true case of memory lane. She held her breath as they climbed the stairs, and when Philippe opened the door to them she was unable to speak. Philippe didn't notice, because he was completely transfixed by Robert. He stood at gaze for what seemed like minutes, and then took

Robert's hand and held it, tears swimming in his eyes.

It was Bernard who broke the silence, introducing Solange and gently ushering Philippe backwards into the sitting room. They had bonded, these two men, Madeleine thought, in the last two days, and Bernard knew how to manage Philippe's emotional enthusiasm. As Philippe recovered his poise, and searched through memory to recognise Solange from the young woman she had been, Madeleine took control of serving small glasses of chilled Banyuls, pulling Robert into the kitchen with her, pointing out the little stove in the corner with a grin of triumph.

There was too much emotion in the room for it to be an easy little gathering at first, but they were saved by nostalgia, as Philippe and Solange revived the past with stories of Luis, Elise and the children, and their rich but frequently almost absurd lives in this little apartment and this little community. Robert bloomed as always, and Madeleine basked in his sunshine. She was more serious than he. She always would be, and she would never have his easy knack of winning over company at the first meeting. It was lucky, she thought, with a private little hug of pleasure, that there was one person for whom she had no rival, someone as serious as her, with a need she could answer just by being herself.

When they returned to the hotel that evening there was a telephone message from Jordi saying he would come to Vermeilla next morning.

'I told you she had made allies,' Bernard winked at Robert.

'We need to see Martin,' Robert reminded her.

'We will. But we can't go until the afternoon, remember, until visiting hours, and anyway, I want you to meet Colette first.'

Philippe had told them that Colette had spent half an hour alone with her two sons that day. He had left them alone and didn't know what they had talked about, but he felt Martin needed to see Madeleine and Robert now. He didn't say why, but they were all groping towards understanding, and for now perhaps it was best just to take those steps without questioning, and see where they led.

And first thing Sunday morning those steps led Jordi to Vermeilla again, where Madeleine had been waiting for him (was she foolish, she wondered?) since early light. She and Robert were standing outside the hotel watching the desultory Sunday morning activity on the quayside. It was too early for the Sunday strollers, and the fishing boats lay at rest at the top of the beach. The bay was reasonably calm, with white flecks where the Tramontane still touched the blue waters, and above them all the clouds had been swept clear away by the wind. They could see for many miles, to a horizon halfway to Corsica, sea meeting sky in an indigo haze.

As they stood silently contemplating, the peace was broken by the put-put of an ancient motor, and Jordi's rickety motorbike chugged around the corner and drew up next to them. Robert looked a question at Madeleine, and she nodded, blushing, before moving towards Jordi, and walking into his embrace. Mindful of Friday's heavy waterproofs and bedraggled hair, she had taken time to dress this morning, choosing an elegant, creamy dress with a low neckline and nipped waist to show off her long, slender figure. She had always known she was pretty, but no one had ever whispered to her before that she was beautiful, or run their fingers through her mane of hair, or kissed her neck until it tingled. The memory set her nerves clamouring, and she wanted to touch his newly shaven cheek. He had even ironed a new shirt, she noticed. Was it for her or her family? Either way, he looked wonderful.

Releasing her, he held a roughened hand out to Robert, who took it surprisingly shyly. He looked very young beside the lived-in Spaniard, but there was an innocence about both of them, thought Madeleine, that they were both quite unaware of.

They walked together along the front, and took coffee by the beach, and then Jordi's restless energy drove them along the cliff path, serene now, with just a vivid breeze, until below in the distance they could see Collioure, with the clock tower standing solo, guarded by the Chateau Royal, in a medley of golden stone.

'This must be the most beautiful place in the world,' said Robert.

Jordi shrugged in a very Hispanic gesture of magniloquence. 'It isn't Spain, and it isn't the Vallespir, but it is pretty enough. When the sun shines it shines too,' he conceded.

Madeleine laughed. 'And amateur artists paint toy pictures of it to sell to tourists, eh Jordi? The Vallespir is magnificent, but Matisse came here before he went to

Céret, and it was here he found his colours. You have to admit that!'

'I admit nothing!' Jordi said, with his arm around her. 'Robert, your sister has arrived here from what sounds like a rather tame England, and I'm afraid it has all rather gone to her head.'

Robert grinned, but came back to Jordi's earlier words. 'Tell me about the Vallespir, and the camps,' he asked.

They talked and walked until Madeleine remembered with a guilty start that they were due to meet Bernard and Solange for lunch.

'And then we have to visit Colette.'

'And Martin? Did you say you were going to see him this afternoon?' Jordi wanted to know. 'I'm glad, but I'll leave you when we get back. I don't think Colette even realised who I was on Friday night, and you don't want to bombard her with more people and memories than you need to.'

'You'll eat with us?' Madeleine urged.

'Yes, *ma belle*, I'll join you for lunch. You can introduce me to your aunt.'

Solange greeted Jordi with her usual calm pleasure, and quelled Bernard's mischievous tongue as she turned her elegant smile to the young man, and talked to him about his work. His prickles had raised slightly in front of Madeleine's sleek Parisian family, but Solange was so natural he had no resistance. Madeleine said little, but watched them all with a glimmering smile. They took time over lunch, but then Jordi insisted on leaving. Solange didn't want to come to the café with them either, but Madeleine begged her to.

'I can't see what my presence can add to the situation, Madeleine. The poor woman will have enough to do handling seeing Robert. It'll bring Luis right back before her eyes. The last she needs is a crowd.'

But Jordi came surprisingly to Madeleine's support.

'I think they need you, Solange,' he said. 'You knew Colette all those years ago, and you're the link to the past. I think your presence will reassure her.'

'She'll hardly remember me,' argued Solange, but her protests lacked conviction. She kissed Jordi on both cheeks, and ushered the others away, leaving Madeleine standing with Jordi by his motorbike.

'Come back soon, young man,' they heard her say, over her shoulder. as she entered the hotel.

'Your aunt is a lovely woman.'

'I know. Jordi?'

'Yes, *ma belle*?'

'If you insist on calling me *ma belle*, I shall have to call you *mon beau*!'

'With pleasure, *carinyo*.'

'Papa used to call me *carinyo*.'

'Because you were his darling.'

'And yours?'

'And mine.' Jordi smiled, and reached out to pull her towards him. 'What were you going to ask me?'

His arms were around Madeleine, stroking down her back, and she had to think for a moment to remember. What had she wanted to say to him?

She shook her head and said, 'Robert can only stay a couple of days, and he thinks I should go back with him.'

Jordi's hands froze, and he pulled her tighter.

'Why? You only came here a week ago. And you only left England a couple of weeks ago.'

'Three weeks,' she corrected him, and then, 'But you're right, and I know, and I don't want to go, but it would only be for a while. You see, there's something wrong about me being here right now. I'm a visitor, in transit, in a hotel, and I was a visitor too in Paris. I left my grandparents' house deliberately deceiving them.'

'They wouldn't have let you go otherwise!'

'I know, but it makes it feel as though I've just done something temporary. Jordi, I need to go, but I'll come back, if you want me to.'

Jordi's hands tightened around her, and he pulled her into a long kiss. Sunday passers-by looked at them, very shocked, and Madeleine wanted to laugh, but for pure happiness. She eased back from his embrace and continued. It was so important to make him understand.

'Robert tells me that he has seen my grandparents and they seem to have aged. They are lonely, I know, and I can't help that. I'm not going to sacrifice my life to stay in their world and marry their choice of "gentleman". But I want to tell them properly, and not run away like my mother did. I think it was her betrayal which made things even worse for them, and all those years they made her pay not just for marrying my father but for abandoning them so publicly. Even if they only care about appearances, I can help them by going back briefly and showing myself locally, making my plans public.'

'They'll never accept you marrying a Spanish potter.'

The words seemed to be ripped from Jordi's throat, and Madeleine looked startled into his face.

'Marry?'

'Yes, Madeleine, marry! Why, where did you think we were going?' There was a challenge in his voice.

Madeleine took a deep breath. He was direct, her man, but to throw a proposal of marriage at her after less than a week, in the street? Only Jordi could do that. She felt an involuntary urge to laugh, in sheer abandonment.

'Jordi, this is a mad road we're going down! You have opened something in life for me that I didn't think could possibly exist. But I've only just discovered that I am an individual and have rights. And whatever I want to do, my grandparents can't stop me. I have some valuable pearls which my mother left me, and I plan to sell them. It's an amazing feeling, to have so much freedom and choice.'

She saw the troubled look in his face, and reached for him.

'I will come back, I promise. I want to see where this crazy road of yours is going to lead us! Like I said, I just need to make things right in England. I don't even need to stay with my grandparents while I'm there. I have cousins in London who have offered me a bed any time, and it would complete things for me somehow to spend some time with them before I come back here. But I must go, and I need some freedom now, after a lifetime when I didn't know the word existed. Then I'll come back, and we can explore this crazy future you're offering me.'

She reached up to stroke his cheek, his hair, the nape of his neck, and pulled his head down towards hers.

A few moments later, Jordi said, 'The cherry festival. Could you come back in time for the cherry festival in three weeks' time? Come here first, Madeleine, and then we'll go to Paris together. I want to get married to you in Paris, in front of all of your fancy relatives, so they don't think we're running away. You can help me build the gallery – I've never been any good at promoting it, and dealing with people. You'll know how, and you know how to talk to people.'

'Perhaps, Jordi. More than perhaps! But just give me a little time, and in the meantime, let's meet for the cherry festival. You can teach me how to dance the Sardane.'

'You promise to be here?' His voice was anxious.

'I promise,' replied Madeleine, and kissed him again. She'd be back, she knew, and with Jordi, but she just needed to be sure she had fully discovered the real Madeleine first.

'Bring your brother to Céret before you leave, won't you? We'll give him a sight of the Vallespir – maybe we can compete with the coast in his eyes!'

'And if he wants to see where the camp was?'

'Then we'll take him there as well. Have courage for this afternoon, Madeleine. You'll be fine now with your new brother.' It was a statement of fact.

'Yes, *mon beau*, we'll all be all right now.'

It was wonderful to have Solange with them that afternoon with Colette. Colette recoiled, as they knew she would, on seeing Robert, and shrank into herself, though it seemed almost impossible for her to shrink any more. The Colette whom Madeleine had met a week ago had been tired but competent, in charge. Now she seemed merely bewildered in the face of events which were too much to handle. Madeleine had the impression that she was just letting life do what it would to her, an injured sea creature at the mercy of the ocean, unsure where she would wash ashore and what the world would look like when she did.

A sister had appeared from somewhere and was running this house of bereavement, planning a funeral, and fielding village visitors. She had the same resigned, patient face as Colette, but she was older, and lacked Colette's essential femininity. She moved between kitchen and sitting room in the traditional long black skirt and scarf of older Catalan women. Colette too was in full black mourning today, with the scarf over her hair, ageing her overnight. Tradition, Madeleine knew, stated she would wear black for seven years. Most women never got out of blacks, once they reached a certain age – there was always another death before the seven years was over.

Colette's sister withdrew discreetly into the kitchen when they arrived, reappearing briefly with coffee, but in fact there was nothing said that she could not have listened to. Colette was now embedded in her silence, and thanked Madeleine for her help on Friday as though there had been nothing but a tragic accident to discover.

'And you found my son, as well, I think,' she added. 'For that I truly thank you. He could not have lain there much longer, they tell me.'

To Robert she said very little, a mere greeting, but her eyes came back to him again and again, almost fearfully, as though a ghost had walked into her home in broad daylight.

It was Solange who made the occasion bearable, reminding Colette of pre-war days, and sitting close in female complicity to talk of their youth, and ancient characters and old village stories. As she asked after Monsieur Le Grand, or old Madame Pierrette who had always caused such havoc at the market, Colette warmed and flowered, and Madeleine was reminded of that day, several years ago, when Solange and *Tante* Louise had worked the same easy magic on her grandmother over lunch in London.

It was hard to come back to the present, but Madeleine had to ask. 'Colette, how is Martin?'

She watched to see whether Colette would withdraw again into her shell, but she looked around quite naturally as she replied, as if to any villager.

'Martin is doing well, thank you, Madeleine. He is no longer so woolly-headed, and he looks well, but he still sleeps a lot. They say he may possibly come home tomorrow.'

'And Daniel?'

'Daniel is the best son a mother could have!' Colette turned half to Solange, as if to share her motherly pride with this woman of her age. 'If he could live at the hospital he would be there with his brother full-time. He's at his vineyard at the moment, thank the Lord. This house is no place for him, with all the people who keep passing by to talk about death.'

'How is he taking his father's death?' Solange asked.

Colette looked down at her hands for a moment, then back at Solange. The answer she gave sounded well rehearsed, but it would do very well for the village, thought Madeleine.

'He's well, thank you. It was difficult, recently, with his father. Jean-Pierre was becoming less well, and more unhappy about being so handicapped in his life. Daniel was so good to him, but in many ways he knows, like me, that this was a blessing. His main concern these last two days has been for his brother.'

She glanced at Robert again as she said this, an unfathomable expression in her tired eyes. He returned the glance, and held her gaze.

'Could we visit Martin, do you think?' They were almost the first words Robert had spoken during this visit. 'Would he accept a visit from us?'

They held their gaze still, and Colette moved her hand towards Robert, pausing uncertain, as if she wanted to touch him, but didn't dare. There was a silence, and then he slowly held out his own hand. Their fingers touched, and he closed his hand gently over hers.

'We don't want to upset him, but we'd like to see him. You know that.'

'Yes. Yes, I know. You are right, I am sure. Why yes, I suppose it is inevitable. Go if you wish, you young people.' The uncertainty in Colette's voice was palpable. Help me, it seemed to say. I don't know the way forward.

Madeleine wanted to answer her, to tell her that all they could do was follow Machado's uncharted road, but she knew that, didn't she? But no stumbling steps – follow Robert, thought Madeleine, he is moving forward for us all.

* * *

And it was Robert, her supposed baby brother, who led the way as they entered the hospital ward later that afternoon – just Madeleine and Robert, come to see the real baby brother they hadn't known existed. As they neared the bed, Madeleine had a sudden jolting memory of her mother lying in the same starched sheets, and that same antiseptic smell. But it was no frail invalid who turned to watch them approach. Martin vibrated health and youth, and looked very out of place in a hospital ward.

He watched with idle curiosity as Robert came towards him, then he saw Madeleine behind, and his whole body stiffened. Robert checked, and turned to Madeleine for confirmation that this was indeed Martin. She nodded, and then moved forward, and spoke rather hurriedly.

'Martin, this is my brother Robert. He came from England to see you. We wanted to know how you were doing.'

Martin looked at them both with something like panic in his eyes, and Madeleine thought, he's just a boy, how is he supposed to cope with this? Then Robert took over. He sat down on one of the bedside chairs, and gestured to Madeleine to take the other chair.

'I bet you're desperate to get out of here,' he said, waving a hand in the direction of the other beds further down the ward. 'I was in hospital once to have my appendix out, and I still hate the sight of the places. But you're going to be a doctor, aren't you? You'll have to get used to the places, then. I thought about studying medicine, but I could never have coped with the chemistry. I had to choose something else.'

His manner was just right, Madeleine realised. He wasn't so much older than Martin, and spoke with a blush and a sincerity that put them on a level. Martin relaxed infinitesimally, and answered in a muted voice.

'What are you studying?'

'Law. I'm in my first year. But you wouldn't want to study law – it's dry and mostly rather boring. I'd rather have studied literature, or history, like Papa, but my grandfather would never have agreed. But he would approve of medicine, and so would Papa. I don't know whether Papa had any medics in his family – we don't know much about his family, really. But Papa certainly wasn't a scientist. He would have loved to have one in the family!'

Martin had no reply to this flow of seemingly innocent disclosure, but Robert just kept on talking, moving on to ask Martin about school, exams, his sports, his friends, and confiding equally from his own side, creating some beginnings of intimacy.

They didn't talk about Jean-Pierre's death, or Martin's accident, and it wasn't until they were leaving, frowned out by a stiff-collared nurse, that Martin turned to Madeleine and spoke.

'Daniel tells me you found me on Friday, you and your friend. I would probably be dead if it wasn't for you. I should say thank you.'

His tone was strained, and Madeleine made haste to answer.

'We spotted a shape across the stream, but it wasn't us who came to find you. It was a team from the village, and Daniel was one of the ones who brought you out. All we did was call for their help. So I would say it's Daniel you should thank, not me!'

'Yes,' the boy's face grew more animated, almost comical, 'and will they let me forget it! Daniel, and Eric and Serge and all the others. They'll be reminding me of it for years!'

'Not if they have any sense! They'll need you one day too, when you're a doctor. Just tell them to mind their manners or they can sing for your help when the time comes! Anyway, they couldn't have gone fishing on Friday night, and they would far prefer to be out there as part of the action than sitting at home listening to the rain! You've given them all something to be heroes about, so just tell them to be grateful!'

Martin grinned at her, a timid schoolboy's grin, and she bent and kissed him on both cheeks, in a gesture both conventional and full of hope.

EPILOGUE

They were due to meet Philippe and Bernard and Solange for dinner that evening, but when they returned to the hotel everyone was out, and with a sigh of relief Madeleine drew Robert up to her room. They hadn't had much time alone.

'I've found the letters Papa sent to *Maman*,' she said, and then watched as he handled the jewellery box, stupefaction juggling with excitement as he lifted off the false bottom. In silence he read the first of Luis's letters, and tears came to his eyes. Like Madeleine four days before, he read and reread each paragraph, taking his time. She watched him closely, but said nothing.

When he reached the second letter, written in the November, one year after their flight from Collioure, it dawned on Madeleine that the letter had been written just at the time Martin had been conceived. Was it a terrible fraud for Luis to write these words of love to Elise when he was sleeping with another woman? Or were the words a call to Elise, calling up her memory to drive away his need for Colette? He had written about his long dark tunnel, and seeing Elise's face at the very end. She looked at Robert, still gently weeping as he read, and she tried not to judge.

When Robert finished the final letter he immediately looked up with a question.

'What was that quote from Voltaire? Do you know?'

'I've found it since. *We are all full of weakness and errors; let us mutually forgive each other our follies – it is the first law of nature.*'

'Mutually forgive! How dare he write this to *Maman*? What did she ever do to be forgiven? There was nothing mutual in this – just our father ruining lives!'

Madeleine was surprised by the level of Robert's anger, and found herself playing Philippe's role of reconciliation.

'What about your anger at *Maman* all these years for her weakness, and for depriving us of our roots? She wasn't perfect either, remember, but if he'd lived Papa knew his bond with *Maman* would survive anything. Everything I've learnt about them makes me realise this. It's all about their bond, that letter, and the words were never meant for us. It makes me realise why *Maman* couldn't share the letters – it feels like the most terrible intrusion reading them, even when they are both dead.'

Robert was silent, and the room was still except for the small movements of his fingers as he read the letters again. Then he sighed.

345

'I can't read them any more right now. Maybe it will become easier over time.'

He leant forward to look at the other letters, which Madeleine had avoided, and read the letter from Philippe telling of Luis's death. Tears came to his eyes again, and he put it to one side decisively.

Madeleine picked up the discarded letters. Leaning forward to put them back in the box, she saw there was one more jagged slip of paper, torn from a small book, which had stuck to the back of the cavity. What next, she wondered? She detached it, and glanced at it warily.

It was a poem from Machado in French translation, one which Madeleine did not remember reading, and underscored heavily was one verse.

> Today in vain you will seek consolation for your pain.
> The fairies have carried off the fibre of your dreams.
> The fountain is silent and the garden is withered.
> There is nothing left today but tears to weep with.
> But weeping is not allowed – silence!

Madeleine read the lines with new tears in her eyes, and then handed the page to Robert.

'My God, Robert! *Maman* put this in here. Imagine living life with such an absence of hope!'

Robert looked numbed. 'Silence – poor *Maman*, she certainly lived her grief in silence. No, I don't think I want to judge either of them, do you? Papa or *Maman*? But we've found them again, at least.'

Madeleine held the little sheet and read the words again.

It was too late for her mother, but life was re-forming here, in the little village where it had all begun. There were other words of Machado's which could take them forward, and as she remembered them she laid her mother's poem back in its secret home.

'*Maman*,' whispered Madeleine, 'We'll make your garden grow again, I promise,' and she wept the tears her mother had been denied.

Author's note

The towns of Collioure, Port Vendres, Céret and Amélie-les-Bains are beautiful and thriving places in Roussillon, France. The neighbouring village of Vermeilla, however, is as imaginary as all the people who live there.

The descriptions of life in 1930s, 1940s and 1950s France are as true as intense research and much listening to wonderful people can make them, and apologies are offered for any inaccuracies.

ACKNOWLEDGEMENTS

Research for this novel has taken me through countless websites, libraries and conversations with those who were there, but I must acknowledge one book which first set me creating this story in my mind, a non-fiction work which truly brings to life the world of Vichy France. Thanks therefore to Rosemary Bailey for her brilliant book *Love And War In The Pyrenees: A Story Of Courage, Fear And Hope*, 1939-1944.

My sincerest thanks also to Louis Baloffi, famously known as Petit Louis, and to Pierrette Périssoud, both of Collioure, for sharing with me so many memories of life from the 1930s to the 1950s.

To discover more great books and to
place an order visit our website at
www.allisonandbusby.com

Don't forget to sign up to our free newsletter at
www. allisonandbusby.com/newsletter
for latest releases, events and exclusive offers

Allison & Busby Books
@AllisonandBusby

You can also call us on
020 7580 1080
for orders, queries
and reading recommendations